THE DUCHESS AND THE INDIGO CHILD

First printing, 2024
Print Edition ISBN: 979-8-9907872-0-9
eBook Edition ISBN: 979-8-9907872-1-6

Cover and Formatting: MiblArt (https://www.miblart.com)
Back Cover Photo: Lindsey Grace Whiddon
(https://www.lindseygrace.com)

Published by:
Maximum Cat Press
Hendersonville, TN
https://www.maximumcatpress.com

To Mom and Dad, for always being my biggest fans.

If it sucked, they'd send flowers.

TABLE OF CONTENTS

PROLOGUE 7

PART ONE 11

CHAPTER ONE: NO SUCH THING AS COINCIDENCE 13

CHAPTER TWO: EIGHT-AND-A-HALF MILLION DATA POINTS 24

CHAPTER THREE: COMPLICATIONS OF COMPLICITY 37

INTERLUDE: SYNCOPE 54

CHAPTER FOUR: A CAPO IN B 56

CHAPTER FIVE: MEA CULPA, SORT OF 68

PART TWO 88

CHAPTER SIX: FAMILY MATTERS 89

CHAPTER SEVEN: GREEN ROOM, YELLOW STRANGER 106

INTERLUDE: ULTERIOR 122

CHAPTER EIGHT: LOOKING INTO THE PRESENT 124

CHAPTER NINE: CRASH AND BANG 138

CHAPTER TEN: SPRING FALLOUT 149

CHAPTER ELEVEN: THE DEEP BLUE WOMAN 163

CHAPTER TWELVE: KALEIDOSCOPE 178

INTERLUDE: GRATUITY 192

CHAPTER THIRTEEN: VIENNA BY THE SEA 194

CHAPTER FOURTEEN: A SECOND SUNSET 206

PART THREE 215

CHAPTER FIFTEEN: SPECIAL INDIGO DELIVERY 216

CHAPTER SIXTEEN: UNPACKING 230

INTERLUDE: IRONY 245

CHAPTER SEVENTEEN: AN UNWILLING GUEST 248

CHAPTER EIGHTEEN: CASUAL CONFRONTATIONS 260

INTERLUDE: VACILLATING 273

CHAPTER NINETEEN: THE QUAY TO SUCCESS 276

CHAPTER TWENTY: LIGHTER THAN AIR 291

CHAPTER TWENTY-ONE: THE HANGOVER 300

CHAPTER TWENTY-TWO: ALONE AGAIN, NATURALLY 314

EPILOGUE 318

ACKNOWLEDGMENTS 321

PROLOGUE

Tajana sat in the back seat of the sedan, wedged uncomfortably between two large men. She could not see their faces—the blindfold ensured that. The deep voices around her spoke in a calm but serious tone, their dialect more Venetian than Triestine. She had no clues to why they abducted her—it was clear they'd singled her out—but causing her harm was not their goal, at least not yet. They grabbed her as she walked up the steps of her building. She used her pepper spray and had thrown at least one punch in self-defense. Without orders to the contrary, she would not be sitting here breathing right now.

It was mild for early January, so they drove through the city with the windows half-open. The growing scent of roasting coffee mixed with salty sea air and diesel exhaust hinted that they were bound for the port. Her years in the coffee trade had finely honed her sense of smell, so she strained to keep her focus on that, to distract from the fear.

A pair of speed bumps taken faster than necessary caused the full sedan to bottom out with a crunch before it came to a stop and her captors pushed her out. She heard the clink and screech of a corroded metal door being opened, and they led her inside what she assumed must be a warehouse near the water. They sat her on a chair gently enough to not hurt her, but emphatically enough to remind her who was in charge. Coffee permeated everything in this place. It was all she could smell, apart from an occasional waft of cheap cologne. There was something familiar about the roast, though. It smelled like…but, no, it couldn't be.

It felt like an hour before they removed her blindfold, but she was sure it had only been moments. In front of her stood an older man in a dapper three-piece suit, looking out of place for the surroundings. Behind him and to the left, another younger man slouched against a support column, his rumpled shirt unbuttoned halfway down his chest. Though he stood in the shadows, she saw a wicked gleam in his eyes. Upon seeing him, she wished she could have the blindfold back. The elder stepped forward to address her, while the others stood around her in a wide circle.

"Good evening," he said, "I'm pleased you could join us this evening, Tajana." It was a cordial greeting, but it carried an air of absolute authority.

"You know who I am?"

"I do."

"Why have you brought me here? Did I do something wrong?"

"Unless you consider family to be a curse, no. You have done nothing wrong apart from being born to the wrong father."

"My father? I don't even know my father!" she insisted. "All I know of him is that I carry his last name. My mother never told me anything else."

"A pity. He was quite a colorful character. Regrettably, he died many years ago, not long after you were born."

She felt a pang of sadness, which caught her by surprise. She'd never met the man, and her mother rarely spoke of him, so it was rubbish to feel anything upon learning of his death.

"Once we figured out who you were, we kept you under observation. Your mother raised you well, given the circumstances."

"Am I supposed to be flattered?" she shouted, then regretted letting her defiant streak show. She would have clapped her hands over her mouth had they not been tied behind her back.

The younger man emerged from the shadows. "You're supposed to be frightened!" He slapped her across the face and immediately raised his hand for another blow. The gentleman grabbed him by the wrist before it could fall.

"Easy, *figlio.* We have no quarrel with this young woman."

"Then why am I here?" she asked. Tears stung her cheek where he'd struck her, but she refused to break.

"You must be intelligent, or our firm would not have hired you, so I will not insult you by lying." He let the words hang in the silent warehouse, waiting for a reaction. There was no mistaking it now. It was *her* roast she smelled. She didn't want to give them the benefit of a reaction, so she inhaled through her mouth to hide her gasp, keeping her face blank. The man continued, saying, "You are here as…an enticement."

"Bait?"

"In a manner of speaking, yes."

"If you have learned so much about me, you would know my mother has almost no money. Not one other person would care enough to pay a ransom for me."

"Ransom? My dear Ms. Nikolić, we have no need for money. We want your sister."

PART ONE

Ajna, or third eye chakra, is the sixth primary chakra in the body. This chakra's color is indigo, a blue hue associated with wisdom and deep inner knowledge. It is the color that opens the consciousness and brings awareness to higher planes and connects us with the spiritual world.

CHAPTER ONE
NO SUCH THING AS COINCIDENCE

ONE MONTH BEFORE THE ABDUCTION...

Monday began much like any other in the residences atop 10 Downing Street, and Michael Hart went to greet his family in the breakfast room. Only six months into his term as Prime Minister, life at Number 10 otherwise bordered on mundane, which disturbed him. A life spent in politics can take its toll on one's soul, but he never imagined he'd become so jaded as to take living at Downing Street for granted. The Christmas decorations were a welcome change, though, and they made him smile each time he walked the hallways. He was looking forward to his first holiday season here.

Since the now-infamous "Purge of Parliament" had seen nine MPs arrested, including the Prime Minister, the public was hungry for change. Hart called for a snap election, which the opposition could not refuse, and his party swept to an overwhelming majority. As he'd presaged, they turned to him to right the ship, which he accepted humbly.

He walked into the breakfast room, still in his pajamas, and kissed his wife and daughter on the tops of their heads. He thanked the staff for his coffee, which was piping hot and to his exact specifications every time, although it made him uncomfortable *having* a staff. Hart had grown up the fourth of five children in a working family from Leeds, so the luxury of leadership suited him poorly. He always relied on the staff for one thing without fail—hygiene. For whatever reason, the residence never felt clean enough for his tastes. The housekeepers, possibly the best in Britain, were meticulous, so he didn't blame them. It must have been something beneath the surface no cleaning product could remove. His predecessor had left the post in ignominy and the ghosts of his indiscretions lingered still.

"Ready for school, Felicity?" he asked his daughter.

She replied with only a grunt, engrossed in a newsprint. She had become more cynical and solitary since turning thirteen, but she had always been an introspective child, and these were not uncommon traits for her age. Her studiousness must have come from her mother—he had never been especially talented in academia. It was rare that he saw her without a book or literary journal anymore, and she made no secret that she aspired to be an author or poet. Once more, he tried to engage her in the few minutes they had together.

"What are you reading?"

"A story."

"I can see it's a story, but what's it about? Who wrote it?"

"Oh, it's ridiculous. You wouldn't be interested, Dad. It's excellent though. I can't put it down."

"Too right, you've not touched your breakfast. You ought to eat something before school."

Felicity shoved half a slice of toast into her mouth without looking up from her magazine.

"You didn't answer me, poppet. I'm interested in everything you do. Give me the quick version."

"Imf amub a mummin hu wivv inna furf."

"Blimey, child, chew your food! We're in Number 10, not

the bloody chippy!"

"Don't get angry with her, dear," Nora Hart interjected.

"She's thirteen. She should have some manners by now. Now, what's this all about?"

"I said it's about a woman who lives in a church."

"Is that all? Nuns have been doing that for centuries."

Felicity huffed at his retort in the typical teenage way that says, "*you just don't get it.*"

"No, Dad, it's not really a church. It only looks like one. She runs a pub and has thieves in and out, and she falls in love with some nerdy computer programmer."

Perhaps the coffee had done its magic, but some part of her explanation connected with an important memory in the back of his mind.

"Does this woman have a name?"

"She calls her 'The Countess', although 'Abbess' might be a better term, don't ya think?"

"Indeed. Felicity, mind if I read that when you're done? It sounds interesting."

"You wot? You don't read unless it's the Financial Times."

"Well, if it interests you this much, then it must be worth a look, eh?"

Nora beamed at her husband, happy to see him take more than a passing interest in their daughter. The Prime Minister smiled back at his family, but he knew he had an important phone call to make...and fast.

The base of a silvery overcast hung just above the windows of the pub, darkening as the afternoon pressed on. The Cathedral

Pub itself was like a speakeasy, hidden in plain sight. If you knew it was there, you were welcome. Mondays were the lightest days up here, but introducing a limited menu brought a handful of additional souls round for a curry. The public at large hadn't caught on yet, but the increasingly unfamiliar faces were causing the current debate between The Duchess and Taylor.

Sebastian Taylor had worked for her companies for several years, but he started bartending in her pub only a year and a half ago. Since then, he'd become a fixture around The Cathedral and the closest thing she could say she had to a proper friend.

"But they all seem to love it," he pleaded. "Why would we stop serving food that people love?"

"Because, as I've been over with you three times already," she groaned, "it's attracting too much attention to my pub."

"So, you'd really stop? Just like that?"

"I've been thinking of something else."

He looked at the ceiling, letting out an exasperated breath. "Of course you have, and you wanted to try to get me angry before you'd tell me."

"You're rather perceptive when you choose to be, Sebastian," she said, smirking as she always did when her manipulation worked.

Taylor no longer grimaced at his first name. Her frequent use of it had inured him, but she was the only person allowed to do it—he made everyone else use his surname.

"Venkata is the key here," she continued. "For one, his two restaurants are impossibly successful. Second, it was his instruction that made the food in the pub so popular."

"Don't sell yourself short, ma'am. Venkata didn't make your menu. Fusing Indian with Croatian was a stroke of genius."

"It seemed only natural."

"Inspired. Name one other Croatian restaurant in the city. Go ahead, I'll wait."

She felt her cheeks get hot and got angry at him for the flattery.

"Anyway," she said, "I decided I would no longer be Venkata's benefactor, but..."

He cut her off. "You're cutting him loose? How could you??"

"Will you let me finish?" she barked. Her stare was severe, and she could almost see him crafting mental sticky notes for further thoughts.

"I will no longer be his benefactor, but his business partner. The menu is unique, good enough to support a restaurant, and he's the perfect person to manage it all. Besides, if we move it away from the pub, it solves our notoriety problem in one go."

"I'd say that was brilliant, but you must tire of hearing it."

"I could stand to hear it once more," she said, flashing a playful smile at him. Before their laughter died away, her mobile rang in her breast pocket. She held up a finger and answered the phone.

"Good afternoon," she said to the caller.

"Duchess, it's me."

"Michael! Good to hear from you. It's been a while. How are you?"

"Preoccupied, as you might have gathered. Turns out, it's not as easy as it looks leading a government. Can we talk in private?"

"Is everything all right, Michael?"

"I couldn't say yet."

"Call me on my private line in five minutes."

She excused herself from her conversation with Taylor and retreated to the office upstairs. Whilst waiting for the phone to ring, she poured a splash of whiskey in a glass and downed it in a single gulp. A concerned call from the Prime Minister signaled trouble, and she needed a buffer. Right on cue, her phone rang. She answered without a greeting, as if to continue where they'd left off.

"What's wrong, Hart?"

"Possibly nothing. Might be everything. Do you know the name Veronica Fancourt?"

"It doesn't ring any bells. Should I?"

"No one called Fancourt in your immediate orbit?"

"None that I can recall, although it would be quite impossible to know every name in every business I own."

"Right, then. A young miss Veronica Fancourt has written a very interesting piece of fiction in one of Felicity's literary journals."

"Fascinating, but I hardly see how that merits the panicked phone call, Michael."

"Then let me fill you in. It speaks of a mysterious woman whom she calls 'The Countess' who lives in a church that isn't a church in the middle of London."

A minuscule pause followed. "Coincidence."

"I thought you didn't believe in coincidence. Anyway, this 'Countess' falls for a computer programmer, whom she calls 'Marvin.' Ring any bells?"

"You have my attention."

"It hints at an arch-nemesis and an office tower, but the publication only contains an excerpt. It won a contest, and I believe the publisher means to release it in its entirety sometime next year."

"And you suspect that there may be additional truth to this fiction?"

"I don't know what transpired between our chat and Owen's arrest, and as we've discussed, I absolutely must not. Based on what I've read, I have no reason to assume that the rest of Miss Fancourt's work is any less accurate."

"You were right to alert me to this, Hart. Thank you. Could you give me the name of this journal? I'd like to have my people do some research."

"It's called *Preeminence*, and it's a teen literary magazine. I believe this was the Fall quarterly issue."

"It's rather fortunate Felicity reads that journal, wouldn't you say? Thank you both."

"One more thing, Duchess. I've seen what you're capable of, but remember, this is a child we're talking about. Tread with extreme caution."

"I appreciate your concern, Michael, but I'm not quite the woman I once was. I will treat the situation with the utmost discretion."

"Cheers. Do pop by Number 10 sometime." He rang off.

Her mind raced in different directions all at once. Before she lost her grip, she reset herself with some calm reassurances. "*Assume nothing,*" she thought. "*Just gather the facts.*"

She unlocked her computer, found the journal with little fuss, and navigated to their back catalog. The contents spilled over her screen in PDF until she found the beginning. "The Countess's Keep" by Veronica Fancourt started out generic enough, but the further she read into the excerpt, the lower her jaw hung.

When she'd finished, a deafening silence filled her office. What shocked her most was that no one in her employ was privy to that depth of detail. Compartmentalization was everything in operational security and was as natural to her as breathing.

The only people who were privy to the complete story were Julia and Martin, but they would pull their own fingernails out in slow motion before they'd betray her. Odder still, why would anyone have told the story to a random teenage girl?

Nothing made the slightest shred of sense, and when she needed sense made of something, there was one person to whom she could turn. As it happened, she'd just left him downstairs in the pub.

Taylor flinched when his employer burst through the stockroom door.

"Find her, now."

"I'm sorry?"

She shoved a small scrap of notepaper into his hand. He looked hard at it, squinting and turning the paper, attempting to decipher her scribble. What he could make out was "VERONICA FANCOURT - PREEMINENCE - FALL EDITION."

"I don't understand, what..." he started.

"I want neither excuses nor delays, Taylor. Find her. Now."

"But there's nothing here."

"Which is precisely why I brought it to you. Off you go."

He sputtered and attempted to complain, but she had already turned away and set to running the pub in his stead. There was nothing else for it but to do as she'd ordered. He grew angry and wanted to refuse the task, but he feared her reproach more and decided he would brood over it later. He boarded the lift and descended to level 10. Though he spent most of his afternoons tending the pub, he had a desk in The Cathedral's management office on the topmost level of the nave.

He unlocked his workstation with his biometric key and stared at the desktop screen, his mind a hopeless blank. He turned his chair away from the screen, staring out the window for several minutes. The enormity of London crashed down on him as he considered his nigh impossible task. Over eight-and-a-half million people lived in the Metropolitan London area, and he had to find one of them, armed with nothing but a name and three meaningless, random words. To call it daunting was a massive understatement.

"There's always Google," he thought, and turned back to his keyboard. He entered the scant information he had and found the excerpt on the journal's website.

"Okay, at least that bit makes sense now," he said. As he read the entry, he realized why The Duchess was so adamant that he find this Veronica person. Though his role had been small, he was aware of the sensitivity surrounding April's events. He returned to the search results but was disappointed to find only a sound-alike match of Veronica Franco, a 16th century Venetian courtesan of some note. According to the Mighty G, even with its limitless reach, the author of this true fiction was null, a ghost.

When he reached that dead end, he considered a business relationship. If this person knew details of the empire's inner workings, perhaps she was on payroll or otherwise associated. He brought up a connection to the main database and searched personnel, vendor certification, and accounts.

"Nada!" he said incredulously. "There must be a record somewhere. Even a pen name should be in a register or something." He concentrated, and it clicked. "The General Register Office, of course!" he proclaimed in victory. "Maybe Adkins will have something."

He dashed down to the command center. Despite his urgency, he resisted the urge to burst in dramatically as analysts working in subterranean closets have a tendency to be jumpy.

"Mr. Adkins, are you there?" he said into the dark, while his eyes adjusted.

"Mr. Taylor!" Adkins responded in a more enthusiastic tone. "I certainly am, sir. How can I help?"

"Do we have anything from the General Register Office? I need to find information on a Veronica Fancourt as soon as possible."

"Did you try Google?"

Taylor huffed. "Don't you think I'd've tried that?"

"Right, sorry." Adkins disappeared into thought for a moment. "I may have an older export somewhere, sir, but we try to stay out of government systems as much as we can. It attracts a lot of scrutiny, as you might imagine."

"I can imagine, and that's a wise policy. Also, Adkins, please stop calling me 'sir.' You know full well I'm a dock worker in the wrong place."

"Have it your way, Mr. Taylor," he replied with a chuckle. "I'll get looking, and if I find anything, I'll let you know."

"My thanks, as always! Have a splendid afternoon."

"Is it afternoon already?" he replied. They shared another laugh and Taylor went upstairs to the plaza level.

As he picked up his coffee, he considered how improbable it was that one of the most impressive private surveillance systems he'd ever heard of had been, so far, useless. There was one other resource he'd yet to tap, so he found a bench near the stream and dug his mobile from his jeans pocket.

"Hello?"

"Martin, it's Taylor. D'ya have a mo?"

"Sure, is it important?"

"Very, it seems. Are you near a secure phone? No mobiles."

"Oh my, that sounds quite serious. I was about to turn off the M4 on my way home. Perhaps I should come to The Cathedral instead?"

"That'd be even better. See you soon."

CHAPTER TWO

EIGHT-AND-A-HALF MILLION DATA POINTS

Martin Alcott was returning from another one of his weekend holidays, though this one had extended into Monday. Ever since The Owen Affair, as he called it, he'd promised himself that he would hop in his car every two weeks, pick a direction, and drive until he felt free enough of himself to stop. When he found the right vibe, he'd hole up at a cozy hotel or promising pub for the weekend. The more remote the village, the better. It was better still if they didn't offer Wi-Fi. He would relax with a good book in the garden, drink himself into oblivion, or both, depending on his mood.

He sailed past the junction that led towards home, called in to work on his day off once again. His mobile rang once more, and he hoped it was Taylor calling to change his mind. No dice: it was his best friend, Maureen.

"Hi, Mo."

"Where was it this time?" she asked.

"Cotswolds. Did you know they have a bird sanctuary there? It was fascinating!"

"Thrilling. You know they have zoos in London, right?"

"It's not the same. I have to get out of the city now and then."

"You never used to."

"Enough of the third degree. What do you want?"

"I haven't seen you in a month and we work in the same bloody building. You owe me a pint and a chat."

"I'd love to, honestly, but I'm on my way to the Cathedral. Duty calls."

"On your day off."

"I know. Before you even say it, I know."

"Do you ever say no to her?"

"It wasn't her this time. Taylor called."

"And who do you suppose told him to call you?"

"You have a strange way of getting somebody to want a drink with you."

"Coffee in the morning, then?"

"Sure, I should be in the office."

"Fine. Don't give her any more than she's entitled to."

"See you," he said, and pressed the end call button on his steering wheel.

As he passed the M25, he allowed himself a second to consider why he needed to leave the city so often. Maureen was right again, and it'd been months since he'd wondered.

The past April, and the May that followed, had all but crushed him.

Initially, the fallout from the operation hadn't affected him, at least not that anyone would notice. Most of his friends assumed he saw it as a job completed and returned to the daily drudgery of running AMWarn. In the few introspective moments he allowed himself, he found it weird how not weird it was. Nevertheless, work was work, and he soldiered on, focusing on the job. One day in mid-May, he was working in the server racks. Without warning, it all crashed on him: the company and his responsibilities, the media and police attention, and the moral quandary of what they'd done. His brain overloaded, glitched, and he broke down. Later that afternoon, Simon found him sobbing in his office, with no idea how long he'd been there. Once he gathered himself together, he ran away to Wales for two weeks. The trip itself was fuzzy in his memory; he figured he must have been catatonic for large segments of it. He returned refreshed, but more wary of the pressures of his new normal. The job hadn't changed, but the implications of it had.

The crux of his collapse was The Duchess. Her advance caught him by surprise, but they both fell into it without hesitation. The weeks that followed were unlike anything he'd experienced in his life. He'd dated and even had some serious relationships in the past, but the suddenness and passion of their connection amazed him. By May, when everything else had cracked, he was well worried. She insisted on him staying in The Cathedral more often and even suggested that he let Zaphod stay there. She claimed she was only joking, but he didn't think it was much of a joke. When he'd returned from Wales, she read him the riot act. He recalled her screeching things like "How dare you?" and "You could have been in danger!" From that point, the relationship cooled and became more professional. He still harbored feelings for her, and they still had their inexplicable mental connection, but he refused to become a trophy in her mansion—another conquest of her empire.

He shook his head, trying to get out of it as he passed through the Hogarth Roundabout onto the A4. He meandered through the suburbs, past petrol stations, nondescript office blocks, and terraced houses. The stop-and-go traffic did little to keep him out of his thoughts, and the dream that awakened him this morning edged into his consciousness.

He'd been cruising along a country road lined with hedgerows bared by the winter. The lane swerved, bobbed, and dove with the topography and a familiar contentment filled him. He smiled as he drove along. It was a beautiful day with brilliant blue skies and nary a soul to interrupt his solitude. As lovely as the view was, he realized it wasn't outside, per se, because he was flying along the lane without a car at all. He crested a hill and down the other side, making his stomach jump like riding a roller coaster. When he reached the bottom, though, the sensation remained. He continued forward along the road, feeling a vague sense of nausea or hunger—he couldn't decide which made the most sense. Though the path ahead was flat, the sensation refused to leave his core. In fact, it was worsening to an ache.

He thought it wisest to stop until the sensation subsided, but he was unsure how without a car. The ache intensified, feeling as if it was pulling at his navel from the inside, and he clenched his abdomen hard. The countryside spun counterclockwise, as if reality were running down an unseen drain. He hadn't yet encountered a car that could barrel roll, so he surmised he must be inside a dream. At this point in most dreams, Martin would awaken surprised and disoriented, before shaking it off. This one, however, was determined to hold on to him longer. He wailed in pain without a sound as his entire self swirled into his own stomach, and he discovered it was not reality, but he who was running down the drain. The pain reached an apex and disappeared in a snap.

His awareness returned, and he saw he was no longer in the countryside, but on the lounge level of The Duchess's cathedral mansion. He spun around, expecting to find her wearing one of her infuriating smirks. Instead, he saw two beings of pure light. He tried to focus on any kind of shape or familiar feature, but the amorphous blobs of brilliance hovered without a whisper six feet in front of him.

"Hello?" he said, or so he thought. His question echoed from everywhere in the room, a reverberation without an original sound.

"OH MY GOD!" the thing on the right shouted, and their intensities tripled. He had to shut his eyes tight to preserve his retinas. Through his eyelids, he saw a bright flash like a camera strobe, and he'd woken up.

He snapped out of the memory, and his eyes refocused in time to hit the brakes, narrowly avoiding a collision with the car in front of him. The burst of adrenaline from the near miss kept him sharp enough for the rest of his trip.

The Cathedral Atrium was like Christmas come to life. Twinkling lights hung from every catwalk, with each strand choreographed to look like snow falling gently from ten stories above. Fresh evergreen swags adorned every stall and storefront, and a cart stood next to the coffee stand, selling hot chocolate, cider, wassail, and gingersnaps. A thirty-foot Norway Spruce stood at the center court, bedecked with fine crystals, mercury glass balls, LED candles, and multicolored large bulb lights. At its base stood a scale model of The Cathedral in gingerbread. The air was thick with the scents of pine, cinnamon, oranges, and cloves. Banners hung from the high ceiling with various holiday wishes printed in languages from around the world. Martin loved the holidays, so he stopped for a mulled cider before heading to Taylor's office.

Simon Mesfin was bored. He enjoyed his job, no question, but there had been far less to do over the last few months.

AMWarn's headquarters had moved to Megalith Tower at the end of August, so he was the only remaining permanent employee in the data center. Sometimes, Martin, his boss, would pop in for a few hours to rewire something or to experiment in his personal lab, but it was just as likely he was trying to keep him company. He was an introvert by nature, but the isolation was getting to him. That's why he jumped when he heard the office door open.

Martin burst through, pallid and wearing a serious expression. The most important thing Simon had learned about his manager was how poorly he hid his emotions. His face wore his mood as explicitly as a sign around his neck.

"All right, Martin?" he asked, though it was perfectly obvious he was not. "What smells like cinnamon?"

"Oh, it's a cider from the atrium," Martin replied, the two questions colliding in a dreadful tangle of logic. He usually knew better than to ask his boss too many questions at once, but he missed this time. "What? No! No, everything is not all right. We have a serious problem, Simon. I've just been upstairs to talk to Taylor, and there's suspicion of a massive leak. Frankly, we need to figure out if we bollocksed something up and fast."

"Why do you think there was a breach?"

"No, not a breach!" he yelled. "A leak. Insider threat. Somebody published a lot of very privileged information in a literary journal."

Simon thought it well out of character for him to yell, but whatever had happened, his stress must be high. "That's tosh. If somebody had that sort of information, we'd have heard something. Blackmail or ransom or some such."

He straightened up. "That's a fair point. Why would someone publish what they knew without trying to extort something?"

"But you still suspect a mole?"

"Believe me, no one outside of our organization knows this much detail."

"What do we do, then?"

"We start with getting every shred of information we can on the publisher. Indigo won't be much help here, I'm afraid."

Indigo was the impossibly clever data gathering system he and Martin had built and tuned over the past year. Its chief limitation was that it still required miles of wiring, dozens of sensors, and software to be installed on pretty much everything connected to the network it was "protecting." Since they had none of that, he thought "won't be much help" was a gross understatement.

Martin continued, "We're going old school here. We just need to find the person. Report what we find upstairs."

"This hacker got a name?" he said, sticking to business. It was the most interesting project he'd had in weeks, so he was itching to jump in.

"Couldn't say it's a hacker, honestly, but this is all too weird. Her name is Veronica Fancourt. An excerpt of her story turned up in the journal *Preeminence*. That's all we have so far."

"Is she an indie author, then? Did you check the socials?"

"Taylor did. He didn't come up with much. She must not be using her real name."

"I can do a quick sweep of subreddits and such. There's also BookSpace."

"BookSpace? I'm not familiar."

"Yeah, it's a new social media made just for authors. I got into some new sci-fi shit and found a ton of recommendations. Only been online since last year." He typed for a few seconds and stated, "I found her."

Martin ran around behind his desk and saw a picture of a rather nondescript gothic-tinged teenager with blue bangs draped over her face, wearing an almost smile. They poked around on the site and were disappointed to find her profile either woefully incomplete or deliberately cagey. All they could confirm was she lived in London and was an aspiring author.

"She's being careful. Not giving too much away," Simon said, his excitement ticking up a notch. "This could be a challenge after all."

"There must be something. Most of the genealogy sites won't give you more than a name if the person's still living. Can we get any vital records?"

"Not without getting into some dark areas. That's not something you'd want me doing on company systems, I'd wager."

"Another fair point. Though, as a security firm, don't you think that'd be something we'd want to do? Ensuring a corporation's data isn't being traded down in the depths would be a valuable service, yeah?"

"I thought you'd say something like that, so I already downloaded the proxy browser."

"One step ahead of me, as usual, mate."

The two dove beneath the surface web into the deeper, darker areas of the information age. Simon used his knowledge of hacker networks, the clicking of his custom mechanical keyboard making the small office sound like a 1960s newsroom. Martin stood behind him with a blank expression on his face—he was in data intake mode. Here and there, he would blurt out a key word or phrase, and Simon would pivot his search to match it.

So far, they had already come up with a middle name, Edwinna, derived from her father's name. Edwin Fancourt was a London solicitor, and they confirmed the connection on his firm's website. His biography page mentioned a daughter, Veronica, and a son, William. They refocused on Edwin and found memberships in various clubs, associations, and philanthropies. His career in corporate governance was beyond reproach, nary an untoward detail to be found.

"I have an address in Hampstead," he said, bringing Martin out of his fugue state.

"I saw it. Thank you, Simon. I understand everything and nothing at all. From what we've seen, there are zero connections to The Duchess, save that we're all in London. How in the name of Linus bleeding Torvalds does a fifteen-year-old girl from Hampstead know anything about anything?"

"Hackers always use aliases. Maybe we haven't found her in the networks yet."

"Keep searching. Take nothing for granted. Not a word of this to anyone but me or Taylor. I'll report upstairs that we have an authentic mystery on our hands, and I doubt it's the kind where it's the old amusement park owner in a mask."

"You wot?"

"Cartoon reference, never mind."

"Is that the one with the talking dog?"

Martin shook his head. "I still have so much to teach you. Let's get a wiggle on."

Francesca poured steamed milk into the coffee, resulting in a design that looked more like a veiny blob than the leaf she'd intended. It would take more practice to improve her latte artwork, but the results were no less delicious. She took her first sip and smiled to herself. Wednesday tasted good so far.

She turned off the espresso maker and opted for the scenic route down to the office, using the grand staircase rather than the lift. It qualified as exercise, in her mind, and could help the caffeine hit her bloodstream a little faster. The first couple of steps were stumbling, but she settled into a cadence down the six flights from the kitchen on B to her office on E level. She alit from the last flight and rounded the corner to enter her office. She pulled the door open, taking another cautious sip of her scalding beverage, and almost spat it out again when she saw the three men sitting at her desk.

"*Majka Božja!* What are all of you doing here?"

Martin startled and stopped pacing around the office. Taylor and Simon looked up in surprise from the chairs opposite her desk. They hadn't seen the hidden door in the wainscoting from which she emerged.

"He let us in!" Simon asserted, pointing at Martin.

She smirked. "No honor among thieves, eh, Simon?"

"Beg pardon?"

"Never mind. Martin, please tell me why you've brought everyone together. It's usually me calling the meetings around here, so next time, at least ring me up first?"

"I'm sorry, Duchess, but we found the information you've been wanting. At least some of it, anyway."

"Couldn't it have waited until a more humane hour? I haven't finished my first coffee yet."

"And miss the sunrise? It's a stunner out there," he replied. He attempted a smirk, but it came off more like a maniacal, sleep-deprived grin.

She crossed the sprawling office into the conference room, where she found the eastern facing windows. She raised the blinds and couldn't help but agree. The sky seemed to shout in violent purple and shocking pink.

"Lovely, but I'm waiting for an explanation of why you're up in my tower before the sun. Information is good and important, but timing is everything, gentlemen. It's too early for riddles. Now get to it."

"For at least two of us, it's not early. It's late."

She looked at Martin and realized he meant it. His eyes looked puffy; his clothes were more rumpled than usual. Simon appeared ready to nod off at any moment in the comfortable chair. Taylor, however, looked fresh as a daisy—it was the middle of his scheduled shift in the command center in the catacombs.

"Up all night again?"

"Since Monday, actually."

"I...er..." she sputtered. Realizing the gravity of the situation, she said nothing else and sat at her desk.

"It's all in that file," Taylor said. "And I'm afraid it's not much."

She opened the file to find a printed screen capture of the girl's BookSpace page, some information on her father and his firm, and a couple of other writing samples she had posted. Simon had also uncovered a copy of her birth record, so they had a full name and birth date, but there was little else.

"So little! Martin, you assured me that people kept complete chronicles of their lives online without even realizing it!"

"That's true for most people, but not a fifteen-year-old. Technically, most social media sites require you to be thirteen, although most kids ignore that. That means almost no history to find. Add a set of overprotective parents, and a child is mostly a blip on the Internet. I suspect that's what's happened here."

"Ah," she said, disappointed. She pushed her glasses to the

top of her head—she hadn't had time to put her contact lenses in yet this morning—and rubbed her eyes.

"It's more what we *didn't* find that was most interesting. The best I can figure, neither this Veronica nor any of her family members have any connection to you or your businesses." Taylor's tone was far too cheerful for this early in the morning, and she glowered at him. She put her glasses back down on her nose, reread the paltry dossier, and frowned.

"That's good news, isn't it?" Taylor asked.

"Not remotely, Taylor. It only raises more questions. It's an impossibility for her to have written this level of detail if she has never crossed paths with us. I don't believe in coincidence, so there must be a reason."

Simon offered nothing but a soft snore. She'd have considered this rude, but she acknowledged the hours he and Martin had put in on this puzzle, so she let it slide.

"What's our next move?" Taylor asked. Martin stood behind him, looking off into the middle distance. She couldn't tell if he was in one of his trances or if he had also fallen asleep standing up.

"I'll have to meet her. In a social setting, of course. We must use extreme care because of her status as a minor. I wouldn't want anyone to get the wrong idea. Her father, being a solicitor, further complicates matters."

She and Taylor thought through their options. Simon remained asleep, and Martin was...somewhere else. She hoped he was also thinking about the problem, else she'd have to get cross with him.

"What have you found about this journal? If they published it, they must know something about it, yes?"

"Erm," Taylor said, caught unawares. "Nothing, I'm afraid.

We only focused on the girl and her father."

"A bit narrow, gents, but it seems the assignment was not as straightforward as I'd hoped. Well done with what you found, though. You came through, as always."

Taylor beamed. Martin came back to his senses at that statement, and said, "Thanks, Duchess."

"All that said, we need to broaden the scope. A plan is brewing. I need contact information for the journal. Don't just tell me to Google it, though. I want more than that. Get me names, get me connections. As a publication, I believe this will be a much simpler assignment and it's far less urgent. Martin, Simon, the pair of you are to go home and get some sleep, and I mean home in a proper bed. No futons. Understood?"

"Right away, ma'am," Taylor responded, and the trio filed out of the office.

She brimmed with confidence as she sat on her swiveling throne. It was a solid plan, and she knew her team could do it. The only question was whether the girl would accept.

CHAPTER THREE

COMPLICATIONS OF COMPLICITY

It had only been ten days since the invitations went out, but the anticipation was making Francesca twitch since the workshop was under a month away. *Preeminence* put forward forty candidates, including Veronica. Martin worked with the journal's team to have the system notify her by email for each RSVP that they received. To date, they'd had twenty-two acceptances, while only two declined because of prior commitments. The responses grew sparse as the days passed, and the one she needed most hadn't arrived.

A rumble and a pair of thumps interrupted her sulking, and today's post arrived via the pneumatic tube system. The delivery tubes were another one of those details she'd insisted upon during the construction of The Cathedral, and it fit her aesthetic to perfection. It was efficient, if outmoded, but the cool quotient was stratospheric, and it never failed to make her smile. The carrier came to rest in its station, and she relieved the capsule of its contents. The mail room was adept at filtering junk and redirecting other corporate correspondence better handled by lieutenants and office managers, but she left explicit instructions that anything from *Preeminence* was to be sent straight to her.

She rifled through the paltry pile and found nothing from the journal, increasing her disquiet. She was about to jettison the entire stack into the bin when the postmark on the last letter caught her eye. The stamp read Trieste, addressed to "The Heiress of Nikolić," care of Five Pence Imports and Shipping. That intrigued her. If few knew her as anything other than The Duchess, fewer still were familiar with her ancestral family name. She inspected the envelope with a mistrustful eye, realizing that anyone with this knowledge was a potential threat. When she felt comfortable that there was nothing but paper inside, she sliced it open with a small knife she kept in her desk drawer and read the letter.

To the daughter of Stjepan Nikolić,

We wish to congratulate you on concealing your identity so well. Few are crafty enough to elude us, but you are unmasked. We have learned enough about you and your businesses to reach you in this manner.

As you are no doubt aware, you are in violation of the terms of the agreement signed by your grandfather, Ljubomir. It states that no Nikolić businesses would, in perpetuity, compete in the import, trade, or processing of coffee in the Free Port of Trieste. Repeated attempts to inform or enforce our domain have been unfruitful to date, so more drastic measures were necessary.

You will present yourself to discuss the matter at the Antico Caffè San Marco in Trieste on Monday the 16th at 20:00. You will come alone, or your dear sister will pay an unfortunate penalty.

There was no signature. Her mind reeled, especially at the last sentence. It was an open secret throughout family circles that her father was a noted philanderer. It would be a greater surprise if she *didn't* have illegitimate half-siblings strewn about Europe. For someone to have made a connection between herself and some young woman in Trieste, though, implied either a formidable adversary or an opportunist overextending themselves.

Her grandfather was also a mystery, having died fifteen years before she was born, and her father did not speak of him. What did he agree to? With whom? They knew her father and that he'd established Five Pence. If they knew of the coffee, they must also be monitoring the contents of her shipments through Trieste, which required resources. Importing coffee was her idea. Her growing interest in the food business and partnership with Venkata led her to become fascinated with coffee culture. It started as a lark, but now her capriciousness landed her most profitable enterprise, and a supposed "dear sister," whom she did not know, in hot water.

"*Sentimental rubbish,*" she thought. "*FOCUS!*"

Her analytical side took over at once, and she calculated potential outcomes and risks. She assessed that, because of proximity, exposure on the Owen Affair was a far greater threat to her in the near-term. Owen's network rivaled her own and, although many languished in prison, there must be loyalists still roaming the south of England intent on revenge. She reread the letter and keyed in on a particular sentence. They'd made repeated attempts, which meant that she may have some time. It was a risk to assume that their patience would hold, but her intuition told her she had one chance remaining with them. Still, something needed to be done. She reached for her desk phone and selected the private line.

"Julia, we have a situation."

Julia Redmond was her most trusted associate, aside from possibly Geoff. In terms of business and solving problems, it was as if they shared a brain. There was no one better suited to handle a problem that required this level of diligence.

"A situation? How bad?"

"Unsure, but it could be serious. Can you be in Trieste by Monday?"

"Might be a wrench, but I'm sure I can manage."

"Good. Try to be there early. I will send you the details, but you must be able to attend a meeting at 8pm local time."

"What's the topic?"

"Something about our recent decision to import coffee has fallen afoul of some old agreement I wasn't aware of. I expect the negotiations should be short once they see reason. Listen to their terms. If it makes sense for us, just accept them. I trust you know what's best for us."

"Yes, of course, ma'am. If you could send me the details?"

"You've heard them, I'm afraid. Anything else I could tell you would be pure conjecture, but I have a feeling they may be patient. I wouldn't take it lightly, but I don't expect trouble."

"I see...erm..."

Hesitancy was uncharacteristic of her most seasoned employee, so she pressed for more. "Was there something else?"

"Can I bring Ian? We were supposed to leave for a skiing holiday on Sunday, and I doubt he'd appreciate a last-minute cancellation."

"Ah, that must be the wrench."

She paused, considering the potential damage of a variable like Ian. She knew little about Julia's fiancé beyond what she or Martin had told her, and limited interactions at The Cathedral. They were engaged in June—she'd asked him, naturally. If she supposed the author of the letter was no amateur or opportunist, they could use him as leverage, and his big mouth could be more trouble than it was worth. *"No, this is just business,"* she thought. *"Don't overthink it."*

"I don't love it, but I'll allow it. When you're done, you can use my villa in Dubrovnik for the rest of your holiday as recompense."

"I'll get started on the bookings at once, and thank you."

As she hung up the phone, a sudden, irrepressible craving for a cappuccino overwhelmed her.

It was cold and breezy in Hampstead, even for January. Veronica Fancourt fastened all the buttons of her cardigan, emblazoned with the crest of her school, St. Catherine's School of the Arts. She loved her school, though it had been an ugly fight with her father to get him to agree to send her there. Her mother had broken the tie by convincing him authors often made legitimate money with the right opportunities and connections.

She jammed her notebooks into her backpack and tried very hard to ignore the 72% mark she'd gotten on her last algebra test. Her father would insist on bringing in a private tutor if he saw it, so she tried to bury it. With limited time to write already, extra schoolwork would leave her with virtually nothing. What she wished for was to set up private sessions with her literature and creative writing teacher, Ms. Corby. No one else had ever been so caring or supportive of her writing. Her encouragement had opened the floodgates, but her recent dreams had provided more than a little inspiration. *"At least the week is over,"* she thought. *"It can't get any worse."*

She followed a group out of the school and across the green. It was a relief when they turned right out of the gate—not in her direction. They wouldn't have talked to her anyway, so she felt no significant loss walking home by herself. She didn't have many friends at St. Catherine's, except...

"Vero, espérame!"

She turned to see her best friend, Beatriz, running up the hill after her. She stopped and waited as her friend had asked, and was happy she wouldn't be walking home alone after all.

"You didn't have to run, Bea. I'm not in a hurry to get home."

"Yeah, well, I didn't want to miss a minute of the moping. I got a 78, so don't worry so much."

She flicked the blue bangs off her face and gave her friend a wry smile. "Maybe we'll end up with the same tutor."

Her statement was intentionally ironic, since Bea had been her Spanish tutor only two years prior. During their first tutoring session, she had used a Pablo Neruda quote for an example, and they became instant BFFs.

"They shouldn't spend so much time on maths. It's a school for the arts!" Bea lamented.

"Ugh, I know. We're never going to use all those letters and Greek symbols, anyway!"

"I know! I'll paint a portrait of the unloved delta!"

"Canción de Cálculo!"

"Neruda would be so proud!"

They laughed at their own wit, crossed the street, and continued up the hill.

"Did you ever hear from the journal?"

"No, nothing. It's been weeks."

"They'll send you something soon, I know it," Bea said, attempting to reassure her. "I still can't believe you came up with something so brilliant!"

"I told you, it sort of came to me. It was so real in my dreams. I couldn't help but write it down."

"They put it in the fall issue! They'd have to want the

whole thing, right?"

Veronica shrugged and didn't respond.

"Abuela is making paella tomorrow. You want to come over?"

"Like I would miss Abuelita's paella! What's the occasion?"

"My uncle and cousins are coming to town. More mandatory family togetherness," Bea said, rolling her eyes. "At least the food will be good."

They reached the fork in the road, waved to each other, and parted ways. Without company, the rest of her walk home became a trudge. The only source of amusement was walking past a compact car parked at the end of her street with a gargantuan man stuffed in the driver's seat. As she rounded the garden wall of #32, it surprised her to see her mother standing at the front door, clearly waiting for her. *"She must have come home from work early today,"* she thought. *"That can't be good."*

"Something came in the post for you today," she said with a grin.

Her mind raced. She wasn't expecting any packages, and her marks weren't due until the end of the quarter. Anyway, the school would have addressed those to her parents, and she guessed Mum wouldn't be smiling.

"What is it?"

"I couldn't resist, so I opened it."

"MOTHER!"

"I won't spoil the surprise, but it's from the journal and it's splendid news!"

She snatched the letter out of her mother's hand, sprinted upstairs, and burst through her bedroom door. Her backpack flew across the room before she flopped face first onto the bed. She savaged the envelope and yanked the letter from inside. It read:

Miss Veronica Fancourt,

The staff of Preeminence Literary Journal wishes to extend to you an invitation to attend our inaugural Young Writer's Workshop. This exclusive event will pair some of the finest young talent in the United Kingdom with best-selling, award-winning, and world-renowned authors, poets, screenwriters, as well as representatives of the publishing industry. It is an honor to announce that our faculty will include celebrated mystery author P. L. Eriksson!

The week-long event will take place February 13-17, 2017 at The Megalith Tower Conference Center, to be followed by an awards banquet on the 18th at The Cathedral Atrium. The Prime Minister, Michael Hart, a generous sponsor of the event, will host the ceremony on Saturday, the 18th.

Please RSVP online or using the enclosed application form no later than January 27th. We look forward to seeing you there!

Warmest regards,
Charles Prescott
Editor-in-Chief
Preeminence

She reread the letter three times, hardly daring to believe it. Scandinavian murder mystery was one of her favorite sub-genres, and P. L. Eriksson was the king in her mind. She was going to meet Per-Lars freaking Eriksson! One hand tried to get to her laptop to fill out the form, and the other attempted to retrieve her mobile from her backpack. Failing at both, she tumbled onto the floor with a round thud.

"Veronica! Are you all right?" her mother shouted up the stairs.

"Fine, Mummy! Did you see who's going to be there??"

"I did. How very exciting for you," she said, attempting to sound interested. "Hadn't you better ask your father, though? He should be home soon."

She didn't answer. Her dad was hard-headed and overprotective, but she knew she could sell him on this. *"No, must call Bea first,"* she thought.

Before her friend could even say hello, she exclaimed, "I heard from the journal!"

"Oh my God, what did they say?"

She read the letter to her best friend, and they both screamed.

Two hours had passed since the post brought the ominous warning, but Francesca had still not received the answer she wanted. That, plus the Trieste situation, whatever it was, increased her stress by an order of magnitude. Though she tried to deny her anxiety, she paced around her office, casting more than occasional glances at her laptop screen for online responses. She had quit smoking months ago, but she worried she wouldn't make it through the weekend without relapsing.

She needed to distract herself somehow, so she focused on the workshop to come. The event had proved fun to plan, and becoming a patroness of the arts was an unexpected thrill. It wasn't uncommon for her to be impressed by her own cleverness, but she'd outdone herself this time. Despite the short notice, she arranged a panel of literary A-listers as faculty for the week-long program. With some generous donations, favors redeemed or promised, and shaking all the right hands, she'd performed a miracle. Success was certain, and the enthusiastic response pleased her, but it was all for naught if Veronica wasn't there or she couldn't get close to her.

She squeezed her eyelids tight in frustration. "*Why don't I have her reply yet?*" she thought.

"Maybe she sent it by post?"

She jumped at the sound of Martin's voice. What was he doing here? With her eyes closed, she'd somehow missed him coming through the main entrance of her office, and was surprised by his stealth.

"You should know better than to sneak up on me like that!" she roared. "What if I'd been armed?"

"Do you often carry weapons on you in your own tower?"

"*Cheeky bastard!*" she thought. With one fluid motion, she opened the top right drawer of her desk, pulled out the knife—her letter opener—and casually embedded it in the wall about a foot to the right of Martin's left ear.

"Now, would you like to tell me why you're here?"

"I, uh…"

He stood wide-eyed and quaking in the doorway, warbly noises spilling from his slack jaw. They sounded like the beginnings of words, but they trailed off after a syllable or two.

"Yes?" she demanded. Her regular playfulness was absent. She could feel her face radiating heat, but her eyes were icy.

"I've forgotten. I, uh, think I'll go have a pint."

He turned and retreated from the office with haste. She could hear the ding of the lift being boarded. She flopped into her desk chair and did some deep breathing exercises to clear the adrenaline from her system. It'd been a long time indeed since she'd snapped like that, and she didn't care for it one bit. She wasn't used to people turning up uninvited in the private areas of her mansion, but she had given Martin a key over the summer. If that wasn't an open invitation to her space, what was? He didn't deserve what she did.

She stood from her desk and pulled the knife from the wall. It took two solid tugs to displace it, illustrating how angry she'd been when she threw it. She dropped the weapon on her desk and was about to hurry down the spiral stairs to the pub when her laptop sounded a new message alert. She sat once more and looked at the screen, finding the message she'd been awaiting. The subject line read, "Veronica Fancourt - YES." A warm wave of relief crashed over her, causing her to go limp in her chair. She opened the message and read the details. It filled in many gaps in their knowledge about the girl, so she needed to get it to Taylor and complete their dossier. First things first, though.

She focused every ounce of her mind on Martin and thought, "*I'm sorry. Please come back.*" She leaned back in her chair and closed her eyes. A terse reply appeared at the edge of perception.

"*Not now.*"

She'd cocked that up in expert fashion, and she would assuredly spend the weekend alone now. At least she had the response she'd been waiting for, so she could relax. She stared at the screen displaying Veronica's reply, and a singular sentence flooded her mind.

"*I'm looking forward to meeting you, Veronica.*"

"So, can I, Dad?" she asked, her fingers crossed behind her back.

"You won't be missing any school?"

"No, it's the week of the spring holidays."

He looked over the letter again. "It must be respectable if the PM will be attending, but I still think it's utter nonsense."

"Dear, the publishing houses are sending representatives," her mother said in her defense. "Don't you think those would be valuable connections?"

"Is any of it valuable? She's gambling with her future, Jeanette. Listen, Veronica, why don't you have a go at something more stable? Perhaps you could pursue a steady job with the banks and write on the weekends?"

"Oh, stop it, Edwin! She's fifteen! She's not taking a job anywhere yet. At least she's not flying off to Ibiza or some such with her friends, like that horrible Worthington girl."

Veronica watched his face, waiting for a hint of his answer. His expression showed that he was in an intense, wordless conversation with his wife. When he turned back to her, she couldn't read him.

"Will you be taking the tube with me?"

"Would we be going the same way?"

"Same train. You'd get off one stop before I change, but otherwise, we can ride in together."

"Wait a mo, does that mean I can go?"

"You'll need connections and an opportunity if you're ever to make money writing, and it sounds like this workshop may give you both. You can go."

She flung her arms around him, then her mum, and dashed upstairs to submit the online form she had already completed. Her stomach dropped when she clicked the button, but it gave her a bigger rush than she'd experienced in her fifteen years. This was happening, and it filled her with a surge of power and confidence. It surprised her how little resistance her father had given to the idea, but she had now submitted the form and paid the fee—he couldn't change his mind.

She closed her laptop, got up from her desk chair, and looked out the window. The giant man from the compact car at the end of her street was walking past their house, looking rather lost. He stopped at their garden steps and looked up at the house—at her. Weird.

She flopped back on her bed with a gigantic sigh, daydreaming about the event to come. Getting an invitation at all was a huge validation of everything she'd worked toward. She stared at her walls, pale pink and bedecked with dust jackets in place of posters.

Her eyes unfocused and her consciousness slipped, like falling asleep except different. Falling awake, maybe? Her pink walls darkened to lavender, as they sometimes did in the fading winter sunlight, but darkened faster still until they were a deep royal purple. The room pulsated with a strange energy, almost electric. Somehow, she was the nexus, and suddenly the universe blossomed from within her.

"I'm looking forward to meeting you, Veronica."

The words reverberated from everywhere and nowhere, spoken by a voice she didn't recognize. She could see nothing but a purple fog, but hints of an office with elaborate wainscoting swam through her vision. A tidy executive desk held a laptop, whose screen showed her own face. A distant wailing of terror rang out across her mind.

The scream panicked her out of her trance. She sat up so fast that she lost her balance for a moment. She gripped the edges of the mattress, worried that if she didn't, she might fall up to the ceiling. Her walls were pink again, even with the light outside still fading.

Oddly, she was more confused than frightened by the

event. The scene reminded her of her recent dreams, but she didn't think she had fallen asleep. Had she? Regardless, she grabbed a notebook and tried to sketch what she had seen. Bea was more the visual artist between them, but her quick drawing of the room she'd seen satisfied her. Maybe it would be enough to explain it to someone else. It also encouraged her to write a few words about it, possibly laying the foundation for a new story.

"Veronica, dinner in ten minutes, dear!" her mother called up the stairs.

"Coming, mummy," she replied. She repeated herself when she realized no sound had come from her on the first try.

Her legs trembled when she stood. As she passed the window toward the bedroom door, she thought she saw the large man lying on his back on the pavement near the garden gate.

The first pint disappeared in three large gulps, and Martin raised his hand for a refill. Taylor, ever the attentive barman, was already pulling another of the same for one of his favorite customers.

"You'll want to take this one slower, mate. It's not a race," Taylor said as a gentle warning. "Something the matter?"

"Dulling my wits," he replied. "At least the ones I haven't been scared out of." Taylor placed the fresh pint in front of him, and he took another mighty swig before continuing. "Taylor, how much do you know about The Duchess? Like really know?"

"She pays me well, and I like my job, but I try not to think about it much. After that other bother this past spring, it seemed safer not knowing."

"A wise approach, all things considered. Here's a helpful tip for you: never sneak up on her. She *really* doesn't like that."

Taylor leaned in close. "That's rather specific. Did something happen, sir?"

"Have you ever felt like your life was in danger?"

"Just once. That one night on the docks. God willing, that's the last time I'm that close to gunfire."

"Trust me. Knives are worse. You can see them coming." He took another sizable drink from his pint.

It didn't take Taylor long to figure it out, and he straightened up. "Right-ho. If you want my professional opinion, sir, finish that one and I'll pour you another, but you should stop there. There's no number of pints wot can make you forget. I find three is enough to make you stop caring."

"Cheers, that's good advice. I'm glad she pays you well, Taylor. You're worth every penny." He raised his glass in salute and downed the rest. His stomach churned from the rapid influx of bitter, so he resisted ordering his third yet. He studied the grain of the bar top, trying to erase the looped replay of the dagger in flight. Although he had been in her employ and good graces for over a year, he sometimes forgot how dangerous she could be.

The saloon doors behind the bar flew open with a crash, attracting everyone's attention. The Duchess had burst through them and was searching the crowd with a wild, unhinged eye. He was about to pull his coat over his face, but she'd already located him.

"Thank Christ you're still here. I need you upstairs right now. It's urgent. Beyond urgent."

"I was about to order another pint."

She came out from behind the bar and draped her arm over his shoulders. He refused to look up again.

"I'm so sorry, Martin. I shouldn't have done what I did. You didn't deserve it and you don't have to forgive me," she said, dropping her voice to a whisper, "but something happened upstairs, and I need to talk to you right away."

Her voice had an odd note to it. When he turned to question it, he saw fear and despair on her face, something he'd never seen before. "Taylor, could you make that pint to go, please?"

He followed her up the spiral stairs to her office. She plopped into her chair and poured a generous portion of scotch into a tumbler with shaking hands. He remained standing opposite her desk in case he required another hasty retreat.

"You look as though you've seen a ghost," he said. "That's a sharp turn from earlier."

"More like a ghost has seen me," she replied in a trembling voice.

"Not sure I follow."

"You know how we can sometimes see each other in our minds? I might have connected with someone else, but it wasn't right."

"Wasn't right? Is any of it?"

"Can you pause your sarcasm, please? I'm serious. I was musing on our young friend, and for a split second, I wasn't in my body anymore. Like someone else was driving. It was terrifying."

"That's never happened before?"

"Never, not even when we first met. I'm sure it lasted only seconds, but it was long enough to wonder if I'd ever return. I thought I'd died until I came back."

"Could Veronica have had something to do with it?"

"I couldn't say anything for sure. All I know is that I was thinking about her when it happened."

"This day keeps getting more unsettling by the minute."

"Don't leave tonight," she blurted. He guessed she was covering her fear with authority, because she softened her tone and tried again. "Please? Stay in the guest rooms if it would make you more comfortable. I don't want to be up here alone."

"You're well and truly frightened, aren't you?"

She nodded.

"Zaphod has enough kibble down to last him the evening. I can at least stick around until you get settled."

She hurried around the desk and squeezed him tight. He returned the embrace, not knowing what else to do. Her full turnaround from furious to vulnerable left him reeling, but he was determined to be here for her. Her breath warmed his chest, and he thought he felt the wetness of tears soaking into his shirt. She looked up at him, her gray-green eyes still damp.

"I'm so, so sorry," she said with a catch in her voice. "I hope you can forgive me." She raised her face to his and kissed him. Martin kissed her back, confused, but not displeased at the turn the evening had taken.

INTERLUDE: SYNCOPE

Geoff staggered to his feet and looked around with bleary eyes. The buzz of the just-illuminated streetlights burrowed through his ears and caused his head to throb. To say he felt disoriented would be insufficient. You might try discombobulated or bewildered, but they also belied his true state of mind. He tried to figure out where he was, why he was there, and who'd been driving the car that'd hit him. No one rushed to his aid, nor was anyone standing about looking guilty over having punched him in the ear. He tried to suss it all out, but his only reward was more pain.

"*What the fuck was that?*" he thought.

He walked back to the car, struggling to piece the events together. Memories eluded him, but he had to try. He remembered looking up at number 32, attempting to be inconspicuous and appear lost. He saw the girl in the window, and she had seen him. With his anonymity blown, he couldn't hang about any longer, so he turned for the car. Three steps later, all he could recall was falling before he blacked out. He weaved his way down the pavement to his car and fumbled with his keys more than once. Perhaps driving was a bad idea?

Stuffed into the driver's seat of his car, he decided, then made a phone call. The Duchess didn't answer her phone, which he found strange. When the voicemail answered, he left his message.

"It's Geoff. No news from the girl. I'm…er…not too well. I think I'll go home now. I'll check in tomorrow. Goodnight, ma'am."

That message would be his last word ever about what happened on Wofford Terrace that night.

CHAPTER FOUR

A CAPO IN B

Ian Waverly had been a salesman his entire career, but international travel was infrequent, to say the least. His work was almost exclusive to the Central London area, but it sometimes took him to exotic locations such as Dublin, Aberdeen, and Cardiff. Early in his career, he'd traveled to Las Vegas for a trade conference, but he loathed everything about it. He adored turning a bad idea into a good time, but Vegas was a bad idea factory suspended over an abyss of regret. The casino didn't hold his interest for long, so he spent the rest of the week in his room eating takeout.

Now engaged to Julia, traveling across borders was a regular occurrence, though he still wasn't used to it. She had taken him to Kingston to meet some of her extended family, and he thought he could get used to life in the Caribbean, apart from the odd hurricane. At present, they found themselves in the back of an average taxi speeding along the coastal road toward the center of Trieste. His first time in Italy was, thus far, unimpressive, lacking the grandeur of Rome or Venice. The coastal cities appeared tired and needed repair, but the mountains were picturesque. Through the trees on his right, he thought he saw the Gulf of Trieste. It was an overcast afternoon, though, making it almost impossible to differentiate the gray sea from the gray sky.

The scenery improved as they entered the center of the

city, dominated by the neoclassical architecture he expected from continental Europe. They drove past the *Piazza Unità d'Italia,* and she pointed out the Grand Hotel, where they would stay for the night. The driver took them around the block, delivered them to the front entrance, and helped them with their bags. She got them checked in and a bellhop took them to their room. As soon as he disappeared, they dropped their bags and started peeling clothing off one another. The one thing they never missed was a chance at christening a hotel room.

Later that evening, they dined at a local osteria walking distance between the hotel and Julia's meeting. Supper was delicious, but a tense quiet enveloped the small table. Ian hated silence, and it had never been a problem between them. Something had been bothering him throughout the trip, but he'd tried to ignore it since she told him about the change of plans. He distracted himself with packing and other preparations, but now that they were here, it wouldn't stay inside him any longer.

"Julia?" he asked.

She held up a finger and put down her fork. Mouth full, it would have been impolite to respond, but she nodded to let him know it was okay to ask.

"Is this dangerous?"

"Of course not. It's only grilled sole."

"Seriously?" he said in a huff. "You're as bad as Martin. I mean this job. This meeting. Should I be worried?"

"Sounds like you'd worry even if I said it's not," she said, taking another bite. He sensed she was avoiding this conversation.

"That implies that you think it is. I've always been able to see through your double-talk and you know it."

She put her fork down and looked him straight in the face. "OK, fine. It's an unknown, right? Unknowns always carry some risk, but you can avoid it if you're smart. The Duchess said they sounded serious, but patient. It's business, isn't it? It's a negotiation. Hell, if she knew you better, she might have sent you instead."

"In that case, we'd be sitting here having a lovely dinner, with the reverse of the same issue. Would you be worried if I were going instead of you?"

"To be honest, no."

"Thanks a lot."

"Don't read too much into this. It's a meeting in a cafe. A public place. You were probably in more danger when you pitched our security system to Owen."

He didn't reply, and though he wanted to stay angry, it's impossible to have a proper sulk over a *crème brûlée*. They completed their meal and walked along the waterfront.

"I'd wanted to go skiing, but this place is rather nice for an industrial city," he said.

"No offense, my love, but I prefer it to all that snow and ice," she replied.

"I've heard good things about the beaches around Dubrovnik."

"Nothing compares to the ones in Jamaica."

"I guess we'll have to see about that in July," he said, musing on their wedding to come.

"I promise to make it memorable."

They finished their walk at the hotel entrance. His worry resurfaced, and he didn't want to let her go.

"Come back soon," he said, and kissed her.

"I'll be back before you know it. It's just a meeting."

He hated watching her walk away, but this was her job, and

he had no choice. There was no way in hell he was going to relax in the hotel room, so he started walking the perimeter of the piazza. He did two laps before his legs had nearly given out and his feet felt like they were on fire. By the time he reached their room, his body was spent, but he couldn't take his mind off her, so he tried to settle down with the book he brought. It wasn't a remarkable book, but it had held his attention well enough on the flight down. Once he found the plot again, it changed his mind enough to stop thinking about his worry. He made it twenty-five pages in before the snoring started.

Julia walked into the cafe, looking around as she walked to the counter. The note instructed her to present herself here at 8:00, but said nothing about with whom she would be meeting. She ordered a simple cup of tea and surveyed the room. Conversations, lively but muted, filled the air almost as much as the warm scent of espresso. As she looked, she spotted a well-dressed older gentleman sitting alone, checking his watch every thirty seconds like, well…clockwork. There was no doubt he was awaiting someone, but whether it was her was a matter of chance. Her drink arrived, and she decided it was a chance she would take.

"May I join you?" she asked, her charm dialed to 11.

"I'm waiting for someone," he said in dismissal.

"I am someone. Perhaps it's me you're waiting for."

He squinted his eyes at her. "You are not the heiress."

"*Heiress,*" she thought. "*This is him.*" She called up the talking points she had discussed with her employer and got to work.

"No, I am not, but I represent Five Pence."

His eyes remained squinted, but she saw a tic in his cheek. "This is unacceptable."

"Sir, I assure you she is treating this with the utmost urgency, but she could not travel on such short notice. I am her second-in-command, and she has asked me to speak on her behalf. I am prepared to 'discuss the matter,' as you said in your letter, and it will be binding."

"You are her second? *Assurdo!*"

"She regrets she was unaware of any agreement regarding her business here, and would never have stepped on your toes, so to speak, if she had known. We are prepared to abide by your terms if you would let us see the contract."

"Contract? This was a gentleman's agreement, and you and your employer are no gentlemen. Her ignorance of it is no excuse."

His casual sexism rankled her, and she toughened her tone. "How can she agree to..."

"You will cease talking at once."

For the first time, he opened his eyes wide, conveying a seriousness she had never seen in her career. His statement was level and calm, but he stated it as a fact rather than a command. She tabled her line of inquiry and let him continue.

"I have informed your local leadership, bribed, threatened, and I have taken someone I assumed to be dear to the family, which was in error. If the young lady were important, I would be speaking with the heiress. Instead, she has disrespected me and her own family."

"Sir, no disre..."

He frowned, and the slight lowering of his head turned his face menacing. "I had not finished, and you will not interrupt me again, yes?"

She only nodded. This time, it had been a command, one she would obey. His threat was nonchalant, as if this were ordinary conversation. It wasn't fear that transfixed her as much as awe. He was accustomed to power and control, and she was altogether out of her depth with him. "*Dammit, Ian. You had to jinx this,*" she thought, fidgeting in her seat.

"My family does not abide disrespect, but my instinct tells me this was not intentional. My letter may not have communicated how grave I consider this to be, so we will give her one last chance." He leaned forward and lowered his voice. "Tell me something, *signorina*. Does she value you?"

She didn't speak. She was pretty sure she knew why he was asking, and the dread rendered her mute.

"A simple yes or no will do, my dear."

She rediscovered enough of her voice to say, "Yes, I am her second."

"Very well. I won't need to assume again."

The gesture he made was all but imperceptible, but she saw it. Before she could react, the men chatting at tables surrounding them had turned toward her. She had walked into a trap. She calculated her odds, and they were not good. The cafe was a landmark, historically significant, and presently packed with bystanders and witnesses. As long as they remained here, she was relatively safe. The only play she had left was to speak her mind, hoping someone might remember her.

"I understand," she said, "but..."

"Do not bother resisting or begging. It would be unbecoming of such a lovely young woman and I prefer not to cause a scene in my favorite cafe."

"I won't, but I would caution you. Don't underestimate The Duchess. She may have unknowingly crossed a line with you, but you are knowingly crossing a line with her."

"It's late and..."

"I had not finished," she said, throwing his threat back at him. "Whatever you think you understand about her, she will be here soon enough to show how wrong you are."

"Have you finished now?" the man said. He looked bored by her act of defiance.

"Yes, sir."

"Then allow me to make something clear as crystal to you, Miss..."

"Redmond, sir. Julia Redmond."

"Miss Redmond," he continued, "The Tessaro family has withstood monarchies and fascist governments, world wars and the European Union, and we continue to own Trieste. Whatever you believe your employer is capable of, it does not impress me. Now, if you would accompany us, our car is waiting."

It was a stormy night in Veronica's dreams early this Tuesday morning, literally. Dark, heavy storm clouds swirled in her subconscious, complete with the requisite lightning. Unusually, though, the lightning flashed in rainbow colors. A shocking orange bolt crossed her thoughts before a deep, foreboding red illuminated the cloud from behind. Ocean blues, royal purples, neon greens, and shimmering gold crackled through her imagination, but rather than thunder, she sensed the faintest traces of words, as if the lightning was murmuring to her.

A red flash mumbled about honor, while the orange bolt demanded she tremble before it. A purple sprite from the top of the cloud asked who she was, but the pulsing navy sky above just wanted to be left alone. The gold jet seemed late for something, but it couldn't remember what. The cloud condensed and drew in on itself like an explosion in reverse until all that remained were two figures sitting quietly in chairs, facing each other. One was black with white eyes, the other its opposite, like yin and yang.

"Help us," the black figure spoke with a sharp crack.

"Or don't. I don't care," the white figure said in a rumble.

Everything flashed in a brilliant yellow-white and her eyes opened to the beginnings of a sunny winter morning. She rolled over to her nightstand and grabbed her dream journal, jotting down everything she could remember.

"*This is going to make a brilliant story,*" she thought.

Bright light caused Ian to squint his still-closed eyes. It didn't add up why it had gotten so bright so suddenly, but it must mean that Julia had returned. His eyes opened a fraction to allow his pupils to adjust, and he prepared to greet his fiancée. When he could open his eyes, he saw the chandelier still glowing above, but its bulbs were not the only source. He realized the light was dawn streaming through the curtains, and he'd slept through the night. His book still rested on his chest as he lay atop the sheets in his clothes.

He groaned before croaking, "Blimey, I slept like the dead. When did you get in?"

When he turned left to greet her, there was no one there. Her side of the bed remained crisp and kempt, suggesting she hadn't come back.

"Julia?" he said, his meek call lost in the quiet emptiness of the suite. He sprang from the bed into the salon, but she was not there either. "Julia! Where are you, love?" he called, much louder this time.

He sprinted back to the bedroom and swiped his mobile off the nightstand, desperate to reach her. To hell with the international rates. Without a ring, the voicemail greeting started, but the voice that greeted him was not hers. He listened to the message, and the panic crawled up his spine.

The effort it took to remain upright was valiant, and he doubted he could maintain it for long. He needed to contact The Duchess, but he had no contact information for her. He flipped to his favorites and mashed his thumb on Martin's face. The line rang four times without an answer. Ian was about to end the call and retry when he heard a click and his friend's hoarse voice.

"Hullo? Ian?"

"Martin, where are you?"

"I was sleeping. It's…what time is it?" he said. Shuffling noises crackled through the speaker. "5:30 in the morning. What's going on?"

"I need you to call The Duchess right now. I'd call her, but I don't have the number."

"What? Why?"

"They took her, Martin. These bastards in Italy have taken my Julia."

"You must be joking."

"Do I sound like I'm joking?" he yelled. "Tell her to call Julia's phone. She'll get everything she needs, then have her call me right after. I need to know what to do. If they hurt her, I'm afraid I'll go mad. At dinner, I told her this was a bad idea. Damn her misguided sense of duty to that awful woman!"

"Settle down, mate. I'll get right on it. Don't worry, she always knows what to do," Martin said, and disconnected.

Ian set his mobile back on the nightstand and tried to calm his heaving breaths. He dashed to the bathroom when he realized that wasn't all he was heaving.

The wave crashed on the beach as Francesca basked in the sun's warmth. She sipped at a drink brimming with fruit and nodded her appreciation to the young, fit waiter who had brought it. A gentle puff of breeze blew her hair back as another wave curled over. She found it incongruous, though, that when this wave collapsed onto itself, there was not a satisfying burst of white noise. This one crashed with a cacophony of bells. The next wave in sequence did the same, and her eyes opened to find herself sprawled out in her king-sized bed, her mobile ringing on the bedside table. She rubbed the sleep out of her eyes and squinted through the morning blur. Without her glasses, she could nearly make out Martin's name on the screen.

"You woke me out of a lovely dream, you know," she said.

"There's an emergency, Duchess," Martin announced, sounding worried.

"If there's something wrong with the servers, I don't see how it merits waking me up. Oh, and by the way, good morning to you, too."

"Ian just called me from Trieste. Julia has disappeared."

"I must have misheard you. It sounded like you said Julia has gone missing."

"That's what he told me. He's a complete wreck."

She sat up fast, fumbling in her nightstand drawer for something with which to take notes. "Now, that is an emergency. What precisely did he say?"

"He said that you should call her mobile, then call him. He needs you to tell him what to do. Here's the number."

She scrawled Ian's number on her notepad. "Thank you, Martin. I'll take care of it right away," she said, and rang off. She gathered herself up, put on her glasses, grabbed her keys, and ran to the lift. Still in her pajamas, she emerged on the office level and ran to her desk. On the secure line, she dialed Julia's number. Her voicemail answered without a ring, and the greeting started in a male voice.

Greetings, Duchessa. Yes, we are now aware of your alias. It is most unfortunate that we did not meet as discussed. Your friend Julia is safe for now, but her continued well-being depends on you. You will meet us in two days' time at the same location and time as before. You...they...will not get another chance. Do not be late. If you'd like, you may leave your response after the tone.

She hung up the line and thought, taking several minutes to process what she'd heard. A wheel of emotions spun in her mind, crossing anger, guilt, revenge, sadness, until it landed on self-doubt. How had she misinterpreted the message so badly? It had so obviously been a threat. She'd put her in tremendous danger, thinking this was merely business, but perhaps that was a vain hope. With Owen out of her hair, she had removed the element of the criminal from her empire, or so she'd thought. Perhaps she had in England, but in Trieste, these were sins of a grandfather she'd never known come to haunt her present.

"A duchess does not dwell. She acts," she thought, and picked up the phone once more.

"Ian, it's The Duchess."

"They took her!" he wailed.

"I realize that, Ian, and I'm sorry. I made an error in judgment and I'm sorry."

"What do we do? How do we get her back?"

"*You* are to do nothing. I will contact the hotel and extend your stay. You will wait for me to arrive. I need to know everything you know."

"Nothing!" he shouted. "I fell asleep, and I woke up this morning with no Julia! There! You know everything I know. Are you fucking satisfied?"

"Shut up!" she commanded. "The only reason I am talking to you right now is because you are important to Julia and Martin, who mean more to me than you ever will." The silence on the line told her she'd gotten through to him, so she continued. "You may be justified in being angry with me, but it solves nothing. I don't give a damn if you forgive me, but you have to trust me."

"I'll help however I can, but there's no chance of the other," Ian said.

"Stay right where you are. You needn't leave the room, and you may order as much room service as you'd like. I'll be there soon to handle my mess in person, as I should have done from the start."

CHAPTER FIVE

MEA CULPA, SORT OF

Martin was still only half awake when the taxi dropped him at Farnborough Airport. He swigged the last of his cappuccino as he stood in front of a terminal building that looked like someone had built it fifty years in the future. The sun wasn't due up for at least an hour, so he stood shivering in the dark outside the entrance, his breath billowing out and mixing in with the fog. *"Hell of a time to fly,"* he thought, and forced himself to go inside. Before he'd taken five steps inside, a man, far too cheerful for the time of day, assailed him, grasping for the small duffel bag he carried. He recoiled by instinct.

"I'm dreadfully sorry if I startled you, sir," the man said, trying to relax him. "I'm the concierge. Which flight are you taking today?"

"Uh..." he uttered, grammar dying on his coffee-coated tongue.

"Are you certain this is your airport, sir?" the man asked.

He thought he detected a note of condescension in the smarmy man's voice. At first, he took offense to his implication that he didn't belong here, but a quick look at his graphic t-shirt, dingy hoodie, and baggy jeans suggested the concierge may have had a point.

"I think it is. The Duchess told me to be..."

The man cut him off. "Ah yes, sir! Your party is awaiting you in the upstairs lounge. I'll take your bag."

"Cheers," he said, and looked around.

"Just up these stairs behind me, sir. You'll see the way. Have a splendid flight."

He plodded up the stairs—his legs were sore from the gym he had joined only last week—and followed the signs to the lounge. The terminal was all but vacant, having only opened fifteen minutes prior. It stood in stark contrast to a 24-hour ant farm like Heathrow, but he guessed these were some of the unadvertised perks of wealth. As he continued past shuttered kiosks, a familiar voice rose above the silence, and he increased his pace toward it.

He rounded a partition wall and spotted Taylor, who was engaged in a heated debate with The Duchess. She looked displeased, but otherwise bright as a button. She wore a lilac skirt suit, with the jacket unbuttoned revealing a pale green blouse beneath, and her hair done up in an efficient bun. Geoff, her gigantic, taciturn bodyguard, stood at her side as always, looking fit to burst out of his gray suit. Two unfamiliar shifty looking men, also besuited, stood behind him, staring him down as he approached. All of them had dressed impeccably despite the early hour, making his shabby attire stand out even worse. The only other exception was Taylor, whose curly hair stuck out wildly from under a slouchy knit cap which clashed brilliantly with his plaid flannel overshirt.

"Martin, glad you could join us. Bit late, aren't you?" The Duchess said as a curt greeting—all business.

"Taxi driver was in no particular hurry. Sorry."

"No matter," she replied, "we'll get right to it, then." She pointed back toward the stairwell and led the group down. He and Taylor lagged behind the other four.

"I guess we missed the memo about the dress code," Taylor said, commiserating.

"Quite," he replied through a yawn. "Have you done this before?"

"Never once. Feeling right out of place here."

"What's this all about, anyway?"

"Dunno, but The Duchess kept talking about Julia. She's in a frightful mood."

"Too right. Late last night, she called saying to be at Farnborough by 7:00 this morning with a couple days' worth of clothes. That was it. I didn't even know this airport existed until I looked it up! You know how she can be."

"Well...I don't, really. She's never asked me to do anything outside The Cathedral. It's my first field trip, so to speak."

He nodded, and they continued following the group ahead. The front group pushed through the doors with purpose, not holding them open for the stragglers. They walked across the concrete apron a considerable number of yards, and Martin gawked like a young man in a confectionery. Aviation had always fascinated him, and he had once considered trying to become a commercial pilot, but the responsibilities were overwhelming for his nervous disposition. The acrid scent of jet exhaust hung heavy under the fog, but something about it always entranced him. They passed under the tail of a larger model and saw their destination.

He admired the sharp nose cone and the aggressive sweep of the sleek business jet. Her livery was two-tone: silver on her belly and a much darker color on the top. In the dark, it appeared black, but the bright apron lights above reflected in metallic amethyst. The vertical stabilizer displayed three purple, spear-like flowers tied in a bundle near the base of their stems.

"Oi, hurry up!" Taylor called from the base of the stairs. He jogged to meet his friend and boarded the jet. It was his first time flying anything but coach, so the level of luxury stunned him. The interior was subdued elegance, with light wood and first-class seating upholstered in deep plum leather.

"Martin, you and Sebastian will sit in the rear seats," The Duchess declared. "I need to confer with my associates during the flight. I will brief you both before we arrive."

Although it communicated all the information it needed to, her statement pierced him. It was devoid of the trademark smugness or even playfulness their banter often contained. It was a dismissal, as if he were an unwelcome burden. "*You asked me to be here,*" he thought, growing bitter. He sat in the seat opposite Taylor, who was beaming.

"This is my first time flying," he said, almost bouncing in his seat. The sulk he'd intended to have when he sat down would have to wait, because he would never miss a chance to live vicariously through someone else's first flight. They talked through taxi, takeoff, and climb, with him explaining every bump and clunk. Taylor was awestricken, watching the sun rise over the Alps to the east. When dawn broke, the seat belt sign went out with a chime. The Duchess wasted no time unfastening her belt and walked to the front of the cabin to address the crew.

"Gentlemen, welcome aboard The Silver Speedwell," she announced with the practiced voice of a veteran flight attendant. "Our destination today, as many of you know, is Trieste, Italy. What you may not know is that we are executing a rescue mission. It will require the utmost delicacy and precision. Each of you aboard today will have a crucial role to play in the next 24 hours. For those of you unaccustomed to this type of work, I won't sugar-coat it for you: this *will* be dangerous. We have very little information about our adversaries, but whomever they are, they have Julia and one other person as hostages."

He gasped, eliciting a raised eyebrow in warning from her before she continued.

"I have discussed plans with Geoff and his team, but I expect you gentlemen in the back are wondering why you're here. Your tasks will be simple, but you may need to adapt to rapid changes in conditions. Martin, you will go to the Grand Hotel to collect Ian. He's been a shambles since Tuesday morning and he's going to need a friend. Mostly, I need you to keep him out of my way. Sebastian, this also involves Five Pence, and few people possess your level of context regarding our shipping business. Go to my office in the city and search the files for any abnormal payments, correspondence, or anything unusual in the months since we've started shipping coffee. My local office manager will assist you."

"You can count on us," Taylor offered.

She frowned and glared at Taylor. "Unnecessary sentiment, Sebastian. If I doubted your capability, I would not employ you." She continued addressing the entire cabin. "Whatever your tasks, you will return to the airport by midnight, ready to depart at a moment's notice. You will follow my instructions to the letter without question. Fail in your mission or to follow instructions, and you will not be returning to London. There is zero margin for error in this endeavor, so no improvising. Am I clear?"

"Yes, ma'am," the crew said in unison, but he shot a panicked glance at Taylor.

"I don't envy those other lads, whatever they're doing," Taylor said. "Sounds like we got the safe jobs."

After he had knocked, he heard footsteps running up to the entryway and hands fumbling at multiple locks. The door opened, and Ian stood behind it with a wild, unhinged demeanor.

"Martin?" he yelped, "The fuck are you doing here?"

"Good to see you too, Fee. You don't look so good."

"I'm going out of my mind, thank you very much. That blasted Duchess has left me here alone for two days and has told me absolutely nothing! It's been radio silence."

"She does sort of do that. Can I come in?"

"Oh," Ian said, realizing that he'd torn straight into his friend in the hallway. "Yeah, sorry."

He followed his friend into the now-disheveled suite. Takeout boxes littered the room, and drawn curtains hid the view for which one paid extra. His friend was in obvious distress, and it was his job to help him, but he had so little to tell him, despite the brief briefing.

"So, er," he said, hesitating because he wanted to treat the situation with care, "what happened?" He winced right after the words came out, knowing he had been anything but delicate. Ian took a sharp breath and he braced for impact.

"We came down here for this business-whatever, and the damned Duchess sent Julia to her meeting, because it was supposed to be simple. We went to a lovely dinner, and we split up. I woke up Tuesday morning, and she wasn't here. I called her mobile, and I got this. JUST LISTEN!"

Ian played the message on speaker, and a chill overtook him. Telephones had always rather freaked him out—horror movies, he guessed—but this took it to a new level.

"No wonder you've been out of your mind!" he exclaimed. "She's told you nothing else since Tuesday?"

"Bugger all, and I'm furious about it." Ian replied.

"Listen, Fee, I can't say I grasp all the reasons she does what she does. I've never known her to do anything *without* a reason, though. Maybe she thought you might bollocks it up somehow if you had more information. I dunno. I'm only guessing."

"It's good to know you both think so highly of me. So, what do you know about all of this? She must have told you something."

"Not much. We're here to rescue her, though. I say 'we,' but she told me that my only job here is to keep you company. I couldn't say what help I'd be other than that, if I'm honest."

"I suppose it's not nothing," Ian said with a resigned exhale. "I need a drink."

"Dude, it's 10:30 in the morning."

"That late already?"

"Why don't we start with a bit of breakfast first?"

"Good idea. I love mimosas."

"You may be missing the point."

"God, I hope not."

"When was the last time you had a shower?"

"Not long after we got here. We both needed a shower after we..."

"Okay, okay! I get the picture. You go clean yourself up and I'll order a tray."

The cafe glowed with a golden, almost sepia tone. The sights, sounds, and smells gave Francesca a disconcerting sense of déjà vu. Since she'd met Martin, and they'd tapped into whatever their gifts were, occasions like this led to uncomfortable questioning. Was it a simple feeling, a premonition, someone else's vision, or some actual memory long forgotten?

No, no more psychoanalysis today. The facts of the matter were plain. She was here for a purpose, and she would do her job.

She was a bit early for the meeting, so she walked straight to the counter and ordered the signature drink of the city: a *Capo in B.* As a frequent visitor to Trieste, she was familiar with all the local customs, especially where coffee was concerned. Her drink was exquisite, and she wanted to learn the secrets of it, but later. There were more important things to consider.

The person or persons who had taken Julia and threatened her business were still a mystery, and that irked her. Regardless, she was determined to gain the upper hand, as she always did. The darker parts of her business brought her no joy, but success was paramount, especially now. She thought back to the words of the advisers who had raised her after her parents died, warning her not to get close to people, lest her enemies use them against her. It never sat well with her. In her heart, she still felt the risk was worth taking.

She noted an older gentleman in the main salon, sitting alone and appearing deeply engrossed in his thoughts. He wore a tailored charcoal gray suit, his silver-streaked hair styled to perfection. Though he must be old enough to be her father, she found him handsome. No, that wasn't quite right—distinguished would be a better descriptor. His mouth turned down at the corners in a sort of contemptuous frown. He looked annoyed to be here. This was no doubt her adversary, but hastening the confrontation was of no benefit. His only advantage at present was that he'd discovered her name, so she waited and used her anonymity to monitor his movements and manners.

His guards were there, as she knew they would be. Anytime

someone included the words "come alone" in a threat, it was certain they themselves would not. It impressed her to a small extent that she could not pinpoint them, but she picked a couple of likely candidates at tables close to him. This was the part of the game she relished. It was chess, albeit with an unconventional board, and he was no amateur. Observation and intuition had run their courses, so the time had come.

"Good evening, *signore,*" she said as she sat at his table, not waiting for the invitation.

"Do I know you?"

"You know my business and have met two of my friends. I am The Duchess."

"*Duchessa,*" he said. "You look nothing like your father."

"I take more after my mother, a tremendously kind woman."

"Your sister resembles your father much more. It is how I discovered her identity."

"Sir, I am here to talk business, not genetics."

"I prefer to discuss history, of which you seem to know nothing. As I told your Julia, ignorance of your family's agreements does not excuse you from them."

"For the moment, let's ignore how unreasonable of a statement that is. I'm curious about this agreement that I am supposed to be aware of. Please enlighten me. You also have me at a loss, sir. Who are you?"

He took obvious offense to her question. "I am Giovanni Tessaro, head of the Tessaro family. You must know of us, yes?"

"I'm afraid I do not, sir."

"*Assurdo!* All this time, you have done business in Trieste and have never heard our name?" He sighed. "It is no matter. I will make many things clear to you, my dear. After the second war, your grandfather, Ljubomir, came to Trieste. He had nothing. The war had taken so much from him. My father financed his affairs for some time while he established himself, cashing in on his old meaningless title. He was a man of his word, however, and paid his debts with us. There was a long peace, even friendship between our families, and we shared much. I remember meeting your father when we were both boys." He paused, lost in memory. "Your father was cruel, even at that tender age. I sensed it in him."

"When was this agreement made?"

"When Stjepan established Five Pence in our port in 1972. He was young and headstrong but posed no real threat to our primary businesses. My father allowed him to trade here in honor of your grandfather, provided he did not encroach on our imports and paid his tithe to his benefactors."

"He paid you for what?"

"Protection. Gratitude. Port tax. Call it what you will. To your own credit, Five Pence has never missed a payment, and we are thankful for your continued patronage."

"Had I known where that 'Port Tax' was going, I might have agreed to meet you on friendlier terms."

"We are still friends, of course. I hope you realize we have done everything according to the rules of business here, and we are not your enemies."

"Continue," she said.

"Your new market has changed the balance. The coffee trade from East Africa is our top import, and we have supplied not only Trieste, but all of Europe for decades. It forced us to act under the agreement your father made those years ago."

"Giovanni—may I call you Giovanni? My father died when I was eight years old. I knew nothing of business or any agreements at that point in my life. When I took control of Five Pence, there were no terms or conditions in any of our files regarding our business affairs here. For months after graduating from business school, I pored over the documentation, trying to familiarize myself with the business I had inherited. I continued to pay the Port Tax because it was reasonable to do so. I did not mean for the coffee imports to compete with anyone's trade. It is an interest of mine, and my intent was to keep quantities small."

"I appreciate the unenviable position you are in, my dear. I do, but the terms were clear. You have crossed the line and it cannot be uncrossed. You will cease the operations of Five Pence in Trieste at once, or you will force us to exact payment from your friends."

She recognized the veiled threat but ignored it. Hostages were dirty business regardless, but he struck her as reasonable, and she thought could work with him.

"I suggest a counterproposal. I will cease all trade in *coffee* through this port and abide by all terms of the agreement henceforth, with my humblest apologies. To prove my sincerity, I will offer you twelve percent in Port Tax. Would that be sufficient atonement?"

"That is a generous offer, *Duchessa,* but I am afraid it is not possible. More than business is at stake here. This is about honor. It is not a class they teach at your Oxford, yes? You will close Five Pence or we close it for you. I will allow you until this time tomorrow to deliver your answer."

"Can you assure me of the safety of your 'guests'?"

His face turned serious.

"Did you not hear me? This is about honor, and you have questioned mine. Do not disrespect me in my city, child!"

"I meant no disrespect, but I am also no stranger to these

sorts of proceedings. Would you allow me to talk to Julia? A gesture of your honor and good faith between us may improve outcomes for everyone."

"You are wise for your age. Something I could never teach my son. *Alessio, il mio cellulare.*"

A man on her right broke off from his conversation, sipped his espresso, and turned toward them. "*Buona sera, Duchessa,*" he said and handed a mobile phone to Giovanni.

"This is my son, Alessio. He is a good boy, but I fear he conducts himself more like your father than myself."

She appraised him to be about her own age, in his late thirties, perhaps. Beneath his expression of utter fealty to his father, there was a diabolic sharpness to his features. She recognized the air of overconfidence and privilege in his attire, with gold chains swinging from his partially unbuttoned shirt. He looked her over, sneered, and returned to his conversation.

Giovanni started the call and issued casual commands to his associates. She tried to eavesdrop on the conversation, but her Italian was terrible, and Trieste had a dialect unto itself. Only a few words connected before he offered her the mobile.

"Two minutes I give, and you will keep the conversation friendly, yes?"

"Naturally," she agreed, taking the phone and pressing it to her ear. "Julia, are you there?"

"Yes, ma'am, I'm here."

"What's your condition?"

"I'm unharmed. They have treated me well, all things considered."

"I'm happy to hear that. I know someone else who will be, too."

"Tell him I'm sorry, will you?"

"Of course. This is all a right spanner, eh?"

"Wrenched it up good," Julia responded, acknowledging the code phrase.

She was betting on them all being reasonably fluent in English, or at least enough to assume they weren't attempting to do exactly what they were now doing. They'd cultivated their code through the years of working together, using a mix of rhyming slang, pidgin, and handpicked nonsense. Through their puzzling conversation, Julia told her everything she could about where they'd taken her. It wasn't enough on its own, but she was sure she could work with it.

At the two-minute mark, he took his device back.

"Thank you for allowing that. My apologies to you and your family for not giving this matter the proper personal attention. I will give you my answer tomorrow as we agreed. Perhaps in the future, we could work together."

"If all else were equal, we would welcome the chance, but this is not so. You are a shrewd businesswoman, and I respect that. The other houses would not respect our leadership if we made an exception now."

"A pity. History is rewritable, Giovanni. Please give my counteroffer careful consideration. It could prove most lucrative for you. You could request the same of all your beneficiaries were you to accept."

She saw his eyes shift to his son for less than a blink, but she could tell she had him thinking. *"Honor is currency here, but Euros spend much easier,"* she thought.

"I bid you good evening," he said, as a formal dismissal from the conversation.

She stood, nodded deferentially to the Tessaros, and walked out of the cafe. Geoff emerged from the shadows and walked beside her. "To the Speedwell, Geoff. We have plans to make."

"You can handle this, yes?" his supervisor asked with a dip of his head. Marco knew this meant there was but one acceptable answer.

"Yes, sir. No problem."

"Your relief will arrive at midnight. You know what to do."

"I won't let you down."

"Good man. See you tomorrow night," the supervisor said, and left for the evening.

The assignment was quite simple: check the perimeter every half-hour and see to the needs of the guests. He had worked security for Tessaro for two years now, but this was a big step up. The elder Tessaro trusted him, and he was a man he dared not disappoint. He tried not to think too hard about why the guests were bound to their chairs, because that was well above his pay grade.

One woman spoke Italian, and he had a brief conversation with her when he brought them both dinner. She only asked to be released once, and he apologized to her for the situation, but she seemed to understand and appreciate his kind treatment. The other woman spoke little, except to ask to be escorted to the lavatory. He guessed she was still in some kind of shock, but she kept watching the door like she was waiting for someone.

The hours neither flew by nor dragged—it was just another night working the warehouse. He passed time scrolling on his phone until he heard a metallic squeak. Was that the door? He checked his watch, but the next shift wasn't due for another fifty minutes. Maybe they got bored and came in early? Had he remembered to latch it when he came in from his rounds? Of course he had. He was green, but he wasn't stupid. He should check it out, but since he was alone, he got his gun out, just in case.

"Massimo, is that you?" he called as he exited the small office. The door creaked, much more open than when he'd left it. He skulked up to it, back against the wall, peering through the dim light. When he reached the door, he closed it with a heavy clank, and a thick arm wrapped around his throat from behind. Another hand closed over his pistol and wrested it from his grip. It all happened so fast that he didn't have time to exclaim his surprise.

"Where are the others?" The voice was growly and, although Marco was not short, it still came from above him. He tried to answer, but the sound that escaped his throat resembled the one bees make when they're displeased about being gargled.

"*Where?*" the voice repeated, and the arm loosened its grip just enough to allow him to speak.

"Midnight," he croaked, his larynx half-smashed.

"It's just you?"

He tried to nod, but the arm squeezed tighter.

"Give this note to your boss," the voice said, stuffing something in his jacket. "Nighty-night."

The blow to the head didn't knock him out completely, but in the dark blur, all he could see was movement. He knew whoever it was would take the women, but he was powerless to stop him now. There would be hell to pay—fired at a minimum—but he figured a quick nap while he waited for his replacements was a splendid idea.

As midnight approached, Martin and his best friend were, to put it mildly, smashed. Ian's thought process was thus: since

The Duchess was footing the bill, and she owed him for pain and suffering, why not take his recompense from her in the form of some very good alcohol? He hadn't protested in the slightest, but insisted they have some food delivered as well, lest they hurt themselves. The meal was unsurpassed, and champagne flowed as champagne does when one is celebrating. They toasted everything under the sun, none more than the purple-tinged cavalry come to save the day. The night had gotten late and neither of them were regular champagne drinkers, so both experienced that moment of drunken introspection, wondering whether they had gone too far. Before he could decide, his mobile rang.

"Hellllo?" he slurred, his tongue sticking to the roof of his parched mouth.

"Didn't I tell you to be prepared?" The Duchess chided. "You're drunk."

"I'm only tipsy," he lied. "Ian's drunk."

"There will be a car waiting for both of you downstairs. You will be in it and en route to the airport in twenty minutes, or I will leave you behind."

"Twenty? That's barely enough time to pack." Sobriety and its friend adrenaline came crashing back into his brain, bringing a dull throb with them.

"I suggest you get started if you'd like a ride back to London. However you sober up, do it fast." The call disconnected.

"We've got fifteen minutes to get out of here, Fee, or we pay our own way home. Duchess's orders."

Ian sat up straight from the bed and ran into the bathroom. Some rather unpleasant noises followed, so he started grabbing anything that didn't belong to the hotel and jamming it into Ian's suitcase. Julia hadn't unpacked; she'd only changed from her travel clothes to business attire, so her bags were easy.

Fourteen minutes later, they stumbled through the lobby, luggage akimbo. A man stood outside the main entrance holding a sign with the name Alcott on it, and they piled in.

"Hold on, *signori,* this will be a fast trip!" the driver said. The tires barked, and they tore through the deserted streets of Trieste. He focused on his breathing as much as possible, trying to hold the contents of his stomach where they belonged. Ian snored in the seat beside him and he cursed his friend's unconsciousness out of sheer jealousy. Twenty-eight minutes and a lot of jostling later, the car screeched to a halt in front of the departures entrance of Trieste Airport. He started digging for his wallet to tip the driver, but the man stopped him.

"No trouble, *signore. La Duchessa,* she has paid me well to get you here. You must hurry!"

"Cheers," he replied, bobbling the suitcases. Ian sprang from the taxi like a man reborn, somehow carrying the rest of the cargo. They were aiming for the main entrance of the terminal when he recognized a man standing next to the door as one of Geoff's team. The man recognized him in return, motioned for them to follow him, and they ran down the concourse to a gate in the chain-link fence. He thought it strange that this unremarkable gate should have a guard, but there he stood. The sentry let them through, nodding to their escort as they ran through. He contemplated how thoroughly different this experience was from their departure from London as they ran across the apron.

"Right on time, gentlemen. Well done," The Duchess said, turning to their escort. "Gustav, throw their luggage in the hold. Our other guests should arrive forthwith. When they do, we'll need to be on our way promptly."

The wiry man grabbed their belongings, flung them through the open cargo door, and closed it. Martin was halfway up the airstairs when Ian shouted, "Julia!" He did a quick about-face, having to grab the handrail to steady himself. He saw Geoff and his colleague running across the tarmac, with Julia and another woman whom he didn't know trailing the men, struggling to keep pace.

"GO!" The Duchess shouted. "We'll have time for reunions once we're in the air."

The crew hustled up the stairs, startling Taylor, who was already aboard and half-asleep in his seat.

"Take any seat and prepare for immediate takeoff," she ordered.

The Silver Speedwell was airborne when his adrenaline wore off. The stress of the race to the airport and the G-forces of takeoff caused him to dash to the lavatory, ignoring the seat belt sign. He clung to the vacuum toilet in nauseous agony for what seemed an hour.

"That much champagne was a poor choice."

The voice behind him caught him unawares, and his head banged against the cabinet with a hollow thud as he turned to find her standing in the doorway. With the job completed and their getaway assured, she showed concern for him, a marked departure from only minutes ago. The Duchess was off duty.

"It was the car ride over that got me," he said, wiping his mouth with his sleeve. "Not sad to be rid of it, though."

She reached into an upper cabinet and grabbed a hand towel. She wet it in the sink, wrung it out, and dabbed his forehead with it.

"I'll get you some still water from up front. The pilots said it should be a smooth flight home, so try to make it back to your seat soon. I have to debrief the team."

"Thanks."

She turned to leave, but paused and said, "I'm sorry if I've been brusque, especially with you."

"No harm done that I didn't do to myself."

"I'll explain it all soon. Take your time," she said, closing the door behind her.

He cleaned up and returned to his seat when he felt ready. Taylor drowsed in the seat opposite him, while The Duchess huddled with Geoff and his team near the front of the cabin. Ian and Julia sat on the plush sofa across the aisle, wrapped around each other in joyous relief, and the other woman they had run up with sat next to them, staring straight ahead. He thought she might be in shock.

"Excuse me, miss. Are you all right?" he asked her.

"I...eh..." she muttered, fluttering her eyes in confusion and realization. He presumed her adrenaline had also worn off.

Before he could ask further questions, The Duchess plopped onto the sofa between the lovebirds and the stranger.

"Do you speak English?" she asked the woman.

"Some."

"Are you all right?"

"No."

"I didn't expect you would be. What's your name?"

"Tajana," she said.

"Lovely to meet you at last, Tajana. I expect we have some catching up to do, but that's for later."

"Duchess, who is this person?" he asked.

"If dear Giovanni is to be believed, Tajana is my sister. Well, half-sister, at any rate."

"Buh...wha..."

"It's unlikely that things will become any clearer now, especially after a couple of intense days. Let's all get some sleep, and we'll sort it out tomorrow."

PART TWO

Indigo Children are children who are believed to possess unusual or supernatural traits or abilities. Some believe that these gifted children are upgraded blueprints of humanity—reincarnated souls that came to earth to challenge old ideas and better all of humankind.

CHAPTER SIX

FAMILY MATTERS

It was clear Giovanni had underestimated her, even despite Julia's warning. She was smarter than Stjepan, more savvy. Worse yet, she played him, and that was difficult to do. The invaders did limited damage to the warehouse, except for the door's lock. The guard was alive, but someone had knocked him unconscious. "*She must not care for the dirty work. That may be useful,*" he thought. Alessio was across the warehouse in an obvious rage, which worried him. He assumed he would grow out of it, but he'd only become more impulsive, vengeful, and cruel. He walked toward his son, disappointed.

"Release him, son. He has told you what he knows."

"But he has not told me what I want to know," Alessio replied. He continued to hold the guard's fingers at an unnatural angle.

"Did you consider that he never saw the intruders?"

"If that is true, he failed at his job and he is of no use to us," he said, and pulled a gun from his waistband.

Though he was nearing seventy years, his mind was sharper than ever, and his reflexes were still quick. He snatched the pistol from his son's hand before he could bring it to bear.

"Fool! I know this man's family, and he has been loyal to us. You will not damage my ears with that vulgar thing in this warehouse."

"Why would you spare this trash?"

"Because the men who did this were professionals, and he

is a mere guard. It would be like you playing football against school children. He is not a failure. I put him in the wrong league." He turned to the young guard who cowered on the floor. "Go home, Marco."

The guard ran out through the destroyed door, clutching his injured hand.

Alessio leaned close to his father. "You've gone soft, papa."

He slapped the back of his son's head. "It is not soft to understand what a man is capable of and forgive him for not being more!" He lowered his voice and continued, "Yes, he failed, but did he not try? The failure is mine. We know so little of this woman, so I relied on my instinct."

"Your instinct was wrong! She has taken our only leverage."

"Her business does not operate as ours does, so I assumed she would concede. I did not think she could find the hostages, let alone try to take them. If I had, poor Marco would not have been their only protection. She is audacious, but leaders admit their mistakes and do not repeat them."

"As you did not repeat the mistake of abducting the wrong woman?"

He glared at his son. "You would do well to hold your tongue, Alessio. I did *not* repeat my mistake, and it brought the heir to us. She is a worthy adversary, but we will prevail as we always have."

"If you had let me run this operation, I..."

"If you had run it, this warehouse would be overrun with more police than I could bribe. You are old enough, but you are not yet wise. Show me wisdom and I will reconsider."

He walked out through the rusty old door, leaving his son to consider his words, but he had some reflection of his own to do. He climbed into the backseat of his car and told the driver to take him home. As they got onto the main highway, he rolled his neck and rubbed his forehead. He'd shown strength to his son in the warehouse because it seemed to be all he understood, but he wasn't wrong, either. He made uncharacteristic mistakes with his handling of the situation. It wasn't his age—he refused to believe that. He concluded it was more plausible that Trieste had become predictable and peaceful over the years through his leadership. No one dared challenge them for decades, so maybe he'd forgotten how to defend the throne. The dynamics of control hadn't changed since Stjepan started Five Pence over forty years ago, so it seemed fitting that it would now be another Nikolić entering the game.

And what to do about Alessio? He was in his late thirties now, so hope was diminishing for him to have an epiphany and mature into the leader he needed to be. As it was, he possessed neither the temperament nor the acumen to run the family anywhere but into the ground. Alessio was his only son. His wife blessed him with a daughter first, but he was proud of them both in different ways. Vittoria was smart like him, and beautiful like her mother, but she'd fallen in love with academics and science, and held no interest in the family name. If his confidence in Alessio was gone, what would become of their legacy and stature?

The future couldn't concern him right now. He reread the note that they'd left with Marco, the guard, at the warehouse.

I regret we were unable to come to another arrangement, but in my world, taking hostages is an ineffective negotiating tactic. Now that the playing field is even, I sincerely apologize for disrupting the status quo. I have ordered all inbound coffee shipments to be returned to their respective points of origin until

I can make other arrangements. Not one bean will pass through Trieste under the Five Pence banner again.

My offer of 12% remains valid, and I welcome the opportunity to do business with you in the future.

Regards,

La Duchessa

He wasn't sure what bothered him more about the note. Was it that his only leverage over her was gone, or was it that her offer made sense? Allowing exceptions to a contract could prove fatal to his reputation, but as he'd told her, there was no contract—only an agreement. He believed her sincerity in her lack of awareness, and he regretted that there was no written contract, but that was not how the port functioned long ago.

No, Five Pence would close, and he knew how to do it. Once they'd shut down, he'd be able to use the additional berths for his own fleet. The car continued up into the hills as Giovanni called the police.

Francesca carried the lattes with great care down the grand staircase to Level D. She had checked in on her guest several times since returning to London, but each time she had either been asleep or staring at the walls, possibly catatonic. It was an act of pure optimism bringing the coffee this time, but she had a hunch her sister would be ready for it. She knocked, but as with each time before, she received no reply. She pushed the door open a crack and noticed that the lights were on. Her guest sat on the edge of the bed, staring out the gothic arched window.

"Good morning," she said with a soft, kind lilt.

No reaction. She stepped closer and saw the woman's nose twitch, sniffing the air before inhaling deeply.

"Yirgacheffe," she said.

"That's right."

"Medium-dark roast. It is single source?"

"Incredible. Right again."

"A lot of studying."

"May I sit?"

Her guest nodded, and she handed her a steaming mug before sitting. They sat quietly watching the clouds for several minutes, savoring the brew, before Francesca broke the ice once more.

"It was Tajana, correct?" she asked.

"Yes."

"I'm not sure I know where to start. It's rare that I'm left speechless, but here we are."

"We are sisters?" Her accent was a curious mix of Italian and Slavic, but she was no stranger to English.

"Half-sisters. It appears we have the same father."

"That is what he said. You are a Nikolić?"

"Here in England, we changed our family name to Nichols, but yes, I am Frančeska Nikolić."

Another pause allowed both women to let that reality sink in.

"How old are you, Tajana?"

"I had my 34th birthday just before they took me. Does it matter?"

"Your...our father died when you were quite young, if my math is correct. I'd say I was sorry that you didn't get a chance to spend much time with him, but I'd be mostly lying. He was neither a kind man nor a good father."

"My mother did the best she could, but he left us with nothing. I grew up hating him for leaving us alone. Now you tell me he was dead most of that time. I don't know how to feel."

"Bitterness is only natural. Your mother must be quite a woman. Is she still living?"

"Oh yes, she had me when she was only nineteen. We share an apartment and she minds my son when I work late."

"You have a son?"

"Yes, Goran. He's eight years old. I've worried about him this whole time. I hope my mother has him safe."

"You'll need to tell me how to contact them, of course, but I'll look into it. I'm sure they're both fine."

"Wouldn't they be watching my family to find out where I am?"

"A wise observation. How would you know that?"

"I watch a lot of movies."

She held back a chuckle. "We wouldn't mention where you were, naturally, but we would tell her you're safe and that we can hopefully reunite you all soon."

Tajana sighed in a way that sounded not altogether like relief. "I'm dying for a cigarette."

"Come downstairs to the pub. I think I can accommodate you."

They went to the lift, and she pressed her bracelet to a pad. It beeped, and she pressed F. With all the people coming and going within her tower these days, the old key system had outlived its utility, and she'd had it replaced in December. They stepped into the deserted pub, the hour far too early for patrons. Sufficient light came in through the windows, but she turned the lights on, anyway. She lifted the bar top hatch and dug around under the counter until she found a box of Dunhills she kept stashed away for "emergencies." She offered the pack and a lighter to her sister—which still sounded weird in her head—and had one herself out of solidarity. Although she'd quit some time ago, it could be a bonding opportunity.

"What is this place?" Tajana asked.

"The pub?"

"All of it."

"Believe it or not, this is my home."

"Don't bullshit me."

She laughed to herself. Her sister was much like her, if a bit less refined. She had grown up without the advantages of family wealth, so her directness was understandable.

"It's not bullshit, but I owe you some explanation. Our father started a rather successful shipping company in the 1970s, and I still run it today. Perhaps you've heard of Five Pence?"

"I heard Signore Tessaro say something about it."

"That, plus some of my other enterprises, has made me quite wealthy. My recent foray into coffee imports crossed some unknown line with dear Giovanni, and he intends to shut me down. He decided that the best way to get my attention was to kidnap you, a sister I didn't know I had. No offense, but I thought it was a bluff."

"None taken. I doubt I would have believed it, either."

"When he realized his miscalculation, he also took Julia, one of my finest employees and a dear friend, and that *did* get my attention. So, we had our little jailbreak."

"How did you find us?"

"I have some talented friends."

The smoke disappeared into the air filters above the bar as the conversation dried up.

"When can I go home?" Tajana asked.

"I wish I had a simple answer for you. If you return to

Trieste before this is all sorted out, it's possible they'd have you killed to save face."

"And my son? My mother?"

"They may not have tracked your family yet, but that's something I'll need to attend to soon. I'll do everything I can to protect them. If they're in imminent danger, I have a safe house up in the hills. They're welcome to stay as long as necessary."

"We can't just sit here! I have a life in Trieste. It is my home, and I will not hide here forever. Where in hell is here, anyway?"

"We're in London."

"Whatever. What will you do to fix this?"

What, indeed? She'd handled events adequately, despite the shaky start, but the game was far from over, and Giovanni remained in the lead. The key problem was how little she knew about her adversary. A brief meeting in a cafe wasn't enough to divine a full motive, so she had to use her best asset—her intuition—and let the researchers do the rest. That also reminded her to call Taylor later and get him started. Her most immediate need was to convince Tajana and build some trust between them. She refused to lie, in keeping with her overall ethic, but she hesitated to tell her the complete truth.

"The first order of business is to secure your family, though I don't think Giovanni would harm them without reason. It's a feeling I get. His sole targets are me and my businesses. The only leverage he'd gain by putting your family in play would be on you, and I'm sure he has surmised that it would get him nowhere. Still, an ounce of prevention is worth a pound of cure."

"What does this mean?"

"I'm sorry, old expression. It means we won't take unnecessary chances. Play it safe." She paused. "The wild card here is his son, Alessio. Something about him unnerves me, but I can't say why."

"He is..." she said, doing some rapid translation in her head. "Hot head? I did not enjoy when he came to visit."

They extinguished their cigarettes, and Francesca changed the subject.

"Is the guest room all right for you?"

"It is a bed and a bath. I sleep when I am tired, and I look out the window. I have not needed more than that."

"Let me show you the rest of the tower. While you're here, what's mine is yours."

The cloud deck covered the windows of Level 48 of Megalith Tower, so when Duncan McCullen looked up from his desk, all he saw was white. The fancy executive office he now inhabited fit him like an itchy shirt. He'd tried adding some personal touches, but that only called further attention to how poorly the environment suited him. He'd grown up in the rough streets of London's East End, a scant two miles from where he now sat, but even that was unrecognizable. Time, more than distance, separated them. His biggest aspiration growing up was to stay out of prison, unlike his father, but a white collar would have been almost as bad.

He stole another glance out of the window, and a wave of claustrophobia crashed over him without warning. As an expert thief, he was certain he wasn't claustrophobic. "Prisons come in all shapes and sizes," he thought. He pushed away from his desk as if repulsed, and hurried out of his office, passing the sign that read, "Duncan McCullen, Chief Security Officer, AMWarn Security Systems." He wasn't sure where he was going, but he needed to escape. The lobby door swung inward past his face and he went to take a step forward. Had he done so, he would have collided with Martin Alcott, who was engrossed in his mobile, blindly grasping for the door handle.

"Martin!" he exclaimed.

"Huh, what?" Martin replied, looking up in shock.

"Blimey, I almost walked straight into you. Look up if you're about to go through a door."

"Oh, sorry, Duncan, I didn't see you there," he said, removing an earbud, having missed the point.

"I can't deal with this place today. Fancy a coffee down in the Arboretum?"

"I could have another cup, sure. Let me put my things down first."

Martin walked to his office down the hall, deposited his belongings, and rejoined his colleague at the entrance. They exited the office into the uninspiring lobby, taking the lift down to 25. The doors slid apart, and they were greeted by the now-familiar smells: humid, loamy topsoil and green vegetation, punctuated with a warm waft of coffee. They emerged into Megalith Tower's newest feature, the Arboretum.

Level 25 had once housed a pair of offices which one might have considered cursed. Instead, it now hosted a lush, tropical rainforest two-hundred-odd feet above the streets of London. The service core containing the elevator shafts, stair column, and lavatory facilities stood in the center, but all the other walls were gone. Although the day outside was gray—they were now below the overcast—brilliant sunlight streamed in from the fixtures overhead. The new owners had spared little expense in this endeavor, opting for a state-of-the-art fiber optic system that concentrated and piped in natural sunlight from the roof to enhance the plants' growth. It was a tranquil and soothing place, not unlike The Cathedral's atrium, but with far fewer distractions.

Paths led away from the lifts in either direction, bisecting the building along the long axis, and connecting with another circumferential one. Narrower paths snaked away from the primary arteries to benches, fountains, statuary, and other such niceties. They exited the lifts and wrapped around behind the service core where the coffee stand lay.

"Two cappuccinos, please," Martin told the barista. He paid, and they both stepped aside to wait for their orders. "So, what's wrong?"

"What am I doing here, Martin?"

"I mean, why are any of us here? It's one of life's great mysteries."

"No, you twit, I mean here in an office. I shouldn't be chief of any-bloody-thing."

"Return question: why do we do this every other Monday morning? You've been saying that shit for months now, and yet you continue to get your job done. I'll grant you this place is rather different from the old shop, but can't you just accept that you actually belong here?"

"I s'pose not."

"Listen, maybe we'll talk to Julia. Perhaps you could work from The Depot more often, but as Chief of Security, you can't avoid office settings altogether."

"Oh, so it's 'The Depot' now? Cor blimey, you could have said 'work from home,' you know."

"Cappuccinos for Martin!" the barista announced. The friends collected their coffees and found a bench on the perimeter path. Perhaps it was fate, but the seat they'd selected was across the path from the terrace door that once belonged to Purple Cube, Ltd.

"If it helps, you can do what I do," Martin continued. "Focus on the tasks. Either you can do them, or you can't. Do you think I ever thought I'd be a Chief Technology Officer? Titles are bollocks anyway. It's just a job to do."

"I like working with the trainees. Degenerates, the lot of them. My sort of blokes."

"See? Focus on that!"

"Okay, okay, you're right. Just in case, same time two Mondays from now?"

"Always," Martin replied, and clinked his coffee cup with Duncan's. "So, how's Tracy coming along?"

"You'd imagine she was building a bloody nest! Never seen so much fuss from her. I can't wait until February when this is all over."

Martin laughed a derisive sort of laugh. "All over? You'll have a new set of problems, Papa!"

"Stop reminding me!" he hissed. "If I'm totally honest, I can't wait to be a father and a better one than me own da. Course, that won't be too hard. What bothers me most is this means the end of me old life."

"How do you mean?"

"Well, even if I could find a job like that, Tracy would never do it again. I'm not even sure I *could* do it without her anymore."

"You're probably right, but how much of a loss is that in the grand scheme? Look around you."

"It's like an itch you can't reach. Sometimes layin' out these offices feels sort of like I'm casing the place, but the payoff aren't the same, is it?"

"I can't pretend to know how you feel. I didn't have to upheave my life completely to be where I am. It's just another day at the office for me."

They sipped their drinks, and a convenient cloud dimmed the ambient light as to punctuate the quiet, until Martin's mobile buzzed in his jacket pocket. He set his coffee down on a rock as he dug around to find it.

"Meet me on 25," read the text from Maureen.

It had only taken Maureen Abernathy three weeks after The Owen Affair to resign her position at AMWarn. Nothing about it ever sat right with her, so she resolved to finish her part in it and walk away. She'd had no prospects when she left, but with a brief stint as CFO on her CV, she was certain jobs would be plentiful. In reality, her former title was less an asset as much as it was an albatross. She hadn't the credentials or length of experience to be a Chief Financial Officer at the larger firms. The C-levels had somewhat of a club mentality, and she was most decidedly not a member, which they'd made altogether clear. Conversely, getting hired as a staff accountant was nigh impossible, as many firms assumed she was overqualified for the position.

"That whore of a duchess ruined my career," she would sometimes mutter, leaving another failed interview.

As the summer waned, the only prospect she looked forward to was the onset of rugby season and her beloved Harlequins. Oddly, it was the first friendly of the season that began the change in her fortunes. Before the match started, she noticed a rather chatty young woman in the row in front of her, cheering on Leicester. Maureen being Maureen, she decided in an instant that she had found her enemy for the afternoon.

It was a fantastic match as the Harlequins and Tigers battled and traded leads. The younger woman slung expert barbs at her, and she always gave as good as she got, but her adversary impressed her. She was blunt, incisive, and her profanity was artful, but she never once made it personal—it was all about the game. The intermission began with Leicester leading and Maureen saying, "Fuck the scoreboard. There's still a half to play," before excusing herself to the loo.

When she exited, her "new friend" was waiting for her outside. She rolled her neck. Whatever was coming, she might not start, but she'd be damned if she wouldn't finish it. To her surprise, though, the woman extended her hand in greeting.

"Nicola. Nicola Cobham. It was a pleasure watching the first half with you."

Maureen was, for once, caught off-guard and speechless. "Maureen Abernathy, likewise."

"You know your rugby, I'll give you that. How long have you been a Quins supporter?"

"All my life, and you?"

"Grew up near Leicester. My dad was a certified fanatic. I try to get here whenever the Tigers are in town."

"Always support your side," Maureen added. "So, you're here in London, then."

"About two years. I moved south after I got my ACA."

"You're joking."

"I beg your pardon?"

"You're a chartered accountant?"

"Yes?" Nicola said slowly, squinting her eyes with suspicion.

"Does your firm have any openings?"

"Eh?"

"I'm an accountant too. Unattached at present, you might say."

"Shame to hear that. I don't think we..." Nicola said before Maureen's mobile rang.

Henry Peel's name appeared on her screen.

"Do you mind? It's an old friend," she told Nicola.

"Not at all. See you for the second half," she replied, disappearing into the crowd.

She checked the time remaining in intermission, decided she had time, then answered.

"Hello Henry, it's good to hear from you!"

"Good afternoon, Maureen. I wondered if you had a moment to talk."

"I'm at a rugby match, but it's intermission. What can I help you with?"

"Nigel has just announced his retirement."

"He what?"

"I'm afraid it's left us in a bit of a bind. I was wondering if you might pop up to Milton Keynes this week to discuss the future."

"Henry, I'm flattered, and I'd love to talk more, but I'm afraid I'm in no position to give this much thought right now. Will there be a party or a send-off of some sort?"

"Planning is already underway, although he caught us rather flat-footed. We were thinking next weekend."

"I'll be there, and we can talk then. Would that be all right?"

"Excellent, thank you Maureen. Enjoy the rest of the match."

She rang off and returned to her seat, thinking less about rugby than before. She and Nicola continued their friendly banter, although less strident than in the first half, and Leicester ultimately prevailed. As the crowd filed out, Nicola turned to bid Maureen farewell, and something connected in her brain.

"Er, Nicola, I wonder if we might have a word, or even a

pint. I think I have a mad idea."

Some eight weeks later, she sat in her new office on the third floor of Megalith Tower. It was only the second full week of operations for Abernathy, Cobham, and Peel, but things looked positive already. Many of Henry Peel's clients followed him to the new firm, and Nicola was a wonderful addition, despite her poor taste in rugby squads. Naturally, when Maureen had discussed the idea with Martin, word got round in certain circles, and they did the lease at Megalith before she realized it, at a significant discount. She'd insisted on a low floor, though, as a skyline view was of little value when she believed her eyes should be on her screen instead.

The office was empty at this hour, and she had just finished the coffee she brought from home. She smacked her lips, tasting the last remnants, and decided on another cup. Checking her watch, she assumed Martin would be in his office upstairs by now, so she sent a text before locking up and heading for the lifts. When the doors opened in the Arboretum, she found him grinning like a Cheshire Cat and holding a cup at arm's length.

"Americano, black. I do sometimes listen," he said.

"How did..."

"Duncan and I have been here for fifteen minutes already. I ordered your coffee when I saw the text."

"Brilliant, thanks!"

"You're welcome, as usual. Rest of the lot not in yet?"

"No, Henry's commute is still murderous until he moves, and Nicola doesn't come in until nine. You said Duncan is here?"

"Yeah, having another crisis of confidence."

"Well, it *is* Monday. I have something for him."

"It's not for him, is it?"

"No, idiot, of course it's for Tracy."

Maureen didn't plan to have children of her own—they were disorderly and unpredictable. When she'd found out Tracy was expecting, though, "Auntie Mo" kicked into high gear and began stocking the flat in Hounslow with every accessory a baby or parent could need. She and Martin rounded the bend in the path to where Duncan was sitting, and she charged at him with a parcel outstretched. He flinched ever so slightly at her approach, unsure if she was about to clout him with it.

"It's a blanket. I know she wants to keep it neutral, so I made it gray with elephants." Although she'd softened toward him, she was not addressing him now as much as she was leaving a message for Tracy at the beep.

"Thanks, Mo, she'll be..." Duncan stopped short. "Did you say you *made* it gray with elephants?"

"And if I did?"

"Since when do you sew?"

"None of your sodding business, Duncan. Give her the blanket."

"I'm with him," Martin said. "All the times I've been to your flat and I've never seen a sewing machine."

"I'm an accountant, thickheads. Fabric is cheaper than premade blankets, so I learned to sew to save them a few pounds. I'm still practicing, but this is my best one so far. There are a couple of burp cloths in there as well."

Various mutterings of astonishment tumbled out of their mouths like marbles until they replaced them with some excellent coffee.

CHAPTER SEVEN

GREEN ROOM, YELLOW STRANGER

Veronica sat spellbound in the last session of the workshop. The week passed in a blissful blur. The auditorium was oversized for the audience of thirty-five, but somehow the panelists made the venue feel intimate. A five-person panel sat on stage, lecturing the young hopefuls. Naturally, P. L. Eriksson was the featured guest, but the speakers also included a screenwriter, an editor from a second-tier publishing house, a literary agent, and an accountant. The accountant seemed out of place, but she supposed famous and successful writers needed someone to mind their fortunes, so it made some sense.

With the last question answered, a round of applause filled the auditorium. The small cohort boarded the lifts for a brief reception on level 25—an *amuse-bouche* for the main event tomorrow. Various gasps, oohs, and aahs filled the lift car as the group caught their first sight of the Megalith Arboretum. The workshop's benefactors reserved the entire level, so they had free rein in the botanical retreat. There was ample room to mingle, enjoy hors d'oeuvres and drinks suitable for the underage crowd, or retreat into the vegetation and work on their final projects. Although she'd made some friends through the event, she opted for the latter and sequestered herself on a rocky outcropping near the center column.

Her fingers danced on the laptop's keyboard as the EDM track blared through her earbuds. She was in the zone. The arboretum filled her with peace and ignited her inspiration, and she knew she'd have to come back here soon. Everything around her radiated a calm green except for the people, who milled about in their pale pinks, fuzzy whites, and powdery blues.

For as long as she could remember, she saw almost all living things in color. It wasn't the colors of their skin or their clothes, but more like a tinted mist that came from within them, surrounded them, and followed them around. Her parents took her to doctors and psychiatrists, and they'd scanned her brain more times than she wanted to remember. Ultimately, they all agreed that she wasn't hallucinating, and that she was "blessed" with synesthesia. They'd stated that, most commonly, synesthetes experienced color in music or numbers, but there had been documented cases of seeing it on people. Her biggest irritation was that she always sucked at visual arts and lacked the skill to paint her unique vision.

Though she hadn't taken her eyes from her screen for some time, she sensed someone was standing in front of her. Annoyed at the interruption, she extracted an earbud and looked up, ready to ask the intruder what their deal was. Before she said a word, she locked eyes with P. L. Eriksson, and the entire English language ran out of her...thinky place.

"You did not want to join in the enjoyment?" he asked. "We thought you may have left."

She stared, gobsmacked. He was not a handsome gentleman, but he exuded confidence, professionalism, and a faint, friendly yellow aura. She realized she was still staring and commanded herself to speak.

"Oh, er, I wanted to get some work done first."

"There's always time to work. Evenings like this are more rare, *ja?*" His accent was not strong, but there was an unmistakable Nordic cadence to his speech.

"*Ja,*" she repeated, before correcting herself. "I mean, yes, you're right." She cursed herself for acting like a star-struck idiot.

"I have enjoyed your work this week. You have a bright future ahead of you."

"Thank you, sir," she squeaked out before her insides turned to mush. Her literary hero had just complimented her writing. She could die happily right this second.

"I will give you some time to gather your things. Please come find me when you are done. I have some people who would like to meet you, I believe."

She nodded and started packing her backpack as he walked away into the improbable jungle. As she zipped her bag and hoisted it onto her shoulder, she felt a warm, prickly sensation on the back of her neck. She rounded to check if someone had snuck up behind her, but she stood alone in the aisle. "*It's nothing,*" she thought, and was about to turn back toward the party. A lift sounded its chime in the lobby behind her, and the prickle intensified. She stared in fascination as a figure emerged from the lift. A glowing figure.

It was like the pale yellow mist around the man was electrified, because he glowed like a low-power neon tube. She'd neither seen nor experienced anything like him, and she stood transfixed. He stepped into the lobby, spotted the sign announcing the level's closure, sagged in disappointment, and left as quickly as he'd arrived.

She stood frozen, stunned. First, her bedroom turned purple, and now she'd seen a glowing yellow man. Why had her life gotten so weird lately? Her neck prickled less and less the longer he was gone, so she decided she'd better return to the festivities. As she walked the path through the foliage, it occurred to her to jot down the experience in her notebook, but she dismissed it out of hand. There was no possible way she could forget it.

The February sun had long since headed west when Martin arrived in the Cathedral Pub. Two regulars, with whom he took great care in avoiding conversation, accompanied him up the tower. Despite recent updates, the pub's clientele had changed little from when he'd first encountered it. He bellied up to the right arm of the wraparound bar but didn't signal Taylor. He was in no hurry to be served, so Taylor, naturally, disappointed him by springing to his service.

"Evenin', Martin. What can I get you tonight? The usual?"

"No thanks, Taylor. Only coffee tonight, please."

"Everything all right, sir?"

"Right as rain, in fact. I'd finished my workday over at the Megalith and stopped at the arboretum for a coffee, but it was closed for a private event. So, I thought I'd pop up here instead."

"One coffee, coming up!" Taylor chirped.

Down the bar, he glimpsed a man glancing at him side-eyed, as if wondering what kind of idiot would come up the tower only to order coffee. In fairness, he didn't know either, because the coffee here was nothing special, and he'd passed several other shops on the way. Another universal sign or premonition, perhaps, but he had a hunch this was where he needed to be tonight.

For once, he sat in the pub without a single care. No one had summoned him here, and nothing was on fire, either figuratively or literally. This Friday had been unremarkable, aside from the minor inconvenience of the closed arboretum. Everything was stable and quiet, and it made him jumpy as all hell. He kept looking behind him, as if he'd lost track of a boomerang he'd thrown.

Taylor delivered his drink with cream and sugar on the side. Martin watched him scan the room, checking his customers before leaning down onto the bar to chat. Fridays could be rambunctious in the pub, but thus far, the crowd was sparse.

"That private event you ran into? That's the workshop The Duchess set up. It's the last night. The big to-do is here tomorrow."

"Oh, right! I totally forgot. I haven't been involved in it."

"Same, but she's been talking about it a lot up the tower here."

He sighed, having run out of small talk. Maybe something *was* bothering him. There were few people aside from Taylor who could appreciate his plight. They had a lot in common as recent additions to the ranks who had stumbled their way into their positions.

"One funny thing happened, though. I got a strange feeling when I walked into the arboretum. Couldn't say what it was, couldn't even say it was bad. There's always been a strange vibe there. It's been better since they converted it, but this was different."

"I'm sure it's nothing. You lot talk about these senses and vibes and all, and I'm sure I'll never understand it."

"Nor do I, Taylor. There have been plenty of times I've wished I could make it stop."

"Has come in handy once or twice, hasn't it?"

"You're not wrong!" he said with a smile and sipped his coffee.

Taylor returned to his duties as more customers arrived, the lift chime ringing every couple of minutes. As he swigged the last of his drink, a warm, satisfied feeling swept over him. He shot an incredulous look at the bottom of his empty cup, thinking that caffeine more often made him jittery than contented. The lift chimed once more, then a voice rose above the crowd.

"I knew you were here."

Martin shot a glance at Taylor, as if to say, "*See?*" He caught Taylor chuckling before he turned to face The Duchess.

"I was expecting company, but it wasn't you. I'm glad you're here, though." She motioned across the room. "A word, if you don't mind, Taylor?"

Taylor finished his pour and walked back to the group.

"I'll be introducing the both of you to someone in a few moments. Best behavior if you don't mind, gents."

"Best behavior?" he asked. "Here?"

"Shush! A dear old friend is stopping by to discuss the event tomorrow. You may know of him," she said with one of her trademark smirks.

As if on cue, the lift sounded its arrival once more. The doors opened, and a hush fell over the crowd. Many customers stared, mouths agape, but a handful became quite interested in their beverages, coat collars pulled up tight.

Michael Hart, Prime Minister of the United Kingdom, stepped into the Cathedral Pub.

"Michael! So good to see you. Welcome! How's the family?" The Duchess said, greeting the PM far less formally than Martin would have thought appropriate.

Hart smiled. "Excellent, Duchess. It's good to see you as well. It's been rather festive at Number 10 of late. Felicity's birthday was last week."

"Happy belated birthday to her, then! She's fourteen now?"

"Impossibly fourteen. She's very much looking forward to tomorrow's event. Might this become a regular occurrence?"

"Might you continue to sponsor it?" she replied with a grin.

"Without a doubt! Felicity would never forgive me otherwise. She's keen to submit an entry next year, but I told her to expect no special treatment because of her last name."

"Then all signs point to yes. It's been a tremendous success, far better than I expected, in fact. If tomorrow goes without a hitch, it's settled."

"Done!" the PM said, shaking her hand.

"Michael, I'd like to introduce you to some associates of mine. This is Sebastian Taylor, one of my senior researchers."

"Taylor, if you please, sir. It's an honor to meet you, sir."

"The honor is mine, Mr. Taylor."

"And this is Martin Alcott, my chief technologist, as it were."

"Mr. Alcott, I've heard so much about you." Hart shook his hand with fervor.

"I hope that's a good thing, sir. It's a pleasure to make your acquaintance."

"Gentlemen," The Duchess interjected. "Shall we discuss some business upstairs?"

"What, all of us?" he asked.

"That was the idea, Martin, hence the use of the plural 'gentlemen.' Maureen is already in the office awaiting us impatiently, as always."

"Who will tend the bar, ma'am?" Taylor chimed in.

"I think it will be in expert hands, Sebastian," she said, pointing behind him.

Where Geoff had come from, he hadn't seen, but there he stood, pulling a pint with a bar towel slung over his shoulder.

"When did he come in?" Taylor asked him, and he responded

with a rapid shake of his head.

Taylor shrugged, and the four unlikely colleagues went up the lift to make plans for tomorrow's event.

The Cathedral Atrium, which one food columnist had recently dubbed "the world's only Michelin Star food court," brimmed with diners in neat queues outside the more popular restaurants. Others milled around through the green spaces, browsing wares at the artisan kiosks, sipping coffees and cocktails. Although cavernous, it had a coziness to it and the mood was very festive indeed.

Adding to the festivity on this night, a low stage backed by a velvet curtain of deep aubergine stood in the center, facing the massive main entrance hall. Rows of folding chairs awaited the audience for the ceremony to come. Participants in the workshop, their families, and the faculty milled about in the area, chatting, shaking hands, and enjoying refreshments.

Michael Hart stood backstage, taking small sips at a glass of white wine. Although a wee nip often calmed his nerves, it would not do for the PM to present the winners of a youth writing competition whilst plastered. Behavior deemed "unbecoming of the office" had been rampant in recent years, and he swore at his appointment that he would bring respectability back to his job. The early months of his tenure had been a testament to his diligence.

The public address system crackled to life, announcing the imminent start of the program and asking everyone to please be seated. His stomach clenched at the announcement, which surprised him. He met with the Queen every week, addressed the Commons and the Cabinet daily, and had been on television countless times. Why should emceeing a small literary event cause him any concern? He took a larger sip of his beverage and a few deep breaths before emerging onto the stage.

Once the applause died away and he got his opening lines out, he forgot all about his nerves. One by one, he introduced the faculty, and they took their seats on stage. He entertained the crowd with self-effacing humor about his poor performance in English classes and the generous use of speechwriters. He also introduced his daughter and hoped aloud they might invite her next year with a knowing glance at the Editor-in-Chief.

"We'd be delighted to have her, sir," Prescott replied with a chuckle, having caught the joke.

He wrapped up his comments and turned over the dais to P.L. Eriksson, who presented the awards for fiction and non-fiction. Although The Duchess had already briefed him on the winners the previous evening, and he was supposed to remain neutral, he still smiled a bit when Veronica Fancourt walked across the stage to collect her Outstanding Fiction Writer award. The awards for poetry and screenplay followed, and Hart took center stage again. He presented the Outstanding Young Author award to the winner of the poetry category and closed the ceremony.

Handshakes and photos followed as the staff changed the seating for the banquet. He sat at the head table with Felicity, who sat beside Miss Fancourt.

"I read your story in the fall issue. It was fantastic!" Felicity said.

"Do you really think?" Veronica replied. She sounded as if she hadn't quite come to terms with her accolades yet.

"Oh yes, I was the one who told Daddy about it. He enjoyed it too, and I think he told several of his friends."

"You're kidding."

"I think you should have gotten the top award."

Felicity's comment rankled him. Miss Fancourt's win was legitimate, and he had to quash any appearance of bias. He hurriedly interjected, "I was told the judging was very close, Felicity. You did a marvelous job, Miss Fancourt. Congratulations."

"Thank you, sir. To win the category was enough of a surprise. I might have fainted if I'd won it all."

After the staff had cleared the dessert away, he stood and tapped his glass with a fork.

"Ladies and gentlemen, thank you all again for coming to this evening's ceremony. Before you leave, I wonder if I could have the winners and their families join me at the front of the stage once more?"

The crowd filtered away until only a small cluster of attendees and family remained. He continued, "There's one more special surprise to go. If you'd all like to follow me, we'll be doing a brief photo shoot for next quarter's cover of *Preeminence.*"

Gasps and excited whispers spread through the crowd, so he knew he needn't convince anyone further. He led the group through the atrium and into a large but cozy alcove. Photographers and officials from the journal had already stationed themselves in the apse recess and welcomed the party.

"Thank you for joining us," Prescott announced. "For the cover, we thought we'd use the ambiance here to give it a Roaring Twenties feel. Authors, if we could have you come over to the seating area, please? The photographers will guide you to your places. Parents and guardians, let us know if you have any qualms about the proceedings. We want everyone to be comfortable. Relax and enjoy the process!"

The photographers took over, posing the rising literary

stars in various thoughtful poses, evoking the sepia-soaked glory of the Bright Young Things.

Politics had never captured Veronica's imagination, because it seemed like it was all her parents talked about. It was only natural that it should be common dinner table conversation, since her father was a high-ranking solicitor in a large multinational corporation and her mother a lobbyist. It didn't mean she had to enjoy it, however. Opinions aside, she knew what an honor it was to be in the Prime Minister's company, even seated at his table for dinner and chatting with his daughter.

As the photographers requested different poses and arrangements, she found it exciting...at first. It was hard to keep her focus on the camera, because she was too busy cringing at her father trying to cozy up to the PM. It was quite a relief when they announced they had all they needed. She exchanged hugs and handshakes with her fellow writers and was about to join her family to leave. A sudden prickle at the back of her neck stopped her in her tracks. She thought, *"That hasn't happened since..."*

Movement caught her eye, and she spied a hidden door opening in the outer wall. The bright yellow man emerged, and this time, she didn't hesitate to approach him. She needed answers.

"Excuse me, sir," she said with confidence. "May I ask you a question?"

"Erm, sure?" the man answered.

"Why are you so yellow?"

"Excuse me?" he replied with slight alarm. He examined his extremities as if she'd told him he was covered with spiders.

"Oh, yeah, you wouldn't be able to see it, but yours is the brightest yellow I think I've ever seen. It's incredible!"

"I'm afraid I don't understand. I think you must have the wrong person."

"No, I'm sure it's you. I saw you yesterday in the Arboretum."

The man's head drew back. He sputtered a bit, looking like he was trying to find a reply, but she didn't give him the chance.

"You were only there for a second, but I felt the same prickle on my neck. How do you do that?"

He continued his confused stammering until her father called, walking over to collect her. "Veronica! We need to be going."

"Veronica? As in Veronica Fancourt?" the man asked.

"Wait, you know me?"

"Yes, er, well, only by name. I'm employed by a sponsor of this event. One of your earlier compositions caught her eye, and she was hoping to meet you this evening if you and your family have the time."

"What's all this?" her father asked, attempting to insert himself between his daughter and the stranger.

"Good evening, sir. My name is Martin Alcott. I was telling Veronica that my employer would like to discuss a possible patronage arrangement with her."

"Is that so? Is she from one of the publishing houses?"

"No, sir. She is, however, a woman of considerable means and a prominent supporter of the arts. If you could spare a few minutes, she would be pleased to welcome you to her lounge upstairs."

She could see her father calculating the situation in his head. His face suggested an unpleasant odor had entered his nose, but she hoped he would agree.

"Fine, but I will allow no one to exploit my daughter. She's only a child, after all."

That infuriated her every time he said it. William was a child, not her. She was almost sixteen now, and capable of choosing her own destiny. She shot a look at her father, laden with as much contempt as she could summon. He smiled a weak smile.

"It's for your protection, sweetheart. When people smell profit, they're prone to doing unsavory things."

"If I may, sir," Mr. Alcott interrupted, "I've been in your position myself, and I appreciate your caution, but no one here would ever dream of exploiting your daughter. Quite the contrary. We want to give her all the support she needs."

His shoulders dropped. "I suppose it won't hurt to chat with this employer of yours."

"Brilliant! Right this way, please," Mr. Alcott said, gesturing them all to the still-waiting lift.

She took the lead, and her family followed with some hesitation. After a few seconds of uncomfortable silence and canned music, the doors opened to a large and comfortable lounge area, where two women awaited them, one of whom was the out-of-place accountant from yesterday's panel. The other was unfamiliar, but a vibrant purple mist surrounded her—a rare color indeed.

"Welcome," the unfamiliar woman said. "My name is Francesca Nichols, chairwoman and CEO of Istria Holdings, one of the gold sponsors of this event. I'm thrilled to meet you all."

She thought she saw Mr. Alcott and the accountant exchange a look, but couldn't imagine what it meant. Before she could introduce herself in return, her father pushed to the front of the group.

"Edwin Fancourt, Ms. Nichols. I'm Veronica's father. I'd like to know what this is all about. It's late, and I want to get my family home."

"Direct, aren't you?"

"I've found it effective in my trade."

"Very well, we shall dispense with the pleasantries. Before you ask, I have no desire to profit from your daughter's talent. That would be unethical due to her young age. I'd like to propose a patronage arrangement. I suspect her talent is limitless, but she could use a hand to guide her through the business of her art."

"Go on," her father said, his interest piqued.

"*Preeminence* has already committed to publishing Veronica's short fiction from this week, and with various publishers in attendance this evening, I expect there will be more to follow. In short, I would like to volunteer my services and resources as her agent, as it were."

"And what would you charge for this service? Ten percent?"

"Nothing. I have no need of a financial stake. I've made my career by investing in the potential of people. The only compensation I'm asking for is the opportunity to work with her. Creative writing has always fascinated me, and I would like to hone my craft alongside her."

"What's the catch?"

"No catches, I assure you," Ms. Nichols stated, before turning to her. "Something about your words moved me, Veronica. I would be honored if you'd share some of your process with me."

It was everything she had ever hoped for. She wanted to leap into the air, cry, or maybe even hug the strange woman, but she tried to remain calm and professional.

"All right."

Her father injected himself into the conversation again. "If she should get a publishing deal, what would be done with any advances?"

"Proceeds from any publications are to be held in trust until her eighteenth birthday. At that point, it will be her choice whether to continue the arrangement. All the contracts are already drawn up for your review, sir. Allow me to present Ms. Maureen Abernathy, principal partner of Abernathy, Cobham, and Peel, who will act as trustee."

The accountant shook her father's hand and handed him a portfolio. There was additional discussion with a lot of terms she had heard her father use and that she had ignored.

"Please give us your decision by next Friday, sir," Ms. Abernathy said.

"Now," Ms. Nichols continued, "I wonder if I might have a word alone with Veronica. My associate, Mr. Alcott, will escort your family back to the atrium."

"See here, now," he protested.

"Sir!" she shouted, defusing him. "Your daughter is perfectly safe here. All I ask is five minutes to speak with her, woman to woman. If she is one second overdue, you may keep Martin."

"Dad, it's all right. I don't mind," Veronica said. "It's only five minutes."

She watched as the others herded her family into the lift until she was alone with her benefactor.

"Thank you for agreeing to stay."

"No problem, ma'am."

"Have you enjoyed your week with us?"

"Oh, indeed! I've met so many wonderful people and learned so much."

"Wonderful. Have you been to The Cathedral before?"

"No, but it's brilliant."

"Are you certain?"

She could tell Ms. Nichols was leading her, but to what, she couldn't figure. "I'm sure I haven't. I think I would remember coming to a place like this before."

"Fitting of a countess, wouldn't you say?"

The question puzzled her. "You mean like in my other story?"

"Precisely. Something to think about. I wonder if you'd be interested in coming back next weekend to discuss that story in deeper detail. I've only seen the excerpt that *Preeminence* published, but I'm fascinated to see where it goes next."

INTERLUDE: ULTERIOR

"Francesca Nichols?" Maureen asked. "All this time, she's been nothing but her royal fucking highness, The Duchess, and this lot turns up and she's Francesca bloody Nichols?" She fumed as she drove them toward home, having agreed to give Martin a lift to the event.

"Believe me, I was as shocked as you. Did she say something about it last night? I'll be honest, I zoned out for chunks of it."

"When did you zone out?"

"I don't remember."

"It's a damned good thing you know how to use a computer, otherwise you'd be no use at all. No, she didn't say anything about using her real name, idiot."

"Why would she do that? She protects her name like a nuclear secret."

"You're the expert on her, you tell me!"

"Well, she doesn't do anything without a reason, but I'll be damned if I can figure this one. I have no gift for strategy. I can't comprehend how she keeps all her lies and half-truths straight. She somehow lives like three separate lives up in that tower."

"You can't even manage one life."

"That's not funny."

"It wasn't a joke. I've been over the paperwork at least ten times, and there's nothing to suggest what she's up to. By the numbers, she means to help this girl, but I don't see how it benefits her."

"All she told me was that she needed to get close to her."

"I don't like it, Martin. She's just a girl, and she doesn't need to get caught up in The Duchess's nonsense."

"I'm with you on that. I felt super icky about making that introduction, but you know how it is with her. When the PM turned up last night, I couldn't say no. I thought she'd been going legit."

"It's legitimate, as far as I can tell, but yeah, it feels terrible and wrong. I suggest we stay the hell out of it as much as we can."

"You read my mind."

"No, I absolutely did not," she replied. This, too, was not a joke.

CHAPTER EIGHT

LOOKING INTO THE PRESENT

It had been a week since the meeting at the end of the writers' workshop, and Edwin had grown rather weary of his daughter's enthusiasm. He loved seeing her happy about anything, especially since she'd grown gloomy in her advancing teens, but he thought she was overdoing it. Every word from her mouth was about the workshop and the upcoming meeting with Ms. Nichols. He, however, trusted her supposed benefactor about as far as he could lift a city bus. No stranger to the world of contracts, he had insisted upon a guarantee of his own: at least one parent must be present at all meetings between Veronica and Ms. Nichols or any of her associates.

"Ronnie, we're going to be late!" he called up the stairs.

"Dad, please don't call me Ronnie anymore. I prefer Veronica, you know that."

"Famous author or not, you'll always be my Ronnie. Let's get going."

Even on a Saturday, driving to The Cathedral from Hampstead took half an hour, leaving them sufficient time to talk. He assumed she would talk about nothing but her excitement about the meeting; instead, she was quiet and pensive in the left-hand seat, saying nothing until they got to Regent's Park.

"Dad? Does Ms. Nichols frighten you a little?"

"Why on earth would you ask that? No, of course not!"

"Oh," she said, and carried on looking out the window.

"Does she frighten you?"

"Maybe 'frighten' isn't the right word, but I got a weird feeling about her and her friend, Martin."

"I can understand that," he said, attempting to comfort her. "I wouldn't say I trusted her, though. You'd do well to stay on your guard."

"Thanks. I mean, thanks for agreeing to all this."

He sighed and paused. He knew what he needed to tell her, but in this moment, it required a lot more courage than he'd guessed.

"Veronica, you've grown up so fast and your talent is astonishing. It's just that your mother and I are from a different world than art and literature and such. I neither understand it nor do I fully approve of it."

He could almost hear her shutting down. "*Shit. Think fast, Edwin,*" he thought.

"But," he continued, "I've not seen you happier than in the last few weeks, and I figure that's worth a couple of Saturdays. I was so proud when you got that award."

"You were? You looked so miserable, like it offended you by even being there."

"I *was* miserable!" he said with a slight chuckle. "But it wasn't for me, was it?"

He glanced at her whilst at the traffic light, and he saw her trying to hide her smile under her long blue bangs.

"An artist's life is hard, sweetheart. We don't want you to have to struggle. And promises of easy money, like this Ms. Nichols is offering, are often false. I couldn't bear to see you get your heart broken."

"Why are you telling me this?"

"Because in a couple more years, you won't let me," he

laughed. She laughed along with him.

They chatted the rest of the way to The Cathedral, probably talking more in those fifteen minutes than they'd done in the two years prior.

He announced their arrival at the main information desk as instructed, and a Mr. Taylor appeared, leading them upstairs. They stepped into the same plush lounge as they'd seen the previous weekend, but this time, Ms. Nichols was the only person there to greet them.

"My friends, welcome!" she said, her arms wide in greeting. "I'm excited to get started today, but first, I've provided some refreshments. Please help yourselves to tea, coffee, scones, croissants, or Eccles cakes. I'm rather fond of black currants, you know. I made them all myself."

He sipped a nervous sip of his black coffee, watching the strange woman who had taken an unlikely interest in his daughter. There were countless comfortable places in the lounge on which to settle; instead, he paced anxiously, a copy of the Financial Times under his arm, studying the surroundings. Small talk and snacks now completed, their hostess asked Veronica to sit with her at a table set up as a makeshift desk.

"Now, what I'm most curious about is what inspired you for the story the journal published? How do you come up with something like that?"

"I can show you my notebooks and dream journals. I brought them all with me," Veronica said.

"Dream journals?"

"Yeah, I dreamed most of it. I'd wake up and write down what I remembered before it disappeared. I had to make up the names, but they fit."

"There was so much detail! It's fantastic."

As he watched them interact, it was becoming obvious that she had indeed read Veronica's work, and it had delighted her. He relaxed by a fraction, considering that perhaps this person wasn't just trying to cash in on his daughter's talent.

"The part that fascinated me most was the church. Your description of it reminded me rather of this cathedral. The similarities are striking. Are you sure you hadn't been here before last week?"

"No, ma'am. Never once."

"You must admit there's a strong likeness to this building, though." Ms. Nichols said.

Something about that phrasing connected in his brain, and he snapped to attention. "Are you suggesting that you're considering suing my daughter for likeness rights? Only the building's owner would have grounds, and this is obviously a work of fiction. Any similarity between people or places is purely coincidental."

"Calm yourself, Edwin," the woman said, condescension very much intended. "I have no interest in suing anyone. Too many lawyers."

He seethed. That was a cheap shot, and she bloody well knew it. She was trying to get under his skin and, although it was working, he wasn't about to let her know that. He clenched his jaw and felt his nostrils flaring.

She continued. "If I had wished to sue either of you, I would not have begun a business relationship with you. I'm merely curious how she could have described *my* cathedral in such painstaking detail if she had never been here before."

"Do you mean..." he said, trailing off in thought.

"Yes, I own The Cathedral, or at least my company does."

"Points well taken. I withdraw my objection."

"Spoken like a gentleman, sir." She turned back to Veronica. "Do you think you can explain it?"

Veronica stared at the floor, as if she'd been caught copying from a classmate's paper. "I can't," she said. "Like I said, I sort of dreamed it. Anyway, putting a pub at the top of a church would be mad!"

Ms. Nichols smirked. "I suppose you're right. Shall we continue?"

This minor diversion dashed any hope he'd clung to for a relaxing Saturday, and he threw his newspaper in the nearest bin.

As the morning passed, Francesca became more and more enamored of the young writer. She'd never encountered someone with whom she formed such an instant connection—not even Martin—and it wasn't just about her writing. They arrived at the same thoughts simultaneously within the first hour, and by 11:00, they were finishing each other's sentences, gasping, and grinning at one another. The minutes flew past as the pair rifled through notebooks, journals, rough drafts, and even some of Veronica's teachers' feedback from school. She shared some of her own writing samples, though they were little more than diary entries, but Veronica was rapt, nonetheless. She kept saying things like, "You really did that?" and "You've been to Moscow? Wow!" For a couple of hours this Saturday, The Duchess, feared woman of business and otherwise, felt like a teenager giggling with a best friend. Edwin sat on the opposite arm of the sofa, occasionally rolling his eyes at the spectacle of it all.

She glanced at her watch, exclaiming, "Oh my!" when she

discovered it was ten minutes to noon. Despite the fun she was having, she had brought the Fancourts here for a greater purpose, and she decided it was time to begin the next phase.

"The morning has gotten away from me. I believe now would be an excellent opportunity to break for lunch," she told the group. "Would anyone care for a curry?"

"I would!" Veronica exclaimed. "You must have read my mind. I was just thinking about curry!" They giggled again.

"How lucky for you! There's a wonderful Indian restaurant downstairs in the atrium, featuring some of the best food in the city. My treat, of course, and then we can resume our session."

"All right," her father grumbled, clearly irritated that this was not the end.

The trio boarded the lift, and she pressed the F button, which did not escape his notice.

"Not the atrium? I thought you said it was downstairs," he said.

"It is. I have one quick stop to make along the way down," she replied. She held back the villainous grin that threatened to cross her face, as it would spoil the surprise.

The doors slid open to reveal the pub in its inimitable glory. Edwin gawped dumbstruck at the sight, while Veronica cupped her hands over her mouth with a sharp inhale.

"It's exactly like I imagined it!" Veronica said. "This is amazing!"

They stepped from the lift into the pub, although Edwin's entrance was more stumbling.

"My dear," she said, "I don't think you imagined it at all, which is why I wanted the chance to collaborate with you. There's something extraordinary about you. Don't misunderstand me, your writing is exceptional, but I suspect there's much more to it than vivid description."

Veronica nodded. "I think I see what you mean, ma'am."

Her father stood behind them, gibbering and pointing at various people and items around the room.

"Ah, dear Edwin. I promised you a curry, did I not?" she announced. "Taylor, the daily special for Mr. Fancourt, please!" She turned back to him. "You'll love it. It's one of my best recipes. Croatian *punjene paprike* but with a curry twist. What could I offer you to drink?"

"Do you serve whiskey here?"

"Naturally! It wouldn't be a proper pub otherwise." She addressed the bar once more. "Please provide our friend with anything he requires from the private stock list. All with my compliments."

"Yes, ma'am," Taylor said. Edwin straightened himself up and took a seat at the bar, and Taylor handed him a small menu card.

"Now, since you're a trifle young for the pub, would you accompany me back up to the lounge? I'd like to talk more about your imagination before we adjourn for our own meal. Would that be all right, Mr. Fancourt?"

"Sure," he said, still stunned.

She escorted her new protégé back to the lounge, and they sat on the great U-shaped sofa. It was time to lay the cards out.

"I need to explain a few things to you, Veronica. Please try not to be upset with me until I've finished."

"All right," she replied.

"All of this was for your benefit. The writers' workshop, the prizes, and the contract were all arranged so I could get close to you and ask you about your writing."

"So, I didn't win anything? It was all rigged?"

"Certainly not! The judging was legitimate. I did not interfere, though I don't believe it would have required much twisting of arms. Mr. Eriksson rather enjoyed your story."

"He did??"

"He made a point of telling me so, in fact. I merely provided the opportunity, but you did the rest yourself." She let Veronica revel in the compliment before getting back to her point. "It didn't feel right coming straight to you and asking what I wanted to ask. With you being a teenager, I'd likely have run afoul of your parents. Now that I know your father better, it's a near certainty. As such, I had a lovely chat with Mr. Prescott from *Preeminence,* and we hatched the idea of the workshop. It was such an enormous success that we plan to make it an annual event."

"Brilliant!"

"I meant every word I said about becoming your benefactor, but there's one condition that was not in the contract. I need to know how you know what you know. When I read your story, it was practically letter-perfect to something that happened here last year."

"That's impossible. It was only a dream, like I told you! That couldn't have actually happened."

"It did, I can assure you. I have introduced myself to you and your family with my real name, but most people only know me as The Duchess, not Countess as you had guessed."

She gasped. "And Marvin?"

"My friend and associate, Martin Alcott, whom you've met. You were nearly spot on with that one."

"What about the rest of it? Like the…um…kidnapping?" she asked, her voice trailing to a whisper.

"All of it happened. I'm sure you now see why I needed to talk to you. There is a remote chance your story could implicate me in a real and dangerous matter. Your imagination is connected to me somehow, and that's a liability."

"I can't turn it off, though. I wish I could sometimes."

"A lament you share with Martin, I suspect. He's rather brilliant, but reluctant to use all of his gifts."

"He's yellow."

Those two simple words put her right off her groove. "I'm...I'm sorry? Yellow?"

"You're purple."

"I don't understand."

"My doctors called it synesthesia. It's like some of my senses got fused together somehow. Some people just look like people, but some people have like a color around them."

"Like an aura?"

"Yeah, but I hadn't seen anyone glow until Mr. Alcott showed up in the arboretum last Friday."

"That's astounding. Do you think it means something?"

"Mean something? No, it's my stupid, broken brain."

"It's not broken, dear. I suspect it is extraordinary, if perhaps misunderstood."

They both lapsed into silent contemplation. She ruminated on what Veronica had said about Martin glowing and wondered what it could mean. Why was he different from any other person she'd met? A strange, uneasy feeling lingered in her stomach as she thought. Her first instinct was to chalk it up to uncertainty, which made her edgy. Too many unknowns had dogged her this year and today arrived with more questions than answers. Every theory she'd postulated about the girl had proven false. Perhaps she was apprehensive about Edwin's reaction when he came to his senses downstairs. The simplest explanation was that she'd still not had lunch.

They were about to adjourn when a chime sounded the

lift's arrival. She prepared herself to explain to Edwin, who was bound to be livid by this point, but Geoff stepped out instead. Relieved, she turned back to Veronica, but the girl was ashen faced and rigid, staring vacantly at her. The instant their eyes met, reality took a holiday with no forwarding address.

Martin steered his sedan through the roundabout and onto the B4000 toward Wickham. He'd booked lodging for the weekend in a nearby village, and looked forward to some quiet solitude, good food, and plentiful drinks in the countryside. With the planning for the writer's workshop, in addition to his regular work, it had been several weeks since his last sabbatical and he was eager to get away. With the money he'd saved from his new pay grade, the car was the one indulgence he'd allowed himself, and he was most grateful for it on holiday weekends. The traffic was light, and the drive relaxed him.

The afternoon sun shone through the bare trees and caused a strobing effect as he drove along. Despite wearing sunglasses, he still had to shade his eyes from the flashing. His stomach grumbled, which struck him as odd. Not thirty minutes had elapsed since he'd stopped for petrol and a snack at Reading Services, so he shouldn't have been hungry already. Even if it proved to be a hunger pang, he planned to gorge himself on the much-touted food at the inn, so he'd have to ignore it for now. Between the random blinking of the sun and his stomach troubles, he felt ill overall and worried that getting sick would ruin his weekend away. In this wooded area, there wasn't much he could do about it, anyway. His head throbbed and his stomach ached, and he tensed his abdomen, trying to dull the worsening pain long enough to get somewhere.

An inexplicable stabbing pain shot through his navel, and he cried out. His eyes shut tight, and all sensation vanished in an instant. No sunlight, no stomach pain, no sound. Was he dead? He opened his eyes—something he could not do if dead—and discovered he was no longer in his car. Or his body.

His consciousness, his Martin-ness, hovered about six feet above the floor of the lounge level of the Cathedral Mansion. Below him, The Duchess and Veronica sat opposite each other, unmoving. Geoff lay splayed across the floor near the doors of the lift. He looked up, and they also floated in front of him.

"What are you doing here?" The Duchess asked.

"What am *I* doing here? What are *you* doing here? *And* down there?" he retorted. "What the hell's going on here?"

"But you can't be here. You're off in the Cotswolds or something, aren't you?"

"Berkshire, but that's not the point. I was driving along, and now I'm here. Floating. In the lounge."

"Veronica?" she asked, turning to the girl, or the essence of her that floated nearby. Her face showed pure terror at the experience. The Duchess, herself, was also terrified, but fear could never withstand reason in her experience. "What were you thinking about just now?"

The girl stammered as she tried to speak. "I…I wa…was thinking about The Countess and Marvin."

The Duchess did a quick bit of mental math and screamed, "OH MY GOD! Think of something else. Anything else! *Hurry!!*"

In his mind, a second sun burst into being six feet above the floor of the lounge level of the Cathedral Mansion. He squeezed his eyes shut tight for a long second. When he opened them again, he'd returned to his car and inhabited his body once more. Then he saw a tree. Then he saw an airbag deploy. Then he saw nothing.

The yellow flash told her he was gone, but she'd expected that to be the end. Instead, Veronica remained floating next to Ms. Nichols—The Duchess—still confused. She recognized the large man who lay unconscious in front of the lift as the same one she'd seen outside of her house the day she got her letter. That had to mean something. What freaked her out more than anything else was seeing herself sitting below... herself. She had heard of out-of-body experiences before, but those stories involved being near death, and her body appeared perfectly safe and healthy.

"I hope he's okay," Ms. Nichols said.

"Why are we up here, ma'am?"

"I haven't a clue, and I'm not used to not knowing. It's only happened once before, when I got your acceptance to the workshop."

This shook her hard. The words came out of her mouth before she realized she was speaking, and it wasn't her voice that said it. *"I'm looking forward to meeting you, Veronica."*

They both gasped, and they were at once back in their bodies. She leaped from the couch as if she'd been sitting on a spring. She took short pacing steps, shaking her hands at her sides, working out whether she was in control of her body again.

"It was you," Ms. Nichols breathed as she too rose from the sofa. "Somehow, it was you. My dear girl, you have a gift, maybe a dangerous one. On that day, from miles away, you *displaced* me from my body."

"What??"

"I'm guessing now, but it's possible that, between the two of us, we displaced Martin from his. That's extremely concerning because he was driving. By concentrating on something else, it seems we released him, but we must find out if he's all right."

She couldn't stop the shaking. It was too much. Yesterday, she was more or less a normal teenager. Today, someone was unironically telling her she ripped a man out of his body with nothing but her mind, like it made perfect scientific sense. At fifteen, she liked to believe she was becoming stronger and more independent, but she was on the verge of crying, and desperately needed a hug from her mother.

"Oh, you poor thing!" Ms. Nichols said and wrapped her up in a hug.

"How did you know?"

"I didn't, but you were shaking so hard, you looked on the verge of collapse. Come sit down."

They sat comforting each other on the massive sectional sofa, then heard a deep, guttural grunt come from the lift foyer. The gigantic man staggered to his feet, confounded, his eyes searching for something on which to focus.

"I know him! He was at my house that day," she said.

"Yes, he was. I had asked Geoff to learn what he could about your family, as discreetly as possible."

"I remember seeing him lying on the pavement like this when I woke up again."

"You mean he'd passed out in front of your house?"

"Yes, ma'am. Is that important?"

"I can't be sure. I'm still trying to make sense of it myself, but when I'm trying to make sense of something, everything is important until it isn't."

She nodded, feeling like she should say more, but unable to.

"What did you think of?" Ms. Nichols asked. She sounded eerily like her mother's friend, the therapist.

"When?"

"When I told you to think of something else, what was it?"

"I sort of panicked. My mind went blank, but I tried to focus on anything but Mr. Alcott."

"Did you see anything?"

"Pardon?"

"Prophetic visions are unsettlingly commonplace amongst my associates, and that might be the maddest thing that's ever escaped my lips. I wondered if you'd had any. I hope you trust me enough to tell me."

She hesitated. She didn't like to talk about the dreams and thoughts she sometimes had, which is why she wrote them. In writing, they were entertaining fictions, rather than the lunacy or fancy that her parents insisted it must be. Considering the extraordinary experience they'd just shared, though, she felt confident she wouldn't be judged for telling the truth.

"I saw a couple of things, but they don't add up. You know how I said you're purple and your friend is yellow? There was someone with a deep blue aura. I couldn't see their face, but it seemed like a woman. Then a big boat blew up in water the same color as the woman. After that, he disappeared."

"A blue woman and an exploding boat?"

"I told you it didn't make sense."

"Has any of this made sense? Was there anything else?"

"I smelled coffee, but that's not a vision. No, nothing else."

"Everything is important until it isn't," Ms. Nichols repeated with a kind smile. "Are you up to eating something? I'm famished, and we should go find your father before he comes to his senses."

CHAPTER NINE

CRASH AND BANG

Francesca scribbled a to-do list on a notepad at her desk. Each time she wrote a line, she thought, "Do this one first," until she added the next one. She was beginning to go in circles, so she reviewed what she had so far:

Find Martin
Exploding Boats?
Blue woman?
How did this all happen?

It was pointless trying to decide which was most pressing, so she started from the top and grabbed her phone. A good leader always delegates, so it was time to call the cavalry.

"Hullo?"

"Duncan, it's The Duchess."

"Oi, Duchess! Been a mo."

"It has, and I'm sorry I haven't checked in. I'd love to chat, but I'm in desperate need of a favor."

"Well, all right! What's the job?"

"Not what you're thinking. I have reason to believe Martin's been in an accident. Don't ask me how I know. He's not answering his mobile."

"He does that, doesn't he? It's likely nothin' to worry over."

"It's more than that. I need you to find him. He said he

was in Berkshire, so start calling all the A&E departments between Swindon and Reading. If you find him, report back to me, and go to him."

"Dunno if you remember, Duchess, but Tracy's right fit to burst. I can't pop off all over the bloody west lookin' for him if she goes into labor!"

"You're farther that way than anyone else I trust. It's important, Duncan!"

"All right, we'll make some calls. You find someone to look after Tracy, or I ain't movin'."

"Fine, fine. Find him first, and we'll figure out the rest."

"Cheers."

She hung up the phone, scribbled another line on her to-do list, reading "Babysit Tracy," and scowled. More problems. She picked up the phone again.

"Taylor."

"Taylor, it's me."

"Aw, shit. Am I late for my shift?"

"What? No, you're not on duty today."

"That's a relief. I'm in no state to tend bar today. Was feeling stressed, so I've been visiting with Jimmy Cliff, if you catch my meaning."

"I'll pretend I didn't hear that. I am your employer, after all. At least you're able to use the phone. I need you to call the dock supervisors in Felixstowe and Trieste right away. Something terrible may have happened."

"How terrible?"

"Start making calls, Taylor. Tell me what you find. Let's hope that it's nothing."

"Irie." Taylor replied with a giggle.

She hung up the phone and rubbed her temples. Why

couldn't anything ever be simple with these people? If Martin weren't missing, she'd be calling him right now, complaining about the rampant lack of professionalism. She might even use some of the profanity she kept stowed away for emphasis. Word association with profanity gave her an idea, so she grabbed the phone and dialed anew. *"I'm going to regret this,"* she thought.

"Whatever it is, the answer is no."

"Hello to you too, Maureen. If you'd already made up your mind, why bother picking up?"

"Because you need to be told no sometimes. None of your other bloody lackeys will say it, so I will."

She sighed. Phone conversations with Maureen were wont to proceed thus and were about as entertaining as attaching a lobster to one's ear.

"I need a favor of you, but it's not for me."

"For who, then? None of this mysterious Duchess rubbish. You want something from me, you tell me straight."

"I had a premonition that Martin's been in an accident. I'm sending Duncan out to find him, but he needs someone to look after Tracy."

"Christ, her due date is Tuesday! You must be desperate."

She paused. "I am. I might be responsible for his injury somehow, and it's eating me up."

"So, you are human, after all. Let Duncan stay where he is. I'll find him."

"Bless you, Maureen. Call Duncan and see if he's had any luck finding him. He's had long enough to make a few calls by now. Let me know when you're with him, whatever state he's in."

"If I find him hurt, you'll have some explaining to do. You'll be lucky to do it with all your teeth, ya cow."

She disconnected without another word, knowing better

than to spar with Maureen. With her response, though, she felt she could consider the first two tasks sorted, even if they had cost her.

The next two items on her list were far more problematic and nothing she could delegate. Veronica's talent was no mere synesthesia, and her visions were more than just dreams. That much was clear. The connection between herself and Martin and his "beautiful mind" was quirky and useful in certain ways, but this was no longer some curiosity. The scope was daunting, the ramifications dire. It had to be identified, itemized, and controlled.

Her mobile rang, showing Davies Lock and Key. The shop downstairs was now AMWarn, but Tracy hadn't had the heart to change the number of the flat.

"What did you find, Duncan?"

"Good news, bad news, Duchess. He was in an accident, and they've taken him to A&E at the Great Western Hospital in Swindon, but he's all right. No major injuries. Maureen is already on her way."

"That's a relief. I'll wait for their call. Thank you so much."

Her mobile beeped. Another call was coming in.

"Must dash. Good luck to you both."

She pulled the phone away and saw that the incoming call was Taylor.

"Give me good news, Taylor."

"Talked to the supervisors in both ports. Nothing out of the ordinary, but I told them to be alert."

She breathed out a long sigh of relief. "At least one thing's gone right today. Enjoy your night off, Taylor. I may need you in here tomorrow to sort some things out for me."

"No problem, ma'am."

One last call to make, the one she dreaded most of all.

"Hello?"

"Mr. Fancourt, it's Ms. Nichols."

"Ah. I think you ought to know, Ms. Nichols, that I'm having grave doubts about this arrangement."

"To be frank, I'd have expected that, given the circumstances."

"What do you want now?"

"I'm calling for two reasons. First, I hope that you and your wife realize your daughter is beyond gifted. She has one of the most creative minds I've come across."

"That's lovely of you to say, but her marks in algebra would suggest otherwise."

"Second, I was wondering if you could bring her round again next weekend. We had a rather productive morning, and I'd like to continue as soon as possible."

"She's been unwell since we left your…well, I scarcely know what to call it. Your establishment? In fact, she's not left her bedroom. I'm disinclined to agree to anything until she recovers and we've talked."

"I'm sorry to hear that, sir, and I hope she feels better soon. Please tell her I called and that I'd like to speak to her?"

"I will tell her you called, but you should be aware I'll be contacting the trustee this week. From what I saw today, things are not what they seemed when we signed the paperwork, and I may insist upon revisions. Good day, Ms. Nichols."

"I understand, and that is your prerogative. Good day, sir."

She cradled the receiver, walked to the center of her office, and loosed a torrent of obscenity that might have made Maureen blush.

The doors of the Emergency Department slid apart, and Maureen stormed through it, more angry than worried. She wanted explanations first, retribution second, and then she might allow herself to worry. The nurse at the admissions desk looked up to greet her but flinched when she stormed up to her station.

"Can I..." she said before Maureen cut her off.

"Alcott. Where is he?"

"You're looking for a patient?"

"Alcott. Martin Alcott. What room?"

"Are you family?"

"I'm his sister," she lied.

"I'll need identification," the nurse said, and Maureen handed her driver's license to her. "Ms. Abernathy?"

"That's right."

The woman looked up at her. It was certain she doubted her story, but she seemed hesitant about pressing the issue.

"It's my married name, all right? Now, where is he?"

"He's in room number five," she replied, pointing down the hall.

Maureen stomped down the corridor, peering through each open door. No one approached her or inquired where she was going, rightly guessing she was in no mood for a chat. When she spotted Martin's room, she rounded the corner and onto its occupant in one seamless action.

"YOU GIT!! How could you crash your car like that?"

"Mo? What on earth are you doing here?"

"She was sending Duncan to find you, but I came instead. That bloody woman said she's responsible for this somehow. If she is, I'll punch her teeth so far down her throat, she'll..."

"All right, enough! I really don't want to hear the end of that. It's my own fault."

"Well?" she said, awaiting an explanation.

"I was driving in the countryside. It was a perfectly normal afternoon. Then I went out of my head and crashed into a tree."

"You spend an awful lot of time out of your head, don't you?"

"I know it sounds absurd."

"Why did she say she was responsible? You'd better start talking, or you'll be the one needing a dentist."

"I've no idea what happened, I swear, Mo. Maybe it was a hallucination. I was driving, and then I was in the Cathedral lounge. I saw The Duchess, Geoff, and that girl, Veronica. Somebody yelled, and I came back to my car just before impact. That's all there is to tell, I promise!"

"Did you pass out or were you daydreaming again? I knew this would all end in tears sooner or later. At least it doesn't seem serious. You look like shit, though."

"Thanks, at least I feel worse than I look."

She glared at him. He seemed to ken she was in no mood for sarcasm.

"They told me I had a fractured collarbone and a mild concussion. I should be able to go home soon."

"You're not going home. You're staying with me until *I* say you're going home."

"But what about..."

"Ian and Julia have the cat. There's not one reason you should be in that flat by yourself until you've healed up a bit. I've had a concussion before. If they don't admit you overnight, there's a protocol for discharge. The doctors should have told you that."

"I'm sure I can..."

"Did it sound optional, arsehole?"

"No, ma'am."

"And how, pray tell, did you imagine you were getting home without a car?"

Martin winced, as if thinking hurt him, which was something she had always surmised. In this one case, it was more likely the head injury, so she'd give him a pass. Now that she'd gotten all the information she wanted, she softened.

"All right, I'm satisfied. You've had a nasty time of it, so relax and let the doctors do their business. If you're here beyond tonight, you'll be flush with visitors as long as you're here. It's all sorted."

"Cheers, Mo," he said, as he lay back in bed. "They called my family in America, but I'm glad I have some family here, too."

She almost smiled, but her mobile rang. She saw Duncan's number on the screen and remembered she had some calls to make.

"It's all right, Duncan, I'm here with him."

"Good, but that's not why I'm calling. We're on the way to hospital ourselves. I think the little one is ready to make his grand entrance a couple of days early."

"Are you fucking serious right now?"

"On my life. Good thing I didn't go out to Swindon today, eh?"

"Get her there fast. Keep me updated." She ended the call before he could say anything else.

"What was that?" Martin asked.

"There's about to be one more bleeding McCullen in the world."

The knock on her bedroom door startled her awake. She heard her mother's voice.

"Veronica, dear, you have a visitor."

She rolled over, groaning, and saw the door creaking open, with Bea peeking around it.

"Ay, Vero. ¿Estás viva?"

"Almost," she replied, sitting up in her bed.

"I haven't seen you at school. Are you contagious?"

"No, I'm not sick. It's hard to explain."

Bea closed the door behind her, set down her backpack, and sat on the corner of the bed.

"Well, try. You must have told your mum something to get out of school for two days."

"I said I got my period. She didn't ask many questions after that."

"Then what was it?"

She wondered how she might put what happened into words in a way that wouldn't send Bea running screaming out of her house. She hadn't realized how much she needed her friend until she arrived, and she didn't want her to leave now. The more she thought about it, the more distraught she became. She felt the tears prickling under her eyelids and her throat tightened.

"I think I'm losing my mind," she said, her voice cracking. She didn't want to break down so soon, but it wouldn't hold back for long. "I might have killed somebody with my mind."

"Now you're not making any sense. How can you kill someone with your mind?"

The first tear escaped her eye, and she looked up. "If I tell you the whole thing, promise me you won't run away."

"Vero, you're my best friend. I wouldn't run away from you. Tell me."

The truth gushed out of her in torrents. Wave after wave of

fear, amazement, confusion, and pain washed over her friend before she restrained herself. Bea's eyebrows danced on her forehead as she tried to process.

"...and I haven't gotten out of bed since," she concluded with a sob. Her stuttering breath was the only sound in the room.

Bea stood up, took a step forward, and wrapped her in the biggest hug she could give.

"I believe you," she said, and Veronica started to cry again.

When her breathing returned to something close to normal, Bea released her and sat down on the corner of the bed again.

"*Dios mío,* it's no wonder you're a wreck," she said. "I didn't know you were psychic!"

"Me either. I mean, I don't know what it was, but it was real, and I'm so scared."

"Did you tell your parents?"

"Are you mad?"

Bea nodded in understanding but said nothing for a couple of minutes. Veronica only sniffled occasionally. Finally, there was one more question.

"Do you think you'll go back there?"

"What? No, no way! Why would I ever go back?"

"Well, she's still supporting your writing, right?"

"Yeah."

"Could it happen again, this thing with your mind?"

"Erm..." she said, staring at the pattern on her duvet.

"I dunno. Maybe you should go back. If you don't, you might never figure out what happened or why, or she won't sponsor you anymore. What do you do if it happens again?"

Her ears got hot, and the tears welled up again. She looked up, but this time, her friend was wearing a wicked grin. She knitted her eyebrows and tilted her head.

"What am I thinking right now?" Bea said, putting her fingers to her temples.

It was the first time she had laughed since Saturday.

CHAPTER TEN

SPRING FALLOUT

Maureen rubbed her temples. Her professionalism was on the edge of slipping, and she was moments from telling Edwin Fancourt exactly how she felt about him. The tension in his office was thick as treacle, and the negotiations almost as sticky. He had insisted on discussing the trusteeship because of recent events, and she'd tried multiple tactics to get him to relent with precious little success. She had one last shot before her temper got the better of her.

"Mr. Fancourt, we've been through this four times now. There are no tricks, no hidden clauses. We all want what's best for Veronica."

"Well, yes, but...have you seen that place?"

"Unfortunately."

"The agreement said nothing about that! What sort of place is that for an impressionable young girl?"

She clenched her abdomen, then exhaled. It was causing her actual physical discomfort to remain calm. She resisted saying what she was about to say, but her disgust for it didn't make it any less true. "There are few better."

"You must be mad. What does that wretched cathedral offer her that a place like St. Catherine's doesn't?"

"Freedom. In that tower, she has complete freedom to realize her potential. Might she be exposed to things she wouldn't otherwise at St. Catherine's or in Hampstead? No question. Is that a bad thing? I'd say that's up to her to decide."

He rubbed his chin. She wasn't sure if it was a promising gesture, but since he didn't immediately bark back at her, it would do.

"Veronica is my first-born daughter, Ms. Abernathy. Can you blame me for wanting to protect her? Can you blame me for lacking trust in this woman who so willingly gives her everything she's ever wanted?"

"No, sir, not one bit. If I may be frank?"

"I'd say you're already well past that."

"If you were to ask me if I trust her on a personal level, I would say no. In business, however, her word is ironclad."

"That's less reassuring than I'd like."

"Best I can offer, I'm afraid. As the disinterested third party, however, I must ensure that both parties remain satisfied. And let me be crystal clear on this point: I couldn't be *less* disinterested. I will not hesitate to tell either of you to get knotted."

"Your candor is refreshing."

"I've been told worse."

"I trust you more than I'll ever trust her."

"Thank you, sir."

"It wasn't a compliment. Given the updated situation, and as I've told you all four times, I will not have my daughter exploited or corrupted. I demand a renegotiation. The current contract is insufficient!"

That was it for her. She was not ignorant of contract law, but he was trying to use his advantage to cover up his insecurities. Her figures were airtight, the contract was more than fair, and her instructions had been clear. Pussyfooting around the subject was no longer an option, and she exploded.

"For whom, exactly, sir?" she shouted, catching him by

surprise. "You have, on more than one occasion, accused Ms. Nichols of trying to profit from your daughter's talent, when it is you and you alone who insisted on higher figures."

For the first time all day, she'd left him speechless.

"Sir, I am trying to be an impartial party here. I hold no allegiance to Ms. Nichols. I'm not terribly fond of the woman, in fact, but according to my figures, she receives not one farthing in profit from this arrangement. The only thing she wants from your daughter is her time."

"Time is money!"

"Do you hear yourself? *Your* time is money, but she is not a commodity to be traded. Her time is hers! I don't have children myself, but I'm sure I wouldn't treat my own this way. You read the contract from stem to stern and signed your agreement. What does *she* stand to lose from this?"

She saw him stewing, angry pink patches blossoming on his cheeks. It was clear he was unaccustomed to dealing with someone as brash as her, but gradually, the offended expression on his face softened.

"Put yourself in my shoes." She didn't care for his condescending tone one bit, but she was content to let him speak his piece. "When she came home on Saturday, something was different. I'm no expert, but I could tell it wasn't right—she didn't leave her bed for two days. As her father, I had to do something, and amending the contract was within my control."

"I'll grant you it's not ideal, but give this another chance, if for no other reason than to save yourself the extra paperwork. If another such event occurs, I'll be on your side—once is an outlier, twice is a pattern. She deserves the chance to do something incredible and right now, this is her best opportunity. In my opinion, sir."

"Please note my objections to Ms. Nichols, but I think you've reassured me, Ms. Abernathy. I must remember I'm a father first, then a solicitor, but it's my way of managing things. I think we'll give next weekend a miss, but I'll bring her round on the 11th."

"Gladly, sir. I will give her your statement and offer a personal warning to her myself. I could even slap her, if you'd like."

"Good heavens, no! Why would I want that?" he said, repulsed.

Maureen leaned forward, putting both elbows on his desk. "I've always wanted to. Could I slap her and *say* you told me to do it?"

She imagined it was going to be difficult walking into The Cathedral again after everything that'd happened, but it was worse when she got there. It took conscious effort to keep her feet moving forward across the atrium, when every synapse was screaming to flee. How could she face Ms. Nichols again or be sure that she wouldn't cause another catastrophe? Her dad tried to be encouraging, but he only stumbled over his words as usual. She was pretty sure he didn't want them to be here either, but he must have gotten some reassurance from somebody. They boarded the lift and used the card Miss White gave them at the concierge desk, ascending directly to the lounge level.

There was no grand greeting or fanfare when they arrived. They found her sitting at her desk, focused on her notes, taking no notice until her dad cleared his throat. She looked up, and her relief at seeing them was unmistakable.

"I'm so glad to see you both," Ms. Nichols said. "Shall we

talk for a bit, or would you prefer to get straight to work?"

"If it's all the same, ma'am, I'd prefer to work," she replied. "I have some new ideas I'd like to show you."

"Mr. Fancourt, you're welcome to stay or relax in the pub downstairs. It's a bit early for a pint, but Mr. Taylor would be happy to serve you coffee or tea."

"Veronica, which would you prefer?" he asked.

"You can go have some coffee, Dad. I think we'll be fine."

"Text me if you need anything," he said, then disappeared down the lift.

"About our last visit," Ms. Nichols said, but she was not yet in the mood.

"So, I've been like *obsessed* with coffee lately. I don't know why."

"That's interesting. Didn't you say you smelled coffee when you were here last?"

"I never used to drink it before, but there's a lovely old place in Hampstead that has the best cafe latte."

"Veronica," she said.

"There's something so wonderful about coffee when it's done right."

"Did you have a latte before coming here today?"

"Two, actually. Why do you ask?"

"You seem a bit jittery," Ms. Nichols said, "and you also seem most determined to not discuss what happened here two weeks ago."

"I can't, not right now. It takes my thoughts into dark places, and I would rather forget it."

"I completely understand, my dear. Maybe let's get you some nice herbal tea, relax, and chat for a bit."

Ms. Nichols led them up two levels to her kitchen, where they made steaming mugs of lavender-chamomile. They settled over the enormous marble island, where her host produced some incredible homemade chocolate biscuits, and she finally felt more at ease being in The Cathedral.

"When did you first know you wanted to be a writer?" Ms. Nichols asked between bites.

"I wrote an entire story when I was seven," she replied, "and my mum told me that people could be authors for their careers. I knew right away I wanted to do that."

"Your mother was encouraging of it? I'd guessed by your father that they wouldn't approve."

"He still doesn't, but Mum and Ms. Abernathy convinced him I'm talented enough to make a living of it."

"You know, I wanted to be an artist when I was that age. My teachers all thought I could, but when my parents died, I had no choice but to follow in their footsteps and take over the family businesses."

"That's sad. You gave up art completely?"

"Not completely. I still paint in what little free time I have, but with my business interests, that's not much. Although I needed information from you, I still wanted to make sure you never had to give up on your dreams like I did."

"You're gonna make me cry!"

They let the moment breathe and sipped the last of their teas.

"What got you suddenly obsessed with coffee? Ordinarily, I wouldn't advise someone of your age to drink it, but it can be rather good, can't it?"

"It started when I was here last time. After everything happened, I thought I smelled coffee, and I haven't been able to get it off my mind since."

"You clearly don't need more today, but perhaps you'd enjoy this new roast I picked up recently," Ms. Nichols said and retrieved a paper bag from a cupboard.

She inhaled the aroma of the beans, and the scent flooded her senses. "That's the same one I smelled two weeks ago!"

"Surely, it's just coffee, isn't it?"

"No, I could never forget it. It has to be the same one! It's like I can almost see the blue woman again."

"That's very interesting."

"Where does it come from?"

"Trieste. A company that I've become interested in learning more about, called Tessa Roasters. I'm sorry to have brought it up. Maybe we could return to the lounge and work on some writing prompts?"

"What did you have in mind?"

"I was thinking I might show you one of my paintings, and you could write how it makes you feel."

"Ooh, that's brilliant! I'd love to see your work!"

Martin's recovery had been smooth, with only a couple of minor painful setbacks along the way. The most painful part, of course, was when he'd roomed with Maureen for a week. If she hadn't gone into accounting, he imagined she'd have made a decent nurse, but a week of her "care" was about all he could tolerate. The first half of March was spent rediscovering the rhythm of living by himself, but a few modifications to the flat let him live comfortably one-armed.

Since the accident, though, parts of his mind seemed closed off or locked, which bothered him beyond measure. It had been almost a full month since he'd felt The Duchess in his thoughts, and he never expected that was something that he would miss.

It was like someone had moved a piece of furniture while he was away. The shift was minute enough to not see, but you bump into it anyway, just because it's out of place.

The silence of his flat was growing quite uncomfortable indeed, so he chose to phone a friend.

"Hello?" the voice answered.

"Hey, Fee," he said.

"Martin! How are you, mate?"

"I'm all right, I guess. Feeling a bit caged today."

"Sorry we haven't been by to visit. We've turned into proper homebodies since Trieste."

"I can't fault you for that. How's Julia?"

"She's her usual lovely self, as long as we don't talk about what happened. I figure she'll process it in her own time."

"No question. She really is as tough as The Duchess, isn't she?"

"Every bit. I try not to think about it too hard. If this is a dream, I don't ever want to wake up from it."

He laughed gingerly. His shoulder still hurt if he overdid it.

"What has you feeling caged?" Ian asked.

"Well, I'm not cleared to drive yet, not that I have a car to drive, so I'm certain I haven't left the flat in days. My life revolves around sleeping, eating, and working. I'm not trying to lay a guilt trip on you or anything, but the last person to visit was Maureen last Saturday, and you can imagine what a treat that was." He couldn't restrain his sarcasm, so he finished his report with, "Apart from that, I'm fine."

The mobile's small speaker crackled with Ian's laughter. "All right, pizza or curry?"

"What?"

"Do you want pizza or curry for dinner tonight?" he repeated, as if talking to a toddler.

"Are you for real?"

"Sure. If I'm honest, I've been cooped up here too. I think Julia can do without me for one evening."

"Cheers, Fee. I didn't mean to sound so pathetic."

"It worked, didn't it? Give yourself some credit. You're still broken and allowed to be pathetic sometimes. Don't make it a habit, though. It's unbecoming. So, which do you want?"

"You should know curry is always my first choice."

"Done. Be there in about half an hour."

"See you soon," he said, and ended the call.

He looked around the apartment, and it appeared bigger somehow, knowing that he wouldn't be alone much longer. He considered tidying up a bit, but it was only Ian coming by, and he was sure he'd understand.

As he threw away the paperboard container from today's lunch, something crept into the edge of sensation, familiar but distant. He tried to focus, but it eluded him, making it unsurprising that the knock on the door startled him so much. It was way too soon for Ian to have arrived with dinner, and he wasn't expecting other visitors. What startled him further, upon peering through the peephole, was seeing The Duchess on the other side of the door, which he opened without delay.

"Er...hi. What are you doing here?" he said in a clumsy greeting.

"I haven't seen or heard from you for a month. Did I do something wrong?"

"Well, come in first. Sorry that the place is a bit of a mess. Cleaning becomes more difficult and less important when you're down an arm."

"I can imagine," she replied, closing the door behind her. "Why haven't you called?"

"I've been busy recuperating and adjusting to a new normal.

Some days, just getting by is hard enough."

"That's not the reason, and you know it."

He hesitated. "No, it's not. It's complicated."

"Enough. With all we've been through together, I deserve better than empty platitudes."

"I'm sorry. I don't quite know how to say it, though."

"Say it, then. I'm not some delicate flower."

"I was scared. Of you. What happened before the accident was terrifying, and I didn't know how to deal with it."

"Come now, Martin. What you went through was extraordinary and traumatic. Not a single, well-adjusted soul could shrug that off. Is that all?"

"Yes, that's all. Why shouldn't it be? Did you get pulled out of your body from fifty miles away?"

"I wasn't fifty miles away, but I got pulled out of my body the same as you. Perhaps you recall? You were there."

"Fine," he said, his voice turning to ice. "You want the whole truth? I thought by not talking to you, I could more easily pretend none of it had happened. It can't have. I need to believe that."

She smirked. His assertiveness hadn't fazed her. "Was that so hard? You could have said so."

"I *did* say so!" he shouted, wincing at the pressure on his still healing shoulder.

"Would it help to know that I've been equally frightened by what happened, but what frightened me more was thinking you wouldn't forgive me?"

He blinked several hard blinks.

"Now that we've gotten that all out, is there anything I can do to help while I'm here? I can be handy sometimes. For whatever it's worth, were you aware I don't employ a cleaning service for my tower? Taylor and the other bartenders help me keep the pub tidy, but I do all the rest of the cleaning myself."

"I suppose it's hard to clutter that much space when it's only you using it."

"Oh, there's been more than me for some time. Tajana and her family were living at The Cathedral until only last week, when they moved into their own flat in Parsons Green."

"Her family?"

"Yes, I got her mother and son out of Trieste a couple of weeks ago. Her mother, Sofija, is a treat. It's a bit like having my mum back, in a way, and little Goran is a sweetheart. I'm not sure what to do with them in the long term, but I'm keeping them here, safe and sound. At least until I'm sure they can return safely."

"I suppose that's a plus. It's been going well, then?"

"Tajana can be standoffish, but so can I, as I'm sure you'd attest. I'm starting to like having people around. Hint, hint," she said with a wink.

"Steady on."

"Tell me where everything goes, and I'll take care of it. Do you want me to make dinner?"

"Well, er, Ian is on his way over with curry. I had just gotten off the phone with him when you arrived."

"Oh, brilliant, then. I'll tidy up and be on my way."

"You needn't do that. I can manage."

"Stop me," she said, kissed him on the cheek, and began clearing rubbish from his coffee table.

"So sorry, *Duchessa*, but they will not let us leave port."

"Nino, the *Servola* was supposed to be in Felixstowe yesterday. Not only is she still in port, but now you're telling me *Barcola* is also being held?"

"*Si, signora.* The GdF have not left our docks for weeks. They insist on inspecting everything inside and out."

"Have they said why?"

"They suspect contraband aboard. That's all they will say."

"Have they found anything?"

"There is nothing for them to find! *Servola* carries only canned tomato products, olive oil, and other foodstuffs. *Barcola* is carrying wholesale goods from China. We have opened every container, but still they will not let us sail."

"I'm sure you've done all you can, Nino. Please continue to comply with them, and I'll do what I can from here. *Chiarbola* and *Scorcola* will remain here in England until we can sort this out."

"*Grazie.*" Nino replied and disconnected.

She placed the phone on its cradle and scanned the contents of her desktop. A small, round glass paperweight caught her eye. She picked it up and hurled it against the wall opposite her desk. It disappointed her when, instead of shattering into a satisfying spray of shards, it only dented the paneling.

Tessaro was behind these administrative delays and, although his creativity and reach impressed her, she'd had enough. *"He must be an expert chess player,"* she mused. She held no sway with the local police, and he had cut off any family ties she might have been able to play. The name Nikolić was now poison in the eastern Adriatic, but she refused to conclude that he had boxed her in.

Sorting out Trieste was bound to be thorny business, and establishing a Five Pence presence in a new port would cost time and money. As it was, she was already losing time and money with her small fleet bound up in red tape. The longer she considered it, the more angry she became. Importing coffee was possibly the least important thing she could do, but now she was determined to continue the business out of sheer spite.

She made more phone calls as the afternoon droned on, trying to circumvent the blockade. She wanted a berth in the Mediterranean, to stay close to both Europe and her sources in Ethiopia. By day's end, she had secured a temporary provisional berth in Port Said, Egypt. She was not admitting defeat in Trieste—that was unthinkable—but Giovanni had made it personal, and he didn't realize how stubborn she could be.

"I need to punch something," she thought. She took the stairs up to her personal gymnasium on Level A, and the ache in her legs cleared her head. As she worked out, the stress flowed out of her with each punch and kick delivered to the heavy bag. Exercise had gotten her through tough times of late, and it centered her like few other things could. As she ducked, bobbed, and jabbed at her target, plans and schemes hatched in her thoughts. Every time she got close to an "aha" moment, though, she calculated how her adversary could parry her maneuver, and she'd throw a haymaker to the bag in frustration. Her knuckles ached from the impacts, even though she'd wrapped and padded them well, so she turned around to try a different activity. She jumped when she saw Geoff standing at the entrance and, by instinct, threw a small medicine ball at him. He deflected it with his forearm and grunted.

"Don't sneak up on me like that, Geoff! Announce yourself when you come up to this level, for God's sake!"

"Beg your pardon, ma'am. Wonder if I might have a word?"

"You're not usually the conversational type. What's on

your mind?"

"The girl."

"What about her?" she asked, unwrapping her fists.

He stared at her, his face rigid as stone, but she thought she saw a tic at the corner of his eye.

"Geoff? Is there something wrong?"

"I'm...er..."

"Just say it, lunkhead. You came to talk to me, remember?"

"I'm frightened of her."

She froze. "Say that again very slowly."

"Seems like a nice girl, but every time I'm near her, my head goes all foggy and I wake up with a headache."

"That lines up with what we experienced in the lounge. Well, Goliath, I believe you've met your David."

"It's no fair to attack someone's mind."

"No truer words have been spoken, I assure you. I doubt it's intentional, but if it makes you feel better, I'll try to keep some distance between the two of you."

"Ta. I won't let you down again."

She was about to let him leave when his reply sank in. "Wait, when did you let me down before?"

"When she knocked me out. Can't do me job out cold."

She reached up to pat him on the shoulder. "You're human, Geoff, and this is beyond all of us. Veronica is a friend. I was never in danger, and you have never failed me. All the same, I won't put the two of you together if I can help it. Will that be all right?"

"Okay," he said. He turned and left without so much as a by-your-leave.

She dabbed herself with a towel, and thought, *"I'm going to need a very stiff drink after all that."*

CHAPTER ELEVEN

THE DEEP BLUE WOMAN

"Done," Veronica announced.

They'd been working quietly together in the library of the Duke Suite on the top floor, Francesca painting while Veronica wrote. Last week had been much the same, after the change of scenery. When she opened up about her own artistic aspirations, the young woman suggested that she should take up painting again during their sessions. It had inspired some of the finest work she'd done in decades, and it gave her a freedom she didn't know she'd missed.

She put down her brush, wiped her hands on a nearby towel, and said, "Let's see, then." Veronica handed her the neatly handwritten page, and she sat down and read. She rarely found herself moved to tears by art, but her eyes welled up as she read the short story based on her own painting. Although it bore little resemblance to what she'd actually painted, the emotions it evoked in her were so powerful, she wondered if subconsciously it was what she'd meant all along.

"It's magnificent, Veronica!" she said, coming to the end with a sniffle.

"You really like it?"

"No, I love it. I can't believe you packed so much into 3,000 words. It's like I was there. Look at me, I'm a mess!" She dabbed her eyes.

"Aww, thank you, Ms. Nichols!"

"It's so polished for only two weeks. Did someone help you edit it?"

"Well, Mum looked over it and corrected a few things."

"You should submit it to *Preeminence* for their next edition. I'll send them a photo of the painting as well. I'll never be able to look at it the same way."

"Oh, I'm sorry!"

"No, dear, believe me, that's a splendid thing. Would it be all right if I gave you a hug?"

"Sure."

They embraced for a few moments, until Francesca pushed her away, looked her straight in the eyes, and said, "You're going to be famous one day, Veronica. I know it."

"Do you really think so?"

"If I have anything to do with it, I'd guarantee it." She chanced a glance at her watch and cursed. "Bloody hell, I'm overdue!"

"What is it?"

"My sister is coming over later for dinner and I should have started by now. I have to clean up fast."

"Is there anything I could do to help?"

"Are you any good in the kitchen?"

"I know how to make Pot Noodle and salad, but Mum never asks for help. She won't even let Dad in when she's cooking."

"Salad! I was thinking a nice rocket salad would be perfect. Toddle down to the pub and see if it's all right with your father. If he'd prefer to go home, I can have you escorted back to Hampstead later."

For the next hour, they cooked together and chatted. She sipped red wine while she made pasta from scratch, and Veronica shaved the Parmesan. They squeezed lemons and laughed as if they'd been friends for years. Once dinner was completed, they loaded the chafing dishes and sent them down to the formal dining room via the dumbwaiter system. She explained how the small lifts could also be warmed or chilled depending on the food being transported, and the younger woman hung on her every word.

"With that sorted, let's adjourn to the lounge. It'll be much more comfortable awaiting our guests there."

"Shouldn't we clean up?"

"You've done enough, dear. I couldn't have done it without you. It's time to relax."

"Tajana, it is almost time to leave. Are you ready?" her mother called from the living room.

She sat on the edge of her bed, seething, yet sad. Her emotions fluctuated by the hour and had done so daily for the two months since arriving in London. It exhausted her. She had some gratitude for what her sister had done for her, like getting her family into England, putting them all up in a posh basement flat in Earl's Court, and arranging private tutoring for Goran. She'd met every need they'd had, and fulfilled many of their wishes, yet she harbored incandescent anger at being stuck here in limbo. Most of all, she was bored—intensely fucking bored with filling her days with chat shows and chess with her mother. She missed the vibrancy of Trieste, despite the most important parts having been imported across the continent.

Her sister—she still had trouble even thinking that—insisted that they not roam about much until she had better measured the scope and reach of Signore Tessaro, but weeks passed with no updates. The only time she ever saw her sister was on Saturday evenings, at the family dinner she insisted on hosting at her mansion in the clouds. Tonight would be the seventh such event, and she'd grown to resent it.

"The driver, he is here! Tajana, do you hear me?"

"Give me a moment," she replied, looking at herself one last time in the bedroom mirror. She wiped her face where the tears had smudged her makeup, but she chose not to fix it. This time, she would not play happy family.

"Your face is a mess," her mother chided. "You should fix it."

"Enough, Mamica. We wouldn't want to keep dear sister waiting," she mocked.

Mr. Jenkins, personal driver of The Duchess, waited at street level with a courteous greeting for the family, as always. Sofija struck up her usual conversation with him, asking how his family was and other pleasantries, but she would neither speak to nor make eye contact with him. In the car, Goran sat up against his mother's hip.

"Are you sad, Mami?" he asked.

"A little, Gogi, and a little mad, too. I'll be fine though. Don't worry."

Her mother and Mr. Jenkins chatted all the way across London while she stewed in her bad mood. They arrived at the main entrance of The Cathedral and walked into the lobby. Miss White, the ever-present concierge, greeted them and picked up the phone to announce their arrival. She nodded twice with a polite, "Yes, ma'am," and shuffled items on her desk. At last, she ended the call and addressed them.

"She's still engaged with a previous appointment. You are to meet her in the lounge, Level D. Here is your keycard."

"Thank you," she snapped, snatching the card from the

receptionist's hand. She could feel the side-eye as they entered the atrium.

"What's the matter with you, Tajana?" her mother asked. "You've been pouting all day."

"Not now."

The trio walked the length of the atrium into the nave lobby and rode up the private lift to the lounge level. When the doors opened, she saw her half-sister sitting on the sofa, conferring with a young girl. They were unaware that anyone had arrived until she cleared her throat, and even surprised herself with how much disdain she packed into her "ahem."

"Oh, good. You're all here. Wonderful. Won't be a mo. I need to finish up with Veronica. Oh yes, introductions! Veronica, this is my sister, Tajana, her mother, Sofija, and her little boy, Goran."

The girl looked up from her notebook and flicked the bangs out of her face. She said, "How do you..." before she froze mid-sentence, stunned.

"Er...pleased to meet you," Tajana replied, unsure how to respond to the partial greeting.

"Veronica, are you all right?" Francesca asked her.

"She's...*deep blue.*"

"Deep..." she repeated before her brain caught up. "Are you sure?"

"Oh, yeah. The little boy is light blue, the other lady is sort of pinkish, but she's deep blue, like the ocean."

"The one you saw before?"

"Has to be."

"Excuse me," Tajana interrupted, "but would you tell me what the fuck you're talking about?"

"Language!" her mother chided. "Your son is here."

She glared at her before turning back to the pair on the sofa, awaiting an answer.

"All of you, please, come sit down. We have much to discuss."

Sofija and Goran moved toward the sofa, but she barred them with her arm.

"No. I've had enough of this cape and knife bullshit."

"I think you mean 'cloak and dagger,'" Francesca said, trying to be helpful.

"Shut your hole!" she shouted. "You have kept us locked up in that flat for two months now. No news, no updates, only a 'family' dinner once a week where you tell me nothing. Tell me everything right now, or send me and *my* family back to Trieste, where we belong."

"Tajana, be grateful to your sister. She has been so kind," her mother offered, attempting to defuse her.

"Grateful for what we didn't ask for, Mami? She owes us an explanation, and I want it now!"

"I understand your frustration. I'd like to paint you the entire picture, but it's…complicated."

"Are we in danger, yes or no?"

"At present, my research suggests there is no danger here in London."

"Is there danger in Trieste?"

"That's harder to say. I still don't know what he's up to."

"Should I go?" Veronica asked.

"Not yet, dear. If this is the blue woman you saw, I need you here."

"What is this 'blue woman'?"

"Veronica has a gift, of a sort. She sees people in colors, and I think it means something. When…" Francesca paused, glancing at the girl, then back to her, making her even more suspicious. "She dreamt about a deep blue woman, and it seems to have been you."

"We're leaving. I've put up with enough nonsense. Come on, Gogi," she said.

"Please stay. We've made a lovely Tagliatelle Bolognese with a rocket and roasted asparagus salad upstairs in the dining room. I think it turned out brilliantly."

"No."

"Give me the weekend, Tajana. If I haven't made it right by Monday, you can all go home. Let's talk over dinner and I'll tell you what I can. You three are the only blood family I have left, and I've grown quite fond of having you here."

"Fine. You're lucky Goran loves spaghetti."

"Actually, it's..." Francesca said, before Veronica nudged her with her elbow, shaking her head vigorously. "Right. Who's hungry?"

"Can you drive?"

"Duchess?" Martin answered, puzzled by her unprompted pop quiz.

"I need you at The Cathedral immediately, if not sooner. Can you drive?"

"Signaling is tricky, but I can manage it. Thanks for loaning me the Audi, by the way. Is it an emergency?"

"It's not an emergency, per se, but it's urgent. There's quite a lot at stake. I need you here in person."

"I was about to heat some dinner. Can it wait until after that?"

"I have Tagliatelle Bolognese almost on the table. Get here as fast as you can."

"All right," he said. He opened his mouth to say more, but heard the call disconnect.

As he collected his keys and wallet, he pondered why he did what she asked without question. A dinner invitation on short notice was one of her least outlandish requests, but it wouldn't have mattered. Perhaps it was some kind of spell or Jedi mind trick, but that struck him as too plausible, given the circumstances. Whatever the reasoning, her cooking was top-notch, sure to be a damn sight better than whatever frozen meal he'd have ended up with, so off he went.

He arrived in the main dining room on Level C a shade over an hour later, but he hadn't expected there to be a crowd already in attendance. Judging by the dishes, he was also the only person who hadn't yet eaten, which he considered somewhat rude.

"Er, hello," he said, failing to grasp much else.

"Martin! You're right on time. Have some pasta."

"Cheers."

"How's your shoulder healing, Mr. Alcott?" Veronica asked, her upper-class manners on display.

"I got here undamaged, so that's good enough for now. Thank you for asking."

He sat in a vacant seat next to her as The Duchess presented him with a plate of savory sauce over what looked like homemade noodles and salad with shaved Parmesan and a lemon wedge.

"It looks lovely," he said, about to tuck in.

The Duchess returned to her seat and addressed the table. "While we awaited your arrival, I enlightened the audience about several important things. Things like how we met before we met and how you broke your collarbone. How you *really* broke your collarbone."

"That's bold," he said between bites. "But if you told them all that, why did you need me here?"

"For starters, my sister won't have a word of it. Second, young Goran here has quite a few questions for you of the 'are you a superhero' variety."

He looked at the boy, who looked back at him expectantly.

"And you wanted me to give a demonstration? Is that it?"

"Nothing that grandiose. I thought that, between the three of us, we could corroborate the story."

He turned to Tajana. "Are you likely to believe it if I did?"

"No."

"See? Please tell me I didn't drive a full hour into the city with one arm on a Saturday night for this."

She scowled. "*You're being completely unreasonable,*" he heard in his thoughts.

"I am *not* being unreasonable," he said.

"*What were you planning for dinner tonight?*" she said without moving her mouth.

"Microwave burrito. What of it?"

The rest of the table stared at him as if his hair had caught fire. As he looked at their faces, he realized she had duped him into demonstrating, after all.

"That was a dirty bloody trick, you know."

She squeezed her lips together, attempting to restrain her amusement. It looked to him like she was trying to play an invisible trumpet. Laughter burst out of her. She, too, must have seen his mental image.

"That's funny, but I played viola," she said once the laughter abated.

"How lovely for you." He was altogether unamused.

Tajana sneered at him, breaking her silence. "All right,

clever boy. What am I thinking right now?"

"It's not like that," he said with an exasperated sigh. "We share a kind of psychic connection. It doesn't work with anyone else, or at least I thought not until we met Veronica."

"Her gifts differ from Martin's, but clearly something has brought us all together," The Duchess said, continuing the explanation. "The one thing of which I'm certain is that none of this is coincidence. The dreams, the visions, the synesthesia. It all points to a sort of prophecy, and you, Tajana, are now a part of it."

"I won't do it."

"Won't do what?"

"Any of it. This is madness."

"She sounds like Maureen," she told him, before turning back to her sister. "Would it change your mind if it meant you could go home?"

She seemed prepared to object, but stopped short. She rolled her eyes before saying, "What are you proposing?"

"I need an insider. Maybe not quite a mole, since you're too well known now, but someone who has seen how Tessaro operates. We have so little to go on, so it's a card I'm willing to play."

"This is a game to you? He stole me and told you he would hurt me if you didn't comply. He would not try this again?"

"My intuition says no. You are no longer of value to him. He'll have you watched, but he has no reason to harm you or your family."

"You are sure of this?"

"I cannot be sure of anything, but my instinct is often accurate in such matters."

"What would I do?"

"If you agree to be my eyes and ears, I can arrange for

your enhanced safety. I may not know everything about how that port operates, but I have resources there and I'm a fast learner. If you'd agree to another week here in London, I'd like to introduce you to a friend of mine who is rather good at pulling threads and connecting dots."

"Threads? Dots? I don't understand you."

"What I mean is, with some information from you and putting my associates in the right places, I believe we can *change* the game, as you put it."

"How?"

"I plan to resume shipping coffee through Five Pence. Your expertise will be a tremendous benefit to my fledgling enterprise, so I'm offering you a position as head of the new import division."

"But coffee is how you crossed him before!"

"Yes, I know, and for the past two months, I've played it safe with Giovanni. Now, I shall kick the hornets' nest. He's trying to harass me out of his way, but he continues to misjudge me."

Martin looked at Veronica, who had taken on a rather pallid countenance. It reminded him of how he must have looked on that fateful day in her office when The Duchess revealed the full depth of her business interests. Instead of sitting idly by, he thought he could help in some small way and pulled her aside.

"Overwhelmed?"

"You might say that."

"You're wondering what you've gotten yourself into, yeah?"

Her eyes shot toward The Duchess and back, and she nodded.

"Not so long ago, I was in your shoes, and it's not as scary as it sounds. If it helps, I've never seen her be cruel or break a promise."

"How would you know?"

"She's...er...well...in a manner of speaking, sort of my girlfriend?"

Her expression shifted from shock to excitement. "Juicy!"

He could feel the blush radiate to the tips of his ears.

Alessio paced laps around the chairs opposite his father's desk. He stole occasional glances at the seat of power, wondering when he would do something. Anything.

"Calm down, boy. Everything is going to plan."

"This is your plan? This woman disrespected you, and you still allow her to ship cargo through *our* port! It is a disgrace."

"What would you have me do, Alessio? Kill her workers? They are Triestino, like us."

"She broke the contract, papa."

"She did."

"Your father would have burned their warehouses. Would you make him proud, papa?"

"I am not my father!" he barked before regaining composure. "She was sincere in not knowing the rules, and I show her mercy for that, but she will honor my terms, whatever she expects."

"Mercy is weakness."

"Mercy is business, my son. Money speaks louder than action. I will take this *Duchessa's* money while I drive her out of our waters. You must be patient."

He realized the ice beneath him was now thin, but he hadn't had his say. He racked his brain for anything he could say that would not further arouse his father's wrath. His tactics made no sense. There was no reason he should give this stranger special treatment compared to the other families.

"I've had enough of patience. I'm going out."

"Where are you going?"

"To see Paolo."

"Good. Maybe he can talk sense to you since you have stopped listening to me."

His father turned back to his papers, and he walked out of the building as fast as he could. He called Paolo Zanetti, his closest associate and best friend since childhood. They arranged a meeting at their favorite bar, and the taxi dropped him at the entrance minutes later. He found him at their regular table, waiting with a beer.

"What's the problem?" Paolo asked.

"My father," he replied, downing half the glass of beer.

Paolo sighed. "Your father is a good man, and you know that."

"My father is soft. I've been saying it since we were boys. Surely, you remember. These Five Pence bastards should be smoldering ashes by now."

"If you burn them all down, what is left?"

"Us. We would own Trieste completely, as we should by right."

"But the government would..."

"The government does not concern me, Paolo! Money in the right pocket takes the fangs out of the police. You should know. You have done it yourself, many times!" He gulped the rest of his beer and signaled the barman for another. "It's time I showed my father what I am capable of."

"He is the *Capo*. What happens if you are unsuccessful?"

"I will succeed. Do not doubt me, or I will find someone else who believes."

"Alessio, you are my best friend. You have been my best friend since we were schoolboys. I know you will succeed. I only wonder what your father will think."

"If I succeed, *no one* will wonder what my father thinks again."

"What are you saying?"

"I'm saying it's time this family had a new *Capo.* What part of that did you not understand?"

"You wouldn't..."

"Stupid! Of course not! It is time for him to retire and answer to me."

"Do you trust me, my friend?"

"Above all others," he said.

"You are a fool. Your father will never answer to you."

He slapped him hard. "I trust you, but I will not listen to disloyalty."

"Is it disloyal to warn you of a mistake you're about to make? If you are intent on making it, I will follow you."

"Good. I am making a plan for how we get rid of this woman forever."

"What of your father?"

"Do not speak of my father again! This is my plan, and I do not care about his. It is time to act."

"What can I do?"

"We need access to the docks at Five Pence. Do we have anyone there?"

"No, and your father has their berths crawling with police."

"That will be a problem, but we are resourceful, are we not?"

"We are. We always have been."

He pulled a small notebook out of his back pocket and started scribbling in it.

"Talk to your team and get me these supplies. I want them by the end of the week."

Paolo looked at the list, and concern crossed his face.

"I hope you know what you're doing, Alessio. I think I do, and you had better be sure."

"Quiet, Paolo. Do what I tell you and don't fail me."

CHAPTER TWELVE
KALEIDOSCOPE

It was another Saturday morning, and Francesca awaited her protégé in the lounge, as usual. She looked forward to their meetings and had made vast improvements in her own creative writing during the five weekends they'd spent working together. This Saturday was different, though, because she had no intention of writing today, at least not creatively. It was only data that mattered.

The friendly chime of the lift sounded the arrival, and Veronica stepped into the room alone. After the first weekend, her father decided he would be far less nervy if he spent a couple of hours in the pub. Her head cocked to the side, and her face scrunched into a question mark.

"I know you must be wondering why they are here today," she announced, gesturing to the cast of characters arranged around the lounge.

Martin and Maureen sat fussing over Tracy and baby Aidan. Simon sat on the other side of Martin, gawking at the lounge. Ian snoozed on the opposite side of the sofa, while Julia sat erect with a clipboard on her lap. Taylor and Duncan played billiards at one of the three tables on the south riser. Geoff stood behind the bar on the north riser, serving Tajana her second Bloody Mary of the morning.

"Yes, ma'am," Veronica said, although the confused look did not leave her face.

"I have some suspicions about your colorful talent, and I asked my other friends, family, and associates to help me test my theories. I hope you don't mind."

"No, I guess not, but what kinds of tests?"

"Only one test, and it could not be simpler. Tell me what you see when I introduce each person, and Julia will note it. Julia, are you ready?"

"Certainly," Julia replied, readying her pen.

"Then we'll begin with me. What do you see?"

"Purple, ma'am. Royal purple."

They continued around the room until they had accounted for everyone. Julia, Ian, and Maureen had no colors. Martin was, as before, a bright pale yellow, and she had already established Tajana's deep blue. Simon was a frosty baby blue, Taylor had a faint greenish hue, and Duncan's mist was pale pink, which bothered him to no end. The ones that fascinated her most of all were Tracy and Geoff. Veronica said neither of them had a color, but she sensed that they still had auras she couldn't see. Tracy radiated heat, which she found comforting, while Geoff seemed to emit raw power, and he was difficult for her to look at.

"Are you all right, Veronica?" she asked.

"I'm fine, but I think I need to sit down."

"By all means, dear. Does it often tire you?"

"No, not usually. I see the colors all the time. I wanted to be sure, so it took a lot of concentration." She took a spot on the corner of the sofa nearest to Julia.

"What troubles me," Francesca continued, "is that there's no commonality, so I can draw no definitive conclusions from it. I was hoping a pattern would emerge—I'm certain there is one."

There was a murmur of hushed conversation, punctuated

by the intermittent sharp crack of billiard balls colliding or the coo of an infant. She reexamined her guests, and the status in the lounge was evidently quo. Everyone appeared to have taken the new information in stride.

"Geoff, would you join us, please?" she called across the lounge.

He dropped his towel on the bar and walked to his employer's side as ordered.

"Please have a seat next to Veronica on the sofa," she directed.

"Ma'am?" he replied.

"Have a seat, Geoff. It's not a trick."

"But..."

"I remember what we discussed, but you needn't worry. It'll be fine."

He did as she'd said, and sat near, but not directly next to, Veronica. He kept his focus on his employer, unsure of what she was playing at. Without warning, the girl leaped toward Geoff and wrapped him in a hug. His surprised grunt caught everyone's attention, and all eyes turned toward them.

"Veronica, why have you thrown yourself at Geoff?"

"It doesn't make sense, but I got this intense urge to hug him," she said without releasing him. "I had this feeling that he needed it. I'm not a hug person, like at all, but I *had* to."

His thick arms hung in the air awkwardly. She studied his face, and it wore an unusual blend of surprise, confusion, and unexpected relief, as if he really had needed it. The quip she'd prepared died on her tongue, though. Before she could say another word, her body went rigid from her feet up, as if being dipped in liquid nitrogen. She closed her eyes and felt herself rise. When she opened them next, she was floating near the ceiling with Martin and Veronica.

"It's happening again," she announced.

"No shit, Sherlock. What gave it away?" Martin replied.

The trio looked below at the commotion now unfolding. They could see their own bodies frozen and staring. Veronica was still clutching Geoff, who was now unconscious. Several attendees were shaking their heads and sticking their fingers into their ears. Ian and Julia were standing, now trying to figure out who to help first, and Maureen slapped Martin's body's face, trying to wake him.

"Oi! Quit that!" he shouted, but she did not hear.

"Keep your heads!" she said to the pair. "At least we're all here together and safe, unlike last time. I'm developing a theory here, but we must end this right away before Maureen becomes more violent."

"Agree! Absolutely agree!" Martin yelped.

"Think of something outside of this room. Picture a tree or rock. Any random object will do, but not a notion of anything or anyone in the lounge. Understood?"

They all closed their eyes, and their consciousnesses drifted downward to the floor. Three sharp inhales and stunned silence suggested the episode was over.

"Someone, please get a towel for Geoff's nose," she said, addressing the trickle of blood that was seeping from his nostril. As soon as they heard her speak, the voices erupted. Most shouted some variation of, "what was that?" with several more descriptive metaphors sprinkled in for good measure.

"Ladies and gentlemen, please calm yourselves! I'm afraid I have no solid explanation to give you for what you've all experienced, but I can hazard a guess. Please take your seats."

Some guests sat, but others, like Maureen and Tajana, remained standing, almost maliciously.

"First, let me be clear that correlation is not causation,

and my thoughts are merely correlative. As some of you may know, Martin and I share a form of a psychic connection. It seems Veronica also possesses this gift, only hers is much more powerful."

"Psychic connection? Are you off your nut?" Ian shouted.

"As you have seen yourself, Ian, it is quite real. If I may continue?" she replied, staring through him. "This is my third time experiencing this phenomenon. Each time, Veronica has been involved, and I'm almost certain that it also involves her proximity to Geoff, which explains his current state. I also believe the episode prior to this one caused Martin's auto accident."

"Why were my ears ringing?" Taylor asked.

"I got dizzy," Tracy said.

She nodded, but did not answer. Instead, she turned to Maureen. "Did you feel anything?"

"Apart from a burning desire to rip your hair out, no. Nothing new there."

"Ian? Julia?"

"No ma'am," Julia answered. "Worry, but no ringing ears or dizziness."

"That confirms my theory, or at least part of it. She identified each of you impacted by this event as having a color. I think it suggests a connection, or at least an openness to it."

"But what does it mean?" Duncan asked.

"That's where I'm still unsure, and it's just as likely that I'm wrong," The Duchess said, raising eyebrows around the room. "To call this 'uncharted territory' would be stretching the metaphor. In the meantime, I think we've had enough data for today. Veronica, Martin, and I have some further talking to do. Taylor, your shift starts in the pub soon. I suggest the rest of you go home and try to enjoy the remainders of your respective Saturdays."

"Just you hang on a minute!" he shouted. "I just seen some spooky shit they don't show on those ghost hunter shows, and you're gonna tell me to 'enjoy my Saturday?' Not a chance, Duchess. Nobody ever took down Geoff before. You say this little girl done it with her brain, and we're s'posed to just accept it?"

"I don't think she meant to," she said offhandedly.

"Weren't what I asked, were it? You brought us up here for your little test. Now you owe us answers."

"I don't have answers yet, Duncan. Only theories, which I've told you. There's nothing else to debate."

"What are we supposed to do, then?" Tracy asked.

"All I can say with any certainty is that the majority of you were unaffected, so you have nothing to worry about," she spoke, trying to be reassuring.

"Unaffected?! That was pretty bloody far from unaffected!" he blurted.

"Enough! What you're supposed to do is go home and take care of your adorable son. I'll tell you something when there's something to tell."

The voices of dissent continued for some time, but one by one, the crowd filtered out by the lift as they either got bored, frustrated, or both. Eventually, the crowd dwindled to Martin, The Duchess, and Veronica. Geoff languished on the couch, still recovering from his latest bout. His nerves were sizzling, so he didn't wait for her to make her customary proclamations after yet another life-changing event.

"Can we please never do that again?"

"As you can see..." The Duchess started, but he was determined to have his say.

"What I can see is what caused me to black out and crash my car. I would like it very much if it never happened again, thank you!"

"You were perfectly safe! You were even conscious, in a manner of speaking."

"Were you or were you not just floating outside of your body? I'm sure I recall the three of us hovering just up there," he shouted, pointing at the ceiling. "That is not a natural state of being!" He'd exhausted his daily supply of fear.

"Enough, Martin! You're coming unglued."

"Oh, you've yet to see me come unglued! I've put up with the impossible time and again in this bloody tower. I've tolerated enough madness to make me question my sanity. Now, you've involved this innocent girl and drawn her into your web of nonsense. I've had my absolute fill, and I will no longer take part!"

"Don't be hyperbolic. You don't mean that."

"Try me."

She stared him down—he assumed trying to discern how serious he was—before she said, "Have you quite finished?"

He found her comment flippant and condescending. He couldn't be certain he was right, but he was justified, and she'd added the final straw.

"I'd say finished is the right word for it," he said, stood up, and took several steps toward the lift.

"Now you're just being melodramatic. If you had let me speak first, I would have said I agreed with you. It is imperative that this, whatever it is, should never reoccur. It is unpredictable, illogical, and perilous."

His sneakers squeaked on the hardwood floors as he spun to face her.

"Don't pander to me, Duchess. I know you, and you're an expert at saying exactly what people want to hear."

"Well, I'm certainly glad you wanted to hear the truth, then."

"Er…I'm going to call my father," Veronica interjected.

"Not yet, dear. We still need to talk," The Duchess said.

"About what?"

"I'm afraid you cannot come to The Cathedral again, at least not until we sort this out."

"What about the writing?"

"We can continue our sessions over video chat, but not here anymore. It's too risky."

"If it's all the same, I'm sorry I caused Mr. Alcott to get hurt. I'm afraid I hurt Geoff too, and I never wanted to hurt anyone," she said, her eyes becoming teary. "I just wanted to write my stories."

"And you will, sweetheart, I promise. I always keep my promises."

She nodded, and the tears fell.

"Now, before Martin leaves in his self-righteous huff, I must ask you both what you thought of to break the connection. It was important last time and I believe it will be important again."

"It was almost the same," Veronica offered. "There was a person, but they were bright orange, like the road workers wear. It was a man this time. Then a ship exploded, just like before."

"Nobody here was orange. I must make note of that. Martin?"

"No."

"What did you see?"

"I don't want to say."

"Come now! You can go home after you tell me."

"How do we know this isn't some sort of virus and we're all going to die in a week?"

"Now you're being absurd."

"I beg your pardon, more absurd than what just happened??"

"I believe you've made that point already," she said, squinting her eyes in warning. "What would give you the idea that it's a virus?"

"Because I saw a person in color too when I closed my eyes."

"But that doesn't happen to you."

"I KNOW!" he yelled.

"Who was it?"

"Who knows? It was a humanoid blob who was blood red, standing opposite a purple blob, which I assumed to be you."

The Duchess switched her gaze between them, making noises that were vaguely word-shaped, but otherwise unrecognizable.

"What's the matter, Duchess? Cat got your tongue? I thought you had to have every angle covered."

Her expression turned sharp enough to cut diamonds. "Shut. Your fucking. Mouth," she spoke through grit teeth. "You are in imminent danger of leaving this cathedral in an ambulance."

"Why? Because I dared question you? You needn't always be The Duchess. You can be human for once. Admit you have no idea how to deal with this. Admit it!"

"I DON'T, ALL RIGHT?"

"Should I go now?" Veronica said.

"Yes, your father should be downstairs in the pub. Go home. I'll be in touch soon."

He watched the girl leave. Once the lift doors closed, he

turned back to The Duchess and met her left hook. It stunned him more than it hurt, but the punch still dropped him to the floor. He looked up to question her, and saw her face contorted with fury, her eyes cold and hard as steel.

"YES, because you dared question me! You think all I do is sit in my ivory tower and give orders? I grew up in this business, and I have hurt, even killed, people in my lifetime. The only reason you're not bleeding right now is because I like you. I may even love you, but I don't take that kind of disrespect, even from you."

"You know as well as I do, I can't leave," he said, rubbing his jaw. "I said it the first time we met: I know too much. But if you expect me to be a loyal lapdog and never question you, especially when it involves my soul or whatever being ripped out of my body, you might as well kill me on the spot."

"Don't tempt me," she said, standing over him. "So, you think know me, do you? Do you also know how much of this is a show? I must appear to be in control at all times, else there will be mass panic and utter chaos. These events require an adult in the room and it's always me. Do you have any idea how tiring it is to be in charge, no matter the situation? Have you ever felt the weight of expectation of having every angle covered, every question answered? Have you, even once, considered how frightening this is for me, you selfish prat?"

He was certain that was the first time she'd ever insulted him, even when he'd deserved it. They stared at each other in a stunned silence. It was only now he recognized her vulnerability. The sudden discovery of family, the dangerous rescue in Trieste, and the looming threat to her empire had cracked the façade and revealed that she indeed had a squishy center. He felt sympathy until he saw her arm move in a flash, and he flinched, bracing for another blow. When it didn't come, he opened his eyes and took her outstretched hand to help him up. She pulled him to his feet and looked at him with a softer expression.

"I called you selfish, but I haven't been a model of altruism either. You've accepted so much without a complaint that I took it for granted. I never appreciated how much it hurt you."

"Even with the broken shoulder?"

"I had to convince myself it was only an accident to relieve the guilt, but I suppose I forgot to reconnect it to what happened here. It ate me up thinking you'd been seriously hurt or worse. I'm sorry."

"You're what?"

"I'm sorry, dammit!"

"Apology accepted, Duchess. That's all I wanted."

The air between them grew heavy and expectant. There was more to say, but neither of them was ready to say it.

"I'm impressed. You've grown much more confident since we met. I find it quite sexy," she told him at last.

"Thank you?"

She raised one of her eyebrows and stepped toward him. "Are you joking? You can't switch gears on me that fast. I'll be downstairs trying to drink this morning away."

Sundays were Taylor's days off, and he enjoyed them as furiously as he could. He worked three jobs for The Duchess, between the command center, the management office, and the pub. It added up to over sixty hours per week, if he did the math and thought about it more than he wanted to. Most times, it seemed like anything but work, tending bar and reading files. By Sunday, however, his body felt like he'd been loading cargo again. His feet and back ached like a veteran coal miner, despite having only just turned 28, and the research left his brain like tapioca pudding. On his only day of rest, he could hardly move, and the weed added to his Sunday inertia as well. His usage of it had increased along with his hours.

Dub reggae pumped through his speakers, although not so loud as to annoy his neighbors. The odd, metallic bangs slipped between the beats, so he didn't notice at first. When they grew louder and offbeat, he thought something must be wrong with his vintage hi-fi. He tried to diagnose the noises until he realized they weren't emanating from the stereo but the door to his flat. A wave of panic dampened his buzz, worrying it might be an angry neighbor or, worse, a constable. He peered through the peephole, and a vague hint of recognition traipsed through the haze. He was sure he'd met the woman before, but nothing else connected.

"Who's there?" he shouted.

"It's Tajana. My sister sent me."

"Who??"

"My sister! Your boss?"

Taylor swam through his syrupy thoughts until he found something meaningful. When it hit, he opened the door.

"Oh yeah," he drawled, "The Duchess's sister. What are you doing here?"

"She told me to come here for research. You are Taylor, yes?"

"That's me, but I wasn't expecting company."

She sniffed the air wafting out of his open door. "If that smell is what I think it is, I should come inside."

Taylor was about to object, but she had already pushed

past him. He shrugged and closed the door.

"I don't mean to be rude, you know," he said, "but couldn't this have waited for tomorrow?"

"My sister says I cannot go home until I tell her what I know about Signore Tessaro, and I want to go home."

"Yeah, but couldn't it have waited for tomorrow?"

"I have waited two months already. I want to go home and you can help me."

"All right, I'll try, but I might not be at my best."

"Then we make it even."

"Pardon?"

"You can share, yes?"

"Share what?"

"Your smoke."

"Oh," he said, but perked up when he understood what she was implying. "Cool! You like dub?"

"What is dub?"

"Oh yeah, you're in for a treat, sister of my boss," he said, and turned the volume up on his hi-fi.

To their credit, in the hour that followed, Taylor and Tajana tried to talk about business, but there was a lot of giggling instead. As the afternoon progressed, giggling gave way to snogging. After that, the evening's research took an exclusive focus on anatomy.

Long after nightfall, their stomachs persuaded them out of his bed, and Taylor ordered in curry. Their buzzes had since faded and the nap re-energized them, so they set to doing some actual work whilst waiting for their food to arrive.

"They really kidnapped you, like in the movies? Bag over the head and everything?" Taylor asked, unable to hide the amazement in his questions.

"No, there was no bag. Only a...how you say...visor? I tried to fight them, but there were too many. I thought they would kill me if I continued to fight."

"And they told you why they'd done it later, yeah?" he continued, taking notes on his laptop.

"Yes, they told me about my sister, but I could tell them nothing about her."

"Why you?"

"He said it was because I looked like my father."

"So, what? He had you picked up at random because you looked like someone he used to know?"

"Not random. I worked for one of his companies."

There it was. Taylor had found his first thread to pull. His questions got more specific, and information flowed from her. In certain moments, she looked astonished to hear the words come out. Their curry arrived, and they talked through mouthfuls of it well into the night. The later it got, he noticed her answers came slower and with more deliberation. He looked at the clock on his laptop and noticed it was one in the morning. He clapped the lid shut, which startled her.

"That'll do for tonight. I'll keep working on it this week, but it should give The Duchess enough to let you go home. Speaking of home, you're welcome to stay here tonight. It's late."

"You're trying to get me in your bed again."

He grinned. "I am, but for sleeping this time. On my honor."

The late hour made the prospect of a taxi unappealing, so she agreed to stay, and they proceeded to his bedroom. Exhausted, inebriated, and full of curry, they both fell fast asleep in seconds.

INTERLUDE: GRATUITY

Maureen detested many things, but she loathed nothing more than working on weekends. She had switched on the telly for early coverage of a Harlequins match, when her work mobile alarmed. It was an email from The Duchess, marked as urgent. She read it, then muttered several unsavory curses before switching the television off again. If she could get it all handled quickly, she wouldn't miss much of the game. She made the call with haste.

"Mr. Fancourt, it's Ms. Abernathy. Sorry to call you on a Sunday."

"We were about to sit for supper, Ms. Abernathy. Can't it wait?"

"I'm afraid not, but I hope to be brief. As the intermediary between the parties, it's my duty to announce that Ms. Nichols has a proposition for you and your family."

"Go ahead."

"I'll read directly from the email she sent me, and you'll also receive copies as per the contract. It says, 'I would like to apologize to both of you for any undue stress or discomfort our rather unconventional working arrangement has caused. To make up for it, I wish to offer your family an all-expenses paid five-day excursion to Trieste, Italy. Trieste is a multicultural city with a storied literary past, perfect to inspire an aspiring young author. Please let Ms. Abernathy know by 21 April, so I can arrange for travel and lodging.'"

"That's incredibly generous of her. I don't believe my firm will allow me to accept such a lavish gift, but I can inquire. Until then, I won't mention it to Veronica. I don't want to get her hopes up needlessly."

"That's very sensible, of course. Your firm may have its own rules, sir, but unless they do business directly with her or her companies, there should be no conflict of interest."

"There's a process, Ms. Abernathy, and I will follow it."

"I'm sure you will," Maureen muttered, quite fed up with his rigidity.

"Is there a problem?"

"Yes, there bloody well is a problem. I'm arguing with you instead of watching my rugby match. You're a solicitor, but you treat your daughter like a client rather than your child. I suggest you pull the stick out of your arse," she growled. "Respectfully, sir."

The line went silent for a moment until she heard a chuckle.

"Perhaps I'm being a little 'extra,' as the kids say," he said between laughs.

"To say the least."

Another thoughtful pause followed. "Tell Ms. Nichols we accept. Anything my company will not allow, I will pay for myself. You're quite right, and we're overdue a family vacation."

"She'll be happy to have your answer, sir."

"Harlequins?"

"That's right," she said, somewhat impressed. "You follow rugby? You're not a Leicester fan like my bloody partner, are you?"

"No, but I rather enjoy the Six Nations."

"Well, it's a big match today, playoffs on the line."

"Then I suggest you return to it. Thank you for the call, Ms. Abernathy."

CHAPTER THIRTEEN

VIENNA BY THE SEA

Taylor drove his semi-plush rental car between the warehouse buildings toward a guardhouse and gate. He took a deep breath and pushed it out to calm his nerves. The security seemed more intimidating somehow in these unfamiliar surroundings, and he wished he was driving up to the gate in Felixstowe instead. The Duchess had assured him they'd accept his badge as valid, even if he hadn't officially been a Five Pence employee for a couple of years. It caused him to sweat, regardless. Conspicuous is as conspicuous does. The road dead-ended at the gate with no easy turnoffs, so he was committed. He lowered his window to speak to the guard.

"Buongiorno, signore. Identità, per favore."

Taylor handed him his badge.

"Good morning, Mr. Taylor," the guard said, realizing that he was English.

"Good morning," Taylor replied. "Could you tell me where the main office is?"

"*Si, signore.* Straight ahead, third building on your left."

"*Grazie,*" Taylor said, spending a solid chunk of his Italian vocabulary, and drove through the now open gate.

He found the administrative building and parked, unbuckling his safety belt with shaking hands. Why couldn't he shake the shaking? The docks are friendly territory and the biggest boss of all had authorized him to visit. He tried pep talks, deep breathing, and had even slapped himself in the face, but the tremors continued. At least the dockside equipment, the sea air, and the purple coveralls of Five Pence Imports and Shipping felt familiar enough to keep him from falling apart.

He straightened his ill-fitting suit, walked inside, and a receptionist greeted him.

"I'd like to speak to the supervisor on duty, please. It's somewhat urgent," he told her and flashed his badge like a police officer.

"Yes, sir. He's on the north dock, loading the *Barcola* this morning. I can have someone take you to him."

"*Grazie,*" he said with a smile, realizing that he would get plenty of mileage out of that one word today. A young man in a purple jumpsuit escorted him out of the building to a waiting utility cart, and the pair drove away past warehouses and container stacks. They conversed little, which worried him further. As if he had space for additional worry, he saw men and women in official-looking windbreakers interviewing workers as they drove past. The cart halted with a lurch near a small crowd of purple-clad workers, and the young man ran over to them. As Taylor stepped from the cart, a man with a deep tan and graying hair approached with his hand extended.

"Mr. Taylor, welcome to Five Pence-Trieste. Your reputation precedes you, *signore*. I am Salvatore Mauro, shift supervisor."

"Pleased to meet you, Salvatore. I have a reputation?" Taylor replied, flattered but confused.

"You do not know? You're a hero on these docks."

He stood dumbfounded, thinking back to what he could have done to merit such a high honor. His counterpart must have sensed this, because he explained further.

"That night, three years ago, they say your quick reactions

saved the *Chiarbola* and many lives. A man of the workers."

"I'm flattered, sir."

"How can I help you today? It is not so often we are visited by a celebrity here."

"Headquarters in London wants to me to ask if anything unusual has happened here. Strange visitors or people spying on our operations."

"Nothing out of the ordinary, I think. One moment," he said, turning to speak with some of his colleagues and subordinates. After some quick conversation, he turned back to Taylor. "No, they have seen nothing. Only the usual spies and watchers."

"I beg your pardon," Taylor said. "The *usual* spies?"

"That is how it has always been. They watch us, we watch them. If you look carefully to your right, you'll see one sitting in his car beyond the fence."

He looked as directed and saw a cheap black sedan parked outside the perimeter fence, windows down. Taylor thought he caught a glint from the lenses of binoculars.

"Who's doing it?"

"We have competition in shipping all across the Free Port, but this one, he belongs to Tessaro."

"Who is Tessaro? I've heard mention of the name, but I know next to nothing else."

"You surprise me, Mr. Taylor. They do not talk of such topics in your Felixstowe?"

"I've been off the docks for a while. I was only a shift supervisor, so as long as the cargo showed up on time, we didn't worry about much else."

"The Tessaro family has controlled the port for decades. In times past, there was much blood spilled in Trieste over rights and control, but the current *Capo* has kept the peace.

They are mafia, yes, but Giovanni is a businessman who values honor. Less fighting has made the docks safer to work. I have been here since the beginning, and I've almost forgotten the old ways, but I do not mourn their loss."

"Felixstowe is a very different place, it seems. You should visit sometime."

"You honor me, Mr. Taylor. It would please me to see it."

"Just Taylor will do fine, Salvatore. Have the spies changed or become more aggressive in any way?"

"Before February, they would appear once or twice a week, but they watch us around the clock now. So do the police."

"I had a feeling when I saw the windbreakers. What can you tell me about them? What is GdF?"

"They are the *Guardia di Finanza*—the Financial Police—and they inspect everything. Every morning, the supervisor shows up with a new anonymous tip, and the inspections start anew. We do not break the law here, and yet they insist we do. It slows us down, and we lose business because our shipments do not arrive on time."

Taylor shuffled his feet, ashamed. "I've heard the chiefs in Felixstowe complain about it. I doubt they know what you're dealing with here, and I'll explain it to them when I return."

"*Mille grazie!*"

"It sounds like harassment, though. Do you think Tessaro is doing this to you?"

"Our boss thinks so, but we don't know why. He bribes the local police—all the families do—but the GdF is an anti-corruption force. He must be paying them well. Before then, he had taken little interest in our operations."

"It sounds like he intends to drive us out of business, though I'm sure headquarters would have guessed that."

"He's succeeding. Enough business, now. Come help us finish loading the *Barcola*! I'm sure you're familiar with her and we could use able hands. She sails for England tonight!"

For at least the third time today, Veronica froze in disbelief at where she was and what she was doing. Things like this didn't happen to ordinary girls like her. Maybe she wasn't ordinary, but it still felt like a fever dream. She imagined one day she'd see Milan or Naples, but like many others, she had never given Trieste much thought. When she received Ms. Nichols's invitation, she balked at it until she did her research. The more she learned about its history, the more her excitement increased, and now she was actually here.

Dad snapped another picture of her posing next to the statue of James Joyce on the Ponto Rosso bridge. Her patience for it was waning, but the thrill of being in Trieste outweighed her annoyance...for now. There was a lengthy walk ahead to the ancient amphitheater, but it was a lovely spring day, and her feet didn't hurt yet. She knew how her father liked to vacation, and he would be determined to see every single attraction in his little book. With the last pictures captured, they continued across the bridge and into the city's narrow streets. After a couple of blocks, they reached a piazza, and her dad pointed them to the left. She was about to follow him across the street when something, or rather a couple of someones, caught her eye.

It was their colors that attracted her attention. They stood out even amongst the hundreds of other people with their faint mists. They were at least half a block away from her, but their auras were unmistakable. One man—she was almost certain they were men—beamed a bright orange. His aura wasn't as luminous as Martin's, but for her to even detect it from that distance, it had to be intense. The second man's color wasn't as distinct, but it was warm and darkish. These characters were important to her story, but she couldn't remember why, and she needed time to think before they disappeared.

"Dad, can we stop at this cafe? My feet are starting to hurt."

"Already?" he protested. "We've only just started and there's a lot to see!"

"I know. That's why I want to stop now, before I get a blister!" She plopped herself down in protest at a small table on the pavement.

"I wouldn't mind another coffee, Edwin," her mother said in support.

"Oh, all right, but we can't stay long, or we'll miss the good light at the San Giusto." Her dad was an avid amateur at photography, and lighting was everything. To miss the "good light" was tantamount to treason.

Her dad and brother stepped inside and ordered drinks and pastries. She watched the orange man and his colleague walk up the opposite side of the street. As they approached, his companion came more into focus. Although nowhere near as bright, he had a murky red color around him. Something about the pair gave her the heebiest of jeebies, but she couldn't explain it, even to herself. As they sauntered past, she strained to get a good look at their faces.

"What a mess," Dad muttered as he set the refreshments down on the table.

"What mess?" Mum asked.

"They're training a new employee behind the bar, and

he had some trouble with the steam. Milk foam exploded all over the place."

She stiffened at the sound of the word 'exploded,' and the vision she had at The Cathedral flooded her thoughts. She'd discovered the deep blue woman in London, but here in the opposite corner of Europe, she found the mysterious orange man from the second vision. There was no doubt it was the same person. She had to let Ms. Nichols know right away, but her dad had forbidden the kids from bringing their mobiles—the international rates were too high for his liking. While her parents sipped at their espressos, she dug the notebook out of her satchel, scrawling notes as fast as her hand would write. She recorded any details that might be relevant: names on street signs, time of day, and any physical descriptions she remembered, like her dream journals.

"Are we all set?" Dad asked, setting down his now empty espresso cup.

She glanced up from her notes—there was about to be a show. She looked at her mother, who was still sipping her coffee, and waited for her eyebrow to raise in warning. It didn't take long, and her father got the unspoken message.

"Oh, right," he said, and set to fiddling with his shoulder-slung travel wallet.

"Veronica, you look as though you've seen a ghost. Are you all right, dear?" Mum asked.

"It'll sound mental, but I saw someone across the street that looked familiar."

"Well, they say everyone has a doppelgänger somewhere. I'm sure it was nothing."

She nodded and stuffed her notebook back into her bag. Rubbing her eyes until sparks flew, she thought, *"I need to contact Ms. Nichols."*

"*Veronica?*"

She opened her eyes and refocused them, staring at her mother. Jeanette Fancourt's mouth was, at that moment, chewing a bit of pastry, unable to speak in polite company. If it hadn't been her mother, then whose voice was that?

"Did you hear something just now?" she asked her younger brother.

"Noisy traffic," William replied. "Why, did you?"

"Forget it."

"Ugh, can you not be a weirdo today?" William moaned. She always found him insufferable, but he'd become exponentially worse since getting in with a snobby crowd at St. Catherine's. Her artiness clashed with his newfound obsession with normality.

"Don't forget, septic breath, we're here *because* I'm a weirdo. We got to meet the PM *because* I'm a weirdo."

"But why couldn't we have gone to Rome or Florence like normal people? Chester's family went to Rome for Christmas last year. This place sucks."

"Because," Dad cut in, "Veronica's talent got us this trip for free. It's not exactly the jewel of Italy, but I find it fascinating. You'd do well to pay attention, William. Let's go, the good light is fading."

Francesca shook her head and wiggled her fingers in her ears in a pointless gesture. She knew where the voice had come from, but she didn't have to like it. It was bad enough that she shared her thoughts with Martin, but that was voluntary, and they'd both learned how to control it to some extent. Veronica's connection was intrusive and much stronger.

If Veronica had needed to contact her, that likely meant news to share, but her broadcast sounded strained and urgent—not good news. "*One thing at a time,*" she thought, turning to her laptop. She wrote an email to the Fancourts, inviting them to dinner this evening on the waterfront. The odds were slim that they'd decline, since they were here at her behest, but not zero. Edwin made plain that he did not trust her in the slightest, and was only going along with their continued association for Veronica's benefit. Maureen had told her that much.

She sat staring out the window of the Trieste office of Istria Holdings, Ltd. It wasn't an inspiring view by any means, but it kept her attention away from the other unpleasantness she was in Trieste to deal with. She looked at the average citizens below, envying the lives that hadn't gone to hell like hers. Giovanni checked her every move, predicted her gambits, and she worried she would resort to something desperate and/or stupid to break the stalemate. Her fraying nerves made her jumpy and depressed. She needed a plan, and soon.

At present, the only thing she could cling to was Taylor's recent report on the Tessaro enterprise. His work with Tajana had paid massive dividends thus far. A nascent plan was forming, but it lacked the weak link to exploit. She needed an insider or a piece of information that even Taylor couldn't glean from public record. What she needed was Indigo, but Taylor hadn't unearthed any sign of a significant online footprint for any of the varied businesses. She needed to discuss options with Martin, but that could wait until she returned to London. There was another connection to try, but she feared little goodwill remained in that relationship.

"*Pronto?*"

"Tajana, it's your sister."

"Oh."

"Don't hang up. I'm sorry I haven't called since you've been back. My business with Tessaro has kept me preoccupied, and I know that's not an excuse."

"It's not."

"How have you found the new job?"

"Coffee is coffee, no matter who's supplying it. I hope you don't think I owe you anything because of it."

She bristled at the implication. True, Tajana didn't owe her anything, but she thought that the things she'd done for her warranted a little gratitude—civility at a minimum. Without her intervention, she'd have returned to Trieste without a job and few prospects. Tessaro, with his limitless influence, would surely have blackballed her from the trade.

"I'm not expecting anything other than an occasional chat and perhaps dinner with your family when I'm in the city. In fact, I was calling to invite you to dinner this evening."

"We have plans."

"I'm planning to go back to London tomorrow. The least you could do is allow me to buy you dinner. You can bring your family if you choose. They're all welcome."

"And then you'll leave me alone?"

"I hope not forever, but yes, I'll leave you alone."

"Fine. When and where?"

"I'll book a table and send you the details."

"Just dinner?"

"And a chat."

"See you tonight," she said, and disconnected the call.

She'd never felt more alone in her life. Even Geoff was absent today, out surveilling Tessaro's many outposts. The small office downtown was usually unoccupied—most of her employees here worked at the port. If she didn't hear a friendly voice soon, she was liable to scream. Her return to London couldn't wait, so she picked up her mobile again, and rang someone who would listen.

"Good morning, Duchess. What can I do for you today?" Martin answered. His cheerful greeting elicited a weak smile, her first of the day.

"Be a friend?"

"I'm happy to do it, but—and I mean no offense—this isn't like you."

"No, it really isn't. I feel so..." she trailed off, looking for the right word.

"Duchess?"

"Lost. I think I've lost the only family member I have. I'm about to lose one of my businesses. Maybe adrift is the right word."

"Christ, that's a lot. I've never heard you so despondent. How can I help?"

"Tell me it's going to be okay, even if that's a lie."

"It's going to be okay, and yes, that's a lie," he said. He paused to see if she would laugh—she didn't. "Jokes aside, I don't know how this ends, but nobody is more capable of putting it right than you. You're a brilliant strategist, so keep doing the next right thing. Put one foot in front of another and let genius happen!"

"A brilliant bunch of nonsense," she said. "But coming from you, it makes me feel better. I'm sorry to put you on the spot like this."

"It wasn't the first time, and I'm sure it won't be the last," he added, chuckling. "Are you still coming home tomorrow?"

Something about the way he'd said "coming home" filled her heart. "That's the plan. Can you be available? I might need a hug."

"As you wish."

"*The Princess Bride*, right?"

"You *have* been paying attention! There's hope for you yet."

She laughed as a single tear escaped from the corner of her eye. "Thanks, I needed that more than you know."

"I live to serve. Anything else?"

"Did you see Taylor's report?"

"Yes, there's not much to go on and it's disappointingly analog. That said, I've been working on some improvements to Indigo that don't require a data center. If there's an opening, we'll find it."

"Let's discuss it over dinner tomorrow."

"Done. See you then," he said, and rang off.

A bit more energized, she started going through the list of some of her favorite and most scenic restaurants.

CHAPTER FOURTEEN

A SECOND SUNSET

The Zodiac's throttle was full speed ahead, and its occupants hunkered down, trying not to be thrown from it in the larger ship's choppy wash. The small engine mounted on the dinghy had only enough power to overtake their target while it still sailed through the Bay of Muggia. Once she rounded the point into the gulf, it would accelerate out of reach, so they couldn't afford to slow.

"We'll get there. Do not fear, my friend," Paolo told Alessio as they caught air off the crest of a wave.

"We have three minutes, Paolo. We need to be onshore in five or we're all dead."

"There he is!"

A metal gangplank hung from the port side, where a man in a purple jumpsuit stood near the end, waving at them. Paolo reduced their speed, maneuvering carefully behind the ship. Their straining outboard would attract attention on deck, so stealth was paramount. He steered up the port side, under the extended walkway, and a thick rope came down toward them. The man above dangled on the rope, climbing downward, hand over hand. Paolo's navigation was expert and, using the inflated sides of the tender as bumpers, he parked them under the descending figure. He continued down until he was only six feet above them, then dropped onto the deck and Alessio steadied them.

"I've got him. Go," he ordered.

Paolo steered a course directly toward the shoreline. When they reached about two hundred yards from the ship, he threw the throttle forward, and the engine roared back to life.

"Is everything done, Fredo?" he asked the man.

"All done," Fredo replied, stepping out of the jumpsuit and flinging it into the inky water.

"Time?"

"One minute, forty-five."

"Will we make it, Paolo?"

"We'll be on land in sixty."

"That was too close," Fredo said. "What took you so long?"

"None of your business! We retrieved you, did we not?"

"You know I would die for the family, Alessio, but not tonight."

Paolo yanked the wheel to the left and sliced the water, bringing the craft parallel to a narrow strip of beach along the coastal road. They drifted to shore, and all three jumped out, pulling their boat up a ramp. They crossed the deserted road into a parking area, and stopped there, panting from the effort.

Fredo looked at his watch and said between gasps, "Five, four, three, two..."

It was a bright, clear evening on the Trieste waterfront, and Francesca awaited her guests, unsure if they would turn up at all. Although all of them had accepted her invitation, their acceptances were strained, if not begrudging, and she figured it was somewhere south of a 50 percent chance they'd come. Several anxious minutes passed, and she watched the reservation time approach with every flick of her wrist.

The first to arrive was Tajana, walking alone across the street. She flicked her cigarette to the curb as she approached, exhaled hard, and stared at her half-sister.

"Well, I'm here."

"I'm glad you came. With what we've been through this year, I don't expect us to be best friends."

"All right."

"I hope that, given sufficient time and less dire circumstances, we could at least be civil to each other as sisters."

"You sound like a politician. When are we eating?"

"When the other guests arrive."

"What other guests?" she asked, annoyed.

"Veronica and her family. You remember them."

She huffed, and Francesca could see her eyes planning an escape route.

"I'll be honest," she continued, "I expected at least one of you to decline, and until they're actually standing here, I can't be sure they'll come. They're good people, and we'll keep the conversation casual. I'm leaving tomorrow, and I expect you'll be rid of all of us for some time."

"It's just dinner," Tajana said in a heavy sigh.

"And a chat."

"You keep saying that. Say what you mean to say or shut up."

"I will, but not now, because it involves young Veronica as well. Some new information has come to my attention, and I'd like a quick word with you both after dinner."

"I knew it! I knew there would be ropes attached."

"Do you mean strings attached?"

"I said what I said. Correct my English again and I will smack that annoying smirk off your face."

"Ah, they're here," she interjected, dying to change the subject.

The Fancourt family walked up to the group, dressed their best. Francesca made the introductions, and they went inside to be seated. Dinner was impeccable, elegant in its simplicity, and the conversation was lively, if guarded. To complete the meal, espresso was served with dishes of gelato in a rainbow of flavors.

She tapped her glass with a fork, and all eyes turned to her.

"I realize it's unconventional to make a toast at the end of a meal, but thank you for taking the time to dine with me tonight. I would like to invite you all to join me for an evening stroll out onto the pier. It's a lovely night, after all, and I'm certain a bit of walking would do wonders for our stomachs."

Edwin would have objected, but the meal had befuddled him too much to fuss. She paid the bill, and they crossed the busy avenue out onto the stone jetty. Eventually, she, Tajana, and Veronica separated from the rest of the group, giving them a few private minutes to talk.

"You said you needed to contact me, Veronica? Why didn't you text me?"

"Dad wouldn't let me bring my phone."

"I respect your father, but that's overbearing."

Tajana rolled her eyes, groaning in realization. "This is another one of those mental things, isn't it? Why did you need me here?"

"I'm not sure why yet, I'll admit, aside from just wanting to see you again before I left Trieste," she said. "This is more of an intuition thing. Veronica, what was it you needed to tell me?"

"Do you remember when I told you about the orange man? I saw him in the city today. It had to be him."

"That's two out of three. Can you describe him?"

Veronica described him and his dark-auraed companion

in as much detail as she could.

"Martin said he saw a blood red man as well. This must mean something."

"Alessio," Tajana said.

"Bless you," she replied.

"No, stupid! You described Alessio Tessaro."

"Which one?"

"The one she said was orange."

"Can you be sure?"

"I'll never forget his face. You don't forget someone who tortures you."

Veronica gasped.

"You said nothing about torture, Tajana! How could you leave that out?"

"I've been trying to forget it, but I think it will take me years of therapy for that."

"I don't like how prophetic your visions have been, Veronica," Francesca said, sighing as she gazed over the dark water. "That only leaves the..."

A bright orange flash near the horizon stopped her words. A split-second later, a shock wave rang across the waterfront, echoing off the buildings. Her spine stiffened, The Duchess took command, and the casual chat on the pier became all business.

"Veronica, go join your family. Tell your father to reschedule your flight out of Trieste for as early as he can. I will reimburse him for any fees, but you must leave Italy immediately."

"Yes, ma'am," she said, and ran off.

She stared at the horizon, where she could make out billowing black smoke illuminated by fire from below. If she hadn't known of the visions, or of her company's shipping timetables, she might have thought little of this unfortunate event. As it was, The Duchess had already pieced the puzzle together. A dark smile crossed her face rather than her trademark smirk. She turned to her sister.

"The game has changed, and he just gave me the upper hand. He has made our feud personal and now I will make him pay."

"Make who pay? How do you know?"

"Giovanni Tessaro. That was my ship that he just blew up in the gulf."

"HOW DO YOU KNOW?"

"Simple. The *Barcola* set sail for Felixstowe only an hour ago—Taylor told me this afternoon. I never imagined he'd go this far—it's out of character for him. He didn't need to escalate. Something is different and I need to talk to my people immediately. Is your car nearby? Can you get me to Five Pence fast? At a bare minimum, we need to start the rescue operation. I have good men on that ship."

"This doesn't concern me! I have had it with this. I want to go home."

"You are an employee of this company, so it does concern you. If this goes unaddressed, Five Pence dies and you're out of a job again. I'm only asking for a ride, after which you may leave."

The two women stared at each other in fierce determination, both standing on principle.

"I'm two streets over," Tajana said. "We should run."

The phone rang on Giovanni Tessaro's bedside table. He saw the name on the screen, muted the television, and answered immediately.

"What is it, Mario?"

"Sir," he said, "there's been an explosion."

"Explosion? Where?"

"In the gulf, sir. In the shipping lane."

"Not one of ours. There's nothing scheduled." He paused and pictured the sailing timetables—he memorized them daily—until a name occurred to him. His face dropped when he arrived at the answer. "*Barcola?*"

"We think so, sir. The police and coast guard are en route to the scene, but we think she will be a total loss."

"Assist in any way we can, Mario. We must assure them we were not involved with this."

"Yes, sir," Mario said, and ended the call.

He called his lieutenants and told them to come to his home. They must hold a conclave at once. His family controlled the port in prosperity and crisis, and he would do his part to protect it. He rolled out of bed at once and changed into one of his best suits.

An hour later, he sat at the head of the table, presiding over the local bosses of the family business. Alessio sat to his right, looking self-satisfied, which unsettled him.

"What has happened?"

"The Five Pence ship, *Barcola,* suffered an explosion in her cargo hold twenty minutes out of port," a man to his left said. "It punctured the hull below the waterline, and she will sink."

"The crew?"

"Only one soul unaccounted for. They fear he was below decks when the bomb went off."

"Bomb? You are sure?"

"No, sir, but we suspect. The GdF inspected everything aboard, as you had directed, *Capo,* and they reported no explosives or contraband in any of the containers."

"One of the other families?"

"We don't know, sir. We have not heard from them yet."

"At least *La Duchessa* will not bother us anymore," Alessio said.

"What do you mean, Alessio?"

"Her fleet is small. This loss and the investigation will end her."

"What makes you so sure? We have suffered worse losses and yet we continue."

"We continue because we are Trieste. Can you kill the city? She is nothing, and she will fold," Alessio said, his chest puffed out.

"Federico, I want you to look into this. Take our message to the families and get them to root out the culprit. If this was a bomb, I want the bastard who put it aboard her ship here."

The man to his left nodded and left the room.

"The rest of you, contact your men. There will be police and investigators everywhere, and it will be too big for our friends to control. Go dark. We must wait for this to blow over."

The other besuited men nodded their assents and filtered out of the conference, chattering amongst themselves.

Alessio stood to leave, but his father grabbed his hand.

"You are proud, my son. Perhaps too proud."

"I am, Papa. Our name will strike fear into the families once more."

"So, you have learned nothing. Fear is useful sometimes, not always."

"Better fear than disrespect."

"Fear breeds disrespect, and you should understand that. You lost your grandfather to the violence that fear breeds. I vowed to end the bloodshed of our past and, for 40 years, I accomplished that and more. My way has made us all wealthy and esteemed in our city."

He stared at his son, recognizing the fire of ambition in his eyes.

"Alessio, I must ask you if you arranged this."

"If I did, why should I tell you, Papa? What would it change? You send aid to our enemy."

"Our family has no enemies in this city, only rivals in business. We have enjoyed unity for decades, and you would end that peace for what?"

"For honor! For the name of Tessaro! The world knows the power of Trieste, but they do not know who made it possible. Even *La Duchessa* did not know our name and showed no deference to her superiors! You are old and incompetent. You allowed our eminence to wither, and it's time you stepped aside."

He stood and slapped Alessio. "Your treachery reveals itself at last."

"She is finished, Giovanni, and I finished her."

He slapped him again. "You will call me *Capo*! I am the head of this family, and I have no intention of stepping aside. You dishonored us all, boy. I had this woman at my mercy, and you gave her everything she needs. She now has sympathy with the government, and the bosses will discover this was no accident. You have given her the advantage."

"Her little enterprise is over. I will destroy her ships until she capitulates," Alessio continued, defiant despite the throbbing red spreading across his cheek.

"Stupid! Who will they turn to when the families swear they are not to blame? They owe us no allegiance beyond the peace I keep. You invite war and ruin to our doorstep."

"They will not find us, Papa. I ensured it."

"Do not call me papa, *child*. I have no son. Leave my home and do not return."

PART THREE

In Wicca, indigo represents honesty, integrity, and spirituality. It also represents our family, the ancestors, and important customs that we keep to honor both. A third correspondence is that of divinatory energy, especially for predicting the future.

CHAPTER FIFTEEN

SPECIAL INDIGO DELIVERY

Martin hurried across the Cathedral's atrium, headed for the apse. The call he'd received sounded quite urgent, and she had been very specific about the time, so he was running late, true to form. He rounded the corner into the apse lobby and almost collided with Duncan, who wore a similar look of concern.

"What are you doing here?" he said, out of breath.

"The Duchess said it was urgent," Duncan replied, wearing a half-grin.

"Yeah, but since when do you come running when she calls?"

"She said there was a job."

"Oh, that'll do it," he said, as the lift arrived.

They boarded and ascended to the Office level, entering the seldom used conference room. They found Simon waiting at the table, looking uncomfortable.

"Martin!" he exclaimed. "I'm right pleased to see you, mate. Why did The Duchess call me?"

"I expect I'll find out the same time as you, Simon. You remember Duncan, yeah?"

"Are you joking?"

"Sorry. I forget sometimes. I thought they were still in Trieste!"

"We are," The Duchess said. Startled, they turned to the head of the table, where her larger-than-life face filled the television on the wall.

"Blimey!" Duncan shouted. "How long have you been there?"

"Long enough to remind Martin that he still needs work on his people skills."

"That'll do, Duchess," he said, abashed and blushing.

"Gentlemen, take your seats. I won't beat about the bush: we're at war."

"War?" Duncan blurted. "I hope you ain't draftin' us!"

"That's precisely what I'm doing, Duncan. In fact, your skills may be the ones I need most of all."

"You wot?" all three said at once.

"I shall load the next one of you that speaks out of turn into Geoff's heavy bag."

"Yes, ma'am," they all said.

"My disagreement with the Tessaro family has escalated, but a strategic error has given me an opportunity. I am taking the fight to them, and I'll need help from each of you if we're to succeed."

"How has it escalated?" he asked.

"The *Barcola,* a ship from my Five Pence fleet, exploded and sank in the Gulf of Trieste last night. It was no accident, and I can prove it."

There was a collective gasp before she continued.

"I cannot prove that Tessaro was responsible, although I'm 99% certain of it. I cannot fathom why he'd make an error of this magnitude, however, which vexes me. It smells of desperation, but he has no reason to be desperate. His tactics had been flawless since the feud began, and he had Five Pence all but buried, so it makes no sense. I believe you all know how I feel about things that make no sense."

"Quite," he said. He made no attempt to hide his rolling eyes.

"Data is security, security is data," she spat back at him.

"Well remembered. I think I see where this is going now."

"Taylor is on his way back to London on the Speedwell as we speak. When he arrives, Martin and Duncan will take his place and proceed to Trieste without delay. I will explain the rest of my plan here."

"You want me to fly??" Duncan said in a panic.

"Don't tell me," she muttered, cradling her forehead in her hand.

"Never once, Duchess."

"Martin, please look after him. I know how fond you are of aviation."

"I can talk his ear off the entire way. That's a right fine bird you have."

"Now I really don't want to go."

"You get to break into one of Tessaro's offices when you get here."

His eyes lit up, and he ceased complaining at once.

"And me, ma'am?" Simon said, far less confident than the others.

"Yes, Simon. I want you to work with Mr. Taylor to coordinate the information gathering. From what we've discovered, the Tessaro network hasn't embraced the information age and, as such, is largely off-grid. It will require keen eyes and tech savvy to solve this riddle."

"Brilliant!"

"If you need Simon, then it's pretty clear why I'll be coming along." Martin said. "I've integrated a couple of new useful tricks into Indigo that might assist."

"Just what I had hoped you'd say," The Duchess said with a smile. "You have four hours to gather what you need. Be at Farnborough no later than 7:00 pm."

"What about Tracy? Aidan isn't three months yet, and she

needs extra help about the place."

"I've sent 'Auntie Mo' on ahead to stay with her, so they couldn't be in more protective hands."

"You're only too right at that. She won't even let me go near them when she's about."

"Do not be late. I know the both of you."

"We won't disappoint you, Duchess," he said, and stood to leave.

"One more thing before you go, gentlemen. Duncan, please instruct Martin on the attire he will need to have available."

"Right-ho. We'll fit him up right."

"Cheers, gents. See you in Italy," she said, and the screen went dark.

"Looks like your beta just got promoted, Martin," Simon said, already heading for the door.

"I suspect you're right. I'll follow you down to the catacombs to get the equipment ready. Duncan, meet me in the atrium in ten minutes."

"I'm stopping in the pub on the way down. I'll need a wallop or two before I get close to an airplane."

Fifteen minutes later, Martin was driving Duncan west toward Hounslow. They drove along without speaking, listening to classic rock on the radio. He squirmed in the right-hand seat, his many questions percolating to a boil. By the time they'd reached Hammersmith, the silence had become intolerable.

"She doesn't mean to dress me in a tuxedo, does she?"

"You think I'm a tuxedo sort, mate?"

"I'm suddenly having grave doubts about this trip."

"You're not the one afraid of flying."

"I'm more afraid of arriving."

Geoff pulled the car into a spot along an industrial lane, between a box truck and a Transit van. "Masks on," Duncan announced, pulling the knitted mask down over his prominent chin. He knew the ski mask was the cliche uniform of the cartoon burglar, but everything else he'd tried made his face break out. Some things were classic for good reason.

He glanced at the novices in the back seat. Through their masks, only their eyes were visible, but they told him everything he needed to know about their readiness. Martin's were as big as saucers, and he looked likely to scream at any second. Tajana's green eyes showed an odd mix of annoyance and boredom. With her other features obscured, she reminded him disturbingly of The Duchess. She was one of a hundred unknowns in this operation, and he'd have preferred to leave her out of it. Since they hadn't had time to do proper research, she was their sole connection to the inside of the facility. His stomach swirled with a mixture of excitement, apprehension, and an acute awareness of how far he was from Tracy. She should be running this job with him instead of these amateurs. At least Geoff was a professional.

"Close the doors softly when you get out. We don't want to attract attention."

"But if the doors don't latch, someone could steal the car!" Martin blurted. He'd noted that Martin's anxiety level directly correlated to the volume and shrillness of his voice. He rubbed his ears before replying.

"It's a rental, Martin. If someone makes off with it, we pay the insurance and do the job."

"Oh. Right."

"Cross the street to the side opposite the streetlights. Stay in the shadows where it's possible. It's not a long way, but we can't risk parking any closer. Are you ready?"

The quartet emerged from their rented sedan, all clad in black. The night was overcast, which was lucky for their plan, but the streetlights blazed overhead in sodium orange. He watched Martin sprint across the street, his head swiveling like a lawn sprinkler. "*Rookies,*" he thought, chuckling to himself as he and the others strolled nonchalantly across the empty lane.

The roastery sat nestled in a heavy industrial area just outside the city limits, a mile and a half from the seaport. No one was about at this hour, which they'd hoped for. They rounded the corner into the unguarded parking area in front of the plant. When he first started planning their excursion, he'd thought it odd that there were no guards until he discovered that there was also a small retail shop at the front. The warehouse area and Tessa's fleet of trucks were fenced off, but the storefront was open to the public. In fact, the satellite map of the address showing the fencing structure had been the genesis of his plan. When they reached the double glass doors, he reiterated their roles.

"I'll get us through the doors we need to get through. Tajana, you tell us where we go next once we're inside. Martin, you set up your techno-thingy when we get there. Geoff..." He paused, looking him over. "You're our Plan B."

Geoff rolled his neck. Duncan wondered if it meant he was preparing for a fight or unhappy taking orders from the likes of him, but it didn't seem worth asking. He'd taken a punch from him once before and was not eager to repeat it.

"Remember, no talking inside if you can help it." He couldn't help himself from adding with a grin, "Especially you, Geoff."

He dug around in his tool bag, selected his alarm finder tool, and traced the top of the door frame with it. With a quick snap of electricity, he knew the alarm was dead. The lock was a simple matter, but Tracy would have opened it much quicker. They scrambled inside, and he locked the door behind them. He scanned the ceiling and found the security cameras, blotting them with his paintball gun, as he always did. With their entrance secured, he allowed himself a deep breath and found the aroma inside captivating.

He surveyed the shop, as he would have on an AMWarn assessment, and regretted not being able to case it beforehand. From his position, he spied four doors scattered around the small store: two were unmistakable as restrooms, another bore a sign in Italian, and the last was unmarked. He made an "eyes on me" gesture to Tajana, then pointed toward the unknown door behind the counter. She nodded. A point at the cameras and an air-drawn question mark only elicited an eye roll from the churlish woman. They followed his lead around the counter, and he led them to the signed door. It appeared to be the retail office, complete with a safe in the corner. His first impulse was to crack it, but that wasn't their mission, and he wasn't sure he could do it without Tracy. While that disappointed him, what they didn't find here concerned him worse. He pushed the office door closed and risked whispering to his party.

"No alarm systems or cameras in here, which means there's a security room or guard shack somewhere." He turned to Tajana. "Do you know where it is?"

"Into the factory and on the right."

"Is it staffed around the clock?"

"How should I know? I was never here this late!"

"Shit," he spat. "If it's staffed, they'll have noticed the paintballs by now. We need to get the cameras down. Be ready, Geoff."

He crept along the wall and cracked the factory door open. His stomach dropped when he saw the pair of flashlights headed in their direction, and he closed the door as silently as he could.

"They're coming," he whispered. He pointed at Martin and Tajana. "You two, into the office. Stay out of sight." They ran off and hid as instructed.

"Geoff, you take the front of the door, and I'll take back. I saw two flashlights, so wait until they're both inside, and we flank them."

They took their positions and waited. The door opened smartly, but not so fast that it would hit him as he stood behind it. Two guards entered, sweeping their torch beams across the ceiling to see what might have gone wrong with the cameras. Upon seeing the paint splatter, the first guard reached for his belt, but Geoff pounced on them both, knocking them to the floor. He clunked their heads together, and they went limp.

"Brilliant! Nice to not be on the receiving end of that." He checked the guards' belts and found a pair of tasers, walkie-talkies, and mobile phones. "Let's hope it was only those two."

He collected the others from the office, and Martin gasped when he saw the prone figures. "They're not..."

"I don't kill nobody 'less they're tryin' to kill me," Geoff grunted. "You got twenty tops before these two wake up mad as hell."

With the guards out of action, they hurried through the factory, still wary of finding themselves on camera. The security room was exactly where she indicated, and they were relieved to find it empty. He wiped the recorders and turned the system off.

"Martin, can you do anything here?"

"I didn't think of hijacking security gear, but I can make

use of it. I brought enough Scouts to blanket the place." Martin replied, getting straight to work behind the rack of recording gear.

"Scouts?"

"New toys. I'll explain later."

He turned to Tajana. "Where are the offices?"

"Second floor."

She was getting right on his nerves. He would have preferred her to be nervous or combative instead of the utter disinterest she showed.

"Done," Martin said, emerging from behind the rack covered in dust.

"Okay, let's all get upstairs."

They hastened up the stairs and into the small office area. She took the lead and took them to her former desk.

"This is where I would sit. Some of my things are still here."

"I know it's tempting, but don't take nothin'," he warned her. "If it's only your things missing, they'll suspect you, which will lead them back to us."

She nodded in sad understanding. Martin, however, was already under her desk checking wiring.

"There's a network hookup, which means there's at least a hub or router here somewhere. We need to find it. I could trace the cables to the servers if I could pop into the drop ceiling. We haven't time to look for a ladder, and I've learnt the hard way not to use a swivel chair as a step."

Geoff held his hands in front of him in a cup, and Martin got the gist. One foot in the catapult, he hurtled upwards, head bursting through the ceiling grid. He shifted his feet to Geoff's shoulders and, after a few seconds, Duncan saw his finger point toward a side wall with an unmarked door. He hustled over to it and picked the lock before Martin had hit the floor.

The server closet was stifling hot, dusty, and only big enough for one person. He saw Martin's eyes widen with excitement before digging around in his small bag and retrieving a device. It looked like a thumb drive with the cover stripped off and several additional components soldered on, which intrigued him. Despite his many attempts, he still didn't get on well with computers, but he adored gadgets.

"I'm guessing that's a Scout. Did you make it?"

"Well, sort of. It's an off-the-shelf board, but I've added some bits and programmed the whole thing," Martin replied.

"Get after it. No time for a presentation."

Martin dove behind another rack and set to work while he checked his watch.

"Geoff, go check the guards. Give us three minutes."

He disappeared down the stairs, and Duncan preferred not to imagine the scene below if the guards had awoken.

"All set," Martin said, dusting himself off again. "With this closet's current state, I doubt anyone will ever know we've been in here."

As the last word left his lips, his foot caught on a cable, ripping it from the rack with a sickening snap.

"BALLS!" he shouted, returning to the back of the rack. "If I can't find where that came from, we're toast. They'll be in here first thing."

His patience finally reached its end, and he started barking orders. "You clumsy git! You got thirty seconds to fix this. Lock the door when you leave." He rounded on Tajana. "On your way. Move it!" They hustled down the stairs, with him muttering, "That bloody fool could bugger up a sunny day."

They got back to the store and found Geoff guarding the

unconscious guards. Martin appeared thirty seconds later.

"It was the dust that..."

"Skip it," he growled. "Out, all of you!"

They burst through the outer door and he once again locked it behind them, seeing the first signs of movement from the guards. "RUN!"

Seconds later, they were piling back into their rental car, which no one had stolen. He could no longer hide his ire, and he unloaded on the rookies, Martin being his first target.

"You tosser! We'll be lucky if she doesn't tie us all to chairs this time."

"Chairs? What the fuck?" Tajana added.

"Relax, I found the right port. They shouldn't see any difference," Martin said, attempting reassurance but missing the mark.

"You'd better hope so. And you," he said, turning his ire on Tajana, "useless as a screen door on a submarine."

"I didn't want to be here," she reminded him.

"You made that right fucking clear! Now, shut your cakehole before I make you walk home. I'm counting on those lads trying to pretend none of that happened. When they find nothing's missing, they'll try to save their jobs, won't they? Get us out of here, Geoff."

London, being two hours behind Trieste, was still bustling. Since it was Saturday, The Cathedral's atrium didn't close for another three hours, but Simon had no use for it tonight. He sat behind his desk in his catacomb office, while Taylor paced in and out. He couldn't guess what had him so agitated, but it was making him nervous, too.

"We should have gotten a message by now," Taylor said. "She shouldn't have gone with them."

"She? The Duchess's sister?" he asked, cracking a smile.

"Erm..." Taylor said, blushing to the tips of his ears.

"Wicked! She's right fit, mate."

"Er, thanks. But then she went home and..."

The desk phone rang, and he was sure Taylor was relieved to not have to finish that sentence. It was obvious he'd caught feelings, but Simon could razz him about it later.

He answered the call on speakerphone, using his default greeting, "AMWarn, Simon."

"The beans are in the roaster, I repeat, the beans are in the roaster," Martin said in a hushed voice.

"Come off it, Martin."

"Oh, fine. It's all done. Not as smooth as I'd have liked, but we managed."

They and Taylor heard Duncan fussing in the background, indistinct but clearly aggravated.

"What happened?"

"I, er, sort of tripped over a badly run cable and, erm, ripped it out of the router."

Duncan's fussing increased.

"Classic. Did you get it back in the right spot?"

"I was lucky no one ever goes in there. It was the only open port without dust in it."

"Wizard!"

"Check for a heartbeat. I deployed Scouts One and Three."

"What's a Scout?" Taylor asked.

"Nifty little device Martin whipped up. It lets us use Indigo on systems where we don't have access to install it, and they communicate back over mobile internet. Unless somebody spots the device, they'll never know we're there."

"A bug?"

"A Scout!" Martin said indignantly. "But, yeah, it's mostly a bug."

"Couldn't they trace it back to us if they found them?"

"They're basically burners. I'd love to get them back, of course, but by the time anyone found them, we'll be long gone."

Simon pulled up the Indigo console on his laptop. He set the filter on the streaming logs for the hardware addresses of the two remotes, and data popped up on his console every couple of seconds.

"We have contact, Martin. Cheers, mate, good job."

"Anything so far?"

"Just heartbeats from Scout One, but I'm getting a ton of binary from Three."

"Yeah, I connected Scout Three to their video surveillance rack, so that'll be video. It probably won't amount to all that much, but I thought you ought to know traffic through Three might be different."

"'Sgood thinking," he replied, impressed.

"Duncan's idea, actually. I'll tell him you said so."

"I'll start fine tuning the filters and building the dashboard tomorrow. I don't expect we'll see any other traffic tonight."

"Cheers. See you when we get back," Martin said, disconnecting.

"How's your Italian, Mr. Taylor?"

"Non-existent," Taylor said. "Whatever did you need me for?"

"The Duchess said these blokes aren't super online, so I reckon all we're gonna find is files. You'll need to tell us what it means, especially the shipping bits."

"That sounds like something I can handle. I've already been digging into Tessa, but I've hit a language barrier, as you said."

"I think I read something in a forum about a new image

translator. You take a picture of the document, the system creates a translated copy, and Bob's your uncle. It's an alpha, but I bet we could work with it."

"That'd be ideal! Indigo would do well with a feature like that."

"Now you're starting to sound like Martin."

"Thanks?"

"Or you could get your girlfriend to help you with the translations." Simon muttered, only just holding back the laughter.

"But she's back in Trieste, and..." Taylor started, before realizing what he'd meant. "Oh, do sod off!"

CHAPTER SIXTEEN
UNPACKING

The Silver Speedwell sailed through clear skies and calm air above eastern France. Francesca was accompanying her associates back to London, feeling optimistic about her recent change of fortunes. She sat in the forward cabin opposite Martin, who was staring out the window as usual. She often envied his naïve, almost childlike sense of wonder that nothing seemed able to shake.

"Martin, you have been at 33,000 feet before," she teased.

"Not over this part of France, and not during the day. The topography is fascinating!" he replied.

"If you've seen one alp, you've seen them all."

"But we're not over the Alps," he said, turning to face her. She saw his face drop when he realized she was having him on. "That's not funny."

She laughed. "It's a little funny."

Geoff sat across the aisle from them, eating an enormous lunch. Duncan stretched across the sofa in the aft cabin, taking a much needed, Xanax-induced nap.

"When will we know something from Indigo?" she asked.

"Hard to say. We're collecting data, and Simon is working the numbers. The real question is whether Tessa is a front. If the roastery isn't where things run through, we might collect petabytes of data that would tell us exactly nothing," he said. His sigh told her he was hoping for something more concrete, since he'd never put himself at this much risk before.

"What's a petabyte?"

"It's 1000 terabytes."

"You know what, never mind."

"Everything is important until it isn't," he said.

"True, but how do you mean? You just said the data would tell us nothing if Tessa wasn't the primary front."

"Maybe it's not the hub, but it's a stop on the way, isn't it? We can see what they're connecting to. Given time, we could lay it all out like a tube map."

"How much time?" she asked, unable to hide her excitement. The prospect of an upper hand that significant had her almost bouncing in her seat.

"I'm going to guess more time than you'll give us."

"I might still surprise you," she said, smirking. "It's too risky to do anything before the investigations are complete, and I'm sure they'll miraculously find no evidence and close the case."

"You don't think they'll find anything?"

"*Barcola* sank in deep water, and as long as it's not a danger to shipping, they won't dedicate the resources to conduct a proper search. They'll play at it for a bit, make a good show, declare it accidental, and move on."

"God, that's depressing."

"Not at all. With the amount of influence the families seem to have in the port, it's in no one's best interest to point fingers. It actually benefits us, because the authorities will keep the families' attentions on them rather than us. We can sit back and play the innocent victims, all while we're running our own investigation."

"I hadn't thought of that."

"That's because that's my job," she said, feeling a wide grin cross her face. "Always double-cross a double-crosser."

Martin pulled a face somewhere between deep concentration and stomach upset. "If the Tessaros are so proper and professional, how do you suppose we'll uncover any connection? Without proof, it's academic at best."

"Because something tells me that Giovanni Tessaro didn't do this. If it wasn't him, perhaps the person who did wasn't as careful."

"Well, if *The Godfather* taught me anything, whoever did this under his nose is as good as dead," he said. He seemed gratified to have connected it to a movie, something familiar, but he maintained his uncomfortable expression.

"That would be my preference," she replied.

He resumed his stare out of the window, becoming very interested in the topography of France again.

"Do you have plans tomorrow night?" she said, changing the subject.

"I rarely do these days. All I do is sleep, eat, and work."

"Perhaps you could do a couple of those at The Cathedral tomorrow evening?"

"What did you have in mind?"

"I thought I'd make dinner and see if Veronica can join us. It seems we have work to do."

"Dinner sounds lovely, but why would you need Veronica? It's a school night, after all. I'm sure her father would never consent."

"Between the two of you, every vision you've had has come true. I need to know what's next."

"Wait, why? You just told me your plans. You're starting an investigation, and we just planted Indigo. Isn't that what's next?"

"Those seeds will bear fruit in time, but I require a strategy for the short term. I need to extend my advantage, and your prescience can provide it."

"Out of the question," he said in a huff.

"I beg your pardon?"

"Listen to yourself, Duchess! You're basing your tactics on hallucinations from a noted idiot like me and a fifteen-year-old girl who has no business being involved in this?"

"You are not an idiot."

"That's also not my point," he replied incisively. "Can I be blunt?"

"Since when do you ask permission?"

"Since you punched me the last time I spoke out of turn."

"Okay, fine, I won't punch you this time." Though she wanted to sound playful, she felt anything but, and her words carried an edge.

"You're hell-bent on revenge, aren't you?"

"I wouldn't call it hell-bent, but it's fair to say I want payback, yes," she said, nostrils flaring.

"It's not like you at all," he continued. "You don't take shortcuts."

"And how is this a shortcut?" The back of her neck prickled like a fuse burning up her spine.

"This psychic nonsense is becoming a crutch for you. It'd be a simple matter if we could just continue predicting the future for you, right?"

That pissed her right off. Martin's newfound assertiveness amused her before, but he was pushing her too far. "You are dangerously close to walking home from here."

"You are dangerously close to child abuse, Duchess. That girl is not another one of your associates to order about. She's scared, and to be honest, so am I. We both told you we don't want to use that power again, or whatever the bloody hell it is.

Are you willing to risk her—to risk me—over a petty grudge?"

"It is NOT petty! He kidnapped Julia! He blew up my ship!" Adrenaline flooded her system, and she wanted nothing more than to punch his presumptuous face, but she'd promised she wouldn't.

"So it's personal, then," he said. "He had you beaten, and you couldn't take it."

He was calmer than she'd have thought possible—or preferred—facing her. Worst of all, he was right. She had let Giovanni under her skin and was grasping for any advantage she could find, propriety and ethics forgotten. Quivering with equal parts fury and fear, she simultaneously wanted to pummel his face until her knuckles bled and hide in the lavatory in a fetal ball. Before she could decide, he reached across the table and cupped her cheek in his hand. She wanted to slap it away, but something stopped her.

"You don't need visions. You're The Duchess. Beat him your way."

"What if I can't win this one? What if he's better than me?"

"Poppycock."

The laughter at his choice of word released the tears she'd been holding back, and she let it all out as they overflew Luxembourg.

Duncan plodded up the back steps to the flat, lightheaded and groggy, despite the tranquilizer wearing off by the time they landed at Farnborough. He was no stranger to drugs. Where he grew up, it would have been a larger surprise if he hadn't dabbled. He'd discovered through his adventures that most substances only made him drowsy, which wasn't much fun, so he usually stuck to bitter. The Duchess insisted he nap on the ride back to Hounslow, which he thought was a cracking idea. He tried to unlock the door, but found it already open, so he let himself in. Tracy sat on the sofa feeding Aidan, and Maureen sipped at a mug of something on the loveseat.

"You look a fucking disaster," Maureen said over her mug.

"Cheers, thanks a lot," he replied thickly.

"What's wrong, babe?" Tracy asked.

"I had a panic attack getting on the plane. They had to knock me out before we could take off."

"Crikey!"

"I hate flying, too," Maureen said. "Thankfully, scotch is a thing that exists. Gotten me through a lot of travel, but it got me kicked off a plane once."

He was too stupefied to smile. He dropped his bag at the door and slumped onto the opposite end of the sofa from his wife.

"How did the break-in go?" she asked. In any other household, this question might have been scandalous. For the McCullens, however, this was their version of "How was the office, dear?"

"Just this side of a catastrophe. Martin nearly cocked the whole thing up tripping over a cable," he said.

"Typical," Maureen added.

"Simon called it 'classic,' but I agree."

"Well, I should leave you three be," she said, gathering her things. "Bye-bye, sweet little Aidan. Don't let your daddy drop you." She gave Tracy a quick sideways embrace and headed out the back door.

"Always a treat, she is," he muttered.

"You know she's just taking the piss. Have you eaten?"

"No, but I can get something myself. Give me a few to

collect my wits. You worry about him first."

"He's not made of glass, Duncan. I'll finish up here and make you a sarnie or something."

"Ta."

"But, really, how did it go?"

"We got the job done, but it was all wrong. We went in with almost no layout. Figured there'd be guards, but nobody knew how many—it was two, by the way. She only told us, 'Find out what you can,' so that was super helpful."

"I never would have taken that job, but you already knew that."

"Geoff handled the guards, so that wasn't a wrench. I definitely prefer him on our side. Martin was a time bomb of nerves, and that sister was useless as tits on a bull."

"How did you do with the locks?"

"You'd have done better, but they were simple tumblers. I remembered everything you taught me."

"Brilliant! I think he's just about had enough," she said, tossing the blanket that covered them into the empty seat between them. She cinched up the front of her nursing bra and pulled her tank top down.

"Burp him while I fix your lunch, okay, love? Roast beef good?" she said, handing the infant to his father.

"Yeah, that'd be brilliant," he said, smiled at her, then turned to his tiny son. "Reckon mine will taste better, mate."

Tracy set to work in the kitchen, and the comfortable silence of home warmed him to his core. A couple of minutes later, a small, wet burp interrupted the quiet.

"Did it scratch the itch?" she asked, cutting to the heart of the matter as usual.

"Yes and no."

"How's that?"

"It felt good to be running a job again, no doubt, but something was missing. We sort of succeeded, but it felt empty."

"Did the newbies spoil it for you?"

"They weren't you," he said as he lay Aidan down in his crib.

"Who else is?" she said with a wink.

"It made me realize something, love. It used to be the thrill of the job, but then I met you. We started working together, and you became my thrill. The job just weren't the same without you."

She turned to put his sandwich on the kitchen table. Her eyebrows rose, crinkling her forehead, and her lower lip quivered.

"That's possibly the sweetest thing you've ever said to me, Duncan McCullen, and that's a long list to top."

He walked to the kitchen and held her tight for a long time, forgetting his lunch.

The mood in the Fancourt household was subdued. No one had spoken much to one another since they'd arrived home from Italy, but no one seemed to mind either. The explosion and their hurried departure had cast a pall on an otherwise enjoyable trip. It was logical that they hadn't talked about it because they'd all rather forget. Regardless, it made Veronica happy to be back in Hampstead, safe in the solitude of her bedroom. She scribbled some thoughts about the trip in her journal.

Not a Joyce fan before this trip, and still not, but developed a respect for the guy. I can see why that city would inspire him. Was getting inspired until the orange man appeared. Why does this crap keep happening to me? Afraid of losing my chance with Ms. Nichols, but afraid every time I'm around her, too. Need to decide which scares me worse soon. Should I just talk to her?

The knock at her bedroom door startled her, and she scrambled to hide her diary under her pillow.

"Come in," she said, trying to steady her voice and nerves.

Her father stepped inside her room with a serious look on his face. Not a promising sign. A lecture was in the offing, something she'd feared since they returned.

"I wondered if you had a moment to talk."

The most terrifying nine words in the language. All she could say was, "Yeah, all right."

"Honey, it's about Trieste. I took your word that we needed to leave, but I think I'm entitled to some answers. You've locked yourself away up here since and said nothing about it."

"It's complicated."

"I racked up hundreds of pounds in airline change fees and hotel stays, so I wouldn't have guessed there was a simple explanation. Was it related to that explosion?"

She hesitated to divulge too much about it, knowing it would only make it worse. "Yeah. Ms. Nichols knew something about it, because she seemed to change after that. She just said we should leave."

"At least she was good enough to promise reimbursement," he said.

She glared at him. "Is the money all you care about?"

"Of course not, but it made my decision easier. I assumed it was some kind of terrorism, so it didn't take much convincing to get us the hell out of there."

She continued her glare. He shifted his weight uncomfortably, as if someone had put worms in his shoes.

"I don't want you to be angry with me, but I don't think we should continue your association with her"

"WHAT???"

"Veronica, try to see my perspective. I've walked past so many red flags because I didn't want to seem like I was, well, being me. Ms. Abernathy convinced me I'd been babying you, so that's why I agreed to the trip at all."

She squinted at him, and he winced, as if waiting for her to blow up at him. She was livid, but also amazed that her dad, of all people, would admit to doing anything wrong. Ever. She decided she would let him keep talking.

"I've worried for a long time that something was off about this. At first, I took her for an opportunist, trying to exploit you and cash in on your enthusiasm."

"But she..." she said, before he cut her off.

"I changed my mind about that, Ronnie. She has genuinely tried to help you, but there's always been an underlying motive—something she wasn't saying, and still hasn't. It's possible she's being sincere, but from my vantage point, you come home a total wreck from that ridiculous cathedral of hers. Now with this free trip ending in a massive fireball, that unsaid something seems dangerous. I've been losing sleep over it, if I'm honest."

She didn't like it, but he had a point. In fact, she really didn't like it *because* he had a point. For her entire life, he'd instructed her on what to do and how to do it, never allowing her to experiment. What he'd said about Ms. Nichols made sense, but she resented being told her business again. Since the workshop, she'd felt important, needed, talented, and authentic—she owned her own destiny. Despite what she had written in her diary only a few minutes prior, her dad's position on the matter filled her with resolve.

"I don't want to give it up," she said.

"But Veronica…" he pleaded, before she cut him off.

"Ms. Nichols and the other people in that cathedral appreciate my talent, rather than just tolerating it."

She'd stung him with that one, she could tell. In an instant, his expression changed from "sensitive dad" to "how dare you."

"We have supported your talent since you could write! We got you into St. Catherine's!"

"Putting me in a school for the arts isn't the same as support. You always tell me how I'll grow out of it and get an actual career one day."

"Art is a hard life. You have too much potential to suffer for it."

"I don't have to suffer if I work with her. This is my decision."

"It is NOT your decision, young lady. You are fifteen, and as a minor, we are still responsible for you. If I say it's over, it's over."

"It's not your decision either, Dad. Where Ms. Nichols is concerned, this is a matter for the trustee."

"Nonsense! You haven't the foggiest idea what you're talking about."

"Do you think you're the only person in this house that can read a contract?" she spat.

"Then you've misinterpreted it."

"*All concerned parties, in the arbitrator's presence, must agree to terminating this agreement.* Did I miss a line?"

"You…" he started, but the rest of his words didn't come. She could see his brows knit in concentration, no doubt trying to remember the details of the trust he'd signed.

"I knew you'd try to cut this off sooner or later, so I made a point of memorizing that part. Go ahead! Make an objection to Ms. Abernathy. I dare you, Dad."

He stammered and puffed, too shocked to form words.

"I'm going to Bea's," she announced, and stood up to pack her backpack.

"You'll do no such thing! Jeanette! Come talk sense to your daughter!" He hurried down the stairs, looking for backup.

She had a narrow window for escape, so she grabbed her mobile from her desk and texted her best friend.

"U home?"

The little bouncing dots appeared right away, followed by the message, *"Sí. Y tú?"*

"Coming over. Dad. Again."

"C U soon."

She grabbed her things and met her mother at the bottom of the stairs. "I'll handle him. Come home after school tomorrow, okay?"

"Thanks, Mum," she said, as she walked down the garden steps.

It was only a fifteen-minute walk to Bea's house, but she was so engrossed in her thoughts, it seemed it had taken an hour. Maybe it had. Time had no meaning at the moment. She could walk the alleyways and paths between their houses blindfolded. When she arrived at the front door of the Crespo-Díaz house, she looked at her watch and saw it had indeed only taken fifteen minutes.

Bea's mum answered the door, looking concerned. *"Vero, qué pasó, mija?"*

"Nothing, I'm fine," she replied. Her response was a polite reflex more than an indicator of her mood. She qualified it by saying, "It's just my dad."

"You can stay tonight if you need to. You're always welcome here. Bea!"

Bea came screaming down the stairs, and the attack hug almost knocked her over.

"Jeez!" she yelped.

"Tell me everything!" She was obviously concerned, but she wanted the story, too.

"Dinner is in an hour, chicas," Bea's mum said before retreating to the kitchen.

The girls ran up the stairs, and Veronica chucked her backpack across the room. She flopped into the desk chair as Bea bounced into her own bed.

"Spill!"

"He said he wanted to me to stop working with Ms. Nichols."

"That's bollocks!"

"Yeah, especially because he can't. I looked at the contract."

"Oh, tell me you threw it right in his face."

"I did. He didn't like it at all, but I had him dead to rights."

"Brilliant!! What happened in Trieste? I thought you were supposed to be there at least two more days."

She recounted the visions, her connection with Ms. Nichols, and the explosion. Bea's expression alternated between excitement at the juiciest gossip of all time and abject horror.

"You witnessed a bombing? I would have run for it."

"It was miles out to sea. We weren't in danger. Is it weird that I was angry she made us leave?"

"Uh, yeah, that's weird. Why were you angry?"

"I dunno. I thought I could help or something."

"How could you help with an exploded boat?"

"I didn't say it made sense. I just hated being dismissed like that. What's more likely is she wanted my family out of her way, which I understand. She probably knew Dad wouldn't let me stay without him, so that was it."

Bea tilted her head, looking thoughtful. She sensed there was something important on her mind, but it was uncharacteristic of her to hold back.

"What is it?"

"After all of this, why would you *want* to stick around? Keep working with her, I mean."

"Are you against me too, Bea?" she huffed.

"No, I'm not, I just don't get it! You almost killed a guy with your mind and now this? Most sane people would run away from that as fast as they could. Why wouldn't you?"

"She believes in me. I know it sounds stupid, but I don't understand why a complete stranger would believe in me more than my own family. She does, and I don't want to give it up."

"Is that enough?"

"Why shouldn't it be? It feels like home. I feel powerful when I'm with her, like I'm allowed to be me."

"Now I get it. You have a crush on Ms. Nichols."

"What? Are you mad? This isn't like school."

"She inspires you, and that's where all the great art comes from. *Puedo escribir los versos más tristes esta noche.* Who wouldn't be attracted to that? How is that not like a crush?"

"You're quoting Neruda at me? You really have gone mad."

"I haven't! It's the same way you make me feel. When I'm with you, I feel confident, like I can do anything," Realizing what she'd just said, she blushed and stared at her bedspread.

She stared astonished at her friend, rolling her words around in her mind. Bea's admission was momentous, and she wasn't sure how to take it. With her emotions already taxed to their limits, it overwhelmed her. She had to say something, but what?

"Bea, I..."

"If all you need is someone to believe in you, I do. Can

that be enough?"

For the second time today, time had no meaning. Her pulse hammered in her ears. She had to break this tension, and she wanted so badly to say something kind or poetic, but words had deserted her.

"Are you jealous?" she finally said with a giggle.

"Yes, I bloody well am! I never see you anymore, even at school. I knew you were upset coming over here, but I wouldn't miss a chance to spend time with you."

Their eyes met, and they both burst into laughter.

"If I ask for a hug, are you going to snog me?" she asked.

"No promises," Bea replied, holding her arms out.

She hugged her best friend hard, and her burdens melted a little. There was at least one person in her world who understood.

INTERLUDE: IRONY

The noisy crowd, televisions, and canned music of the pub were a comforting cacophony—a respite from the thoughts swirling through Martin's head. He and Maureen sat at the bar, staring straight ahead. He felt certain she was a fraction of a second from turning on him and starting her tirade, and whatever she had to say was likely to be true. What he couldn't see was, rather than picking her moment to assail him, she had disappeared into a replay of last year's Champion's Cup final on one of the pub's many televisions. This was her local in Twickenham, and rugby was literally everything here.

"I know what you're going to say," he said, unprompted.

She didn't reply.

"Yes, I got myself into this, all right? I know I have no one else to blame."

Still nothing.

"What really chaps my arse is that it seems like she's not listening to me. I've stood up to her, I've made myself clear, and it doesn't get through. She's determined to do things her way. Veronica doesn't deserve to be a pawn in this, and neither do I! I believe I've earned better than that. She doesn't take unnecessary risks as a rule, so why can't she see what she's walking into? It's like I'm screaming into the void."

Maureen sipped her pint and continued to not reply.

"Have you heard me at all or are you just another void?"

he said, growing petulant.

"I've heard every word," she said, without turning to him. "I just don't care."

"Oh, well, thanks very much. My apologies for wasting your time."

"It sucks, doesn't it?"

"What?"

"Not being listened to when you're trying to stop a friend making a mistake," she answered, keeping her focus on the television.

"Bloody well right, it does! It feels like..." he ranted, then stopped in sudden realization.

She made an exaggerated turn toward him. If she'd been wearing glasses, she'd have been looking over the tops of them at him.

"Well, I...I mean..."

"Say it. Say you finally understand, ye bastard."

He attempted to avoid her condescending stare, but nobody was coming to his rescue and there was no escape. "Fuck," he muttered.

"There it is," she said, returning to the match.

He took a solid pull from his pint glass and gestured to the barkeep for another round. "My turn," he said.

"In more ways than one. This is what it's been like being your friend all these years. I do my best to save you from yourself, but there comes a point where I have to let you do whatever idiocy you're diving headlong into and be ready to collect the pieces when it goes wrong. You've never had to do it for me because I never take risks."

"That sounds horrid."

"Which part?"

"The not taking risks part. How do you have fun?"

"Evenings here or watch old movies at home. I'm allergic to fun otherwise."

"Is there a cream for that?"

"I'm exaggerating, you nitwit!" she barked. "You still don't see it, do you? The Duchess is determined to fight this fight with or without you, and if she hasn't heeded you yet, she won't. If you care as much as I suspect you do, be there for her. Be ready to collect the pieces when it all goes to shit. That's what you do."

He drained his glass. "How did you get so wise, Confucius?"

"A decade and a half of watching you make an arse of yourself."

"I'm sorry?"

"You should be. But it's also been worth it," she said, with a warm look and a half smile. "Wanker."

He scooted his stool closer to hers, laid his arm over her shoulders, and they proceeded to get monumentally pissed together, hip to hip.

CHAPTER SEVENTEEN

AN UNWILLING GUEST

Simon was bored...again. For over four weeks now, they'd collected a steady stream of uninteresting data from Tessa Roasters, the Scouts having been undetected. It had gotten so bad that he imagined scenarios of the handful of desktop IPs racing each other, each packet pulling that workstation into the lead. He and Martin had gone on various snipe hunts and chased many wild geese, tracking down external addresses that were innocuous. The longer it went on, the more he became convinced that Tessa Roasters was, in fact, nothing more than an artisan coffee maker of modest renown.

Martin's latest enhancements to Indigo helped a lot, as well. Three times a day, he would pull a report of the most recent unknown addresses inbound and outbound. He would look over the reports and WHOIS information, mark them as reviewed, and they would disappear forever into the database, gathering incrementing counts and digital dust.

As the end of his Friday shift approached, he thought he'd get a head start on the weekend and do the day's final review a bit early. His report had a couple of new addresses registered to the most popular of the social media sites, so he combined those records. Then there was a manufacturer's website wherein someone was looking at replacement parts, which elicited a yawn. Alarm bells rang inside his head, however, when he spotted an outbound connection to a cloud service provider.

"They don't use cloud, do they?" he said aloud, though he was alone in his office.

His White Hat training kicked in and he dove into the packet data. Based on what he saw, someone from the office was uploading a file to some remote storage location. He traced the packet chain back to the first in the series, and easily spotted that it was a PDF document, based on the file headers. That was one of the first tricks he'd ever learned as an amateur. Since Martin had gotten the Scouts inside the network, there was no encryption to crack, and he could sequence and piece together the contents of the file. Once he'd cleaned up some corruption around the splits, he displayed the document—an invoice. As he read through it, he noticed a line item that made him curse and reach for his phone.

"Alcott."

"It's Simon. You need to get to the office straight away. Bring the boss."

"You found something."

"More than 'something,' mate. Some numpty at Tessa just gave us the keys and all."

"Track down who it was. I'll call The Duchess. I'll be at The Cathedral fast as I can get there," Martin said, ringing off without another word.

He set straight to work, tracking down everything he could find about the source of the file leak. Despite its tiny size, the Scout device was a complete functional workstation in its own right, and they had preloaded it with all the tools they might need. He barged his way into the directory server and dug up the details of the workstation. The primary user on it was 'pzanetti,' which led him to Paolo Zanetti in the user directory. The name matched the invoice, so this was who he needed to investigate. But who was he? The directory listed his title as "*Vicepresidente dell'Attuazione,*" which Google translated to Vice President of either Implementation or Execution. Given what he knew of their less legitimate enterprises, that gave him a nasty knock.

Next, he connected to what he'd guessed was the office's mail server—he was right again, of course—and looked into the account. He saw a handful of recurring names, since Tessa's staff was small, and it looked as if Mr. Zanetti managed a team of four. He ignored several messages containing reports and status updates, which he found mundane and uninteresting. The one that caught his eye was from an address marked "A. Tessaro" hosted by a local provider in Trieste. He opened the message, but it was just a request to meet at their local for a beer. He scribbled the details on a notepad, hoping he would have time to do additional sleuthing before the brass arrived.

The Duchess arrived first, and he stood up so fast, he almost upset his energy drink.

"Oh, bollocks," he muttered before issuing a proper greeting. "It's good to see you, ma'am."

"Good evening, Simon," she said. "Thank you for sacrificing some of your Friday night for this. Can you tell me what you've found?"

"Yeah, but, er...I'd be happier if Martin were here to translate for me."

"Have a go. I've learned quite a lot from him these last couple of years. Nowhere near your level, but I may know more than you imagine."

He stumbled through explaining the particulars to his highest supervisor, but she seemed to understand most of it and was unafraid of asking questions along the way. He'd gone on for ten minutes or more before Martin rushed into the office, sweaty and panting.

"Sorry, got here fast as I could. I'd got as far as King's Cross when you called," he said.

"Ammonium nitrate," she said in her matter-of-fact style. Simon thought it was an unusual way to greet him. Without context, she might as well have said, "Good evening, Martin. Pink flamingo."

"Huh?" Martin said, missing it entirely, as he expected.

Simon came to his rescue. "That was what I found. They uploaded an invoice to a storage bucket that had quite a large amount of ammonium nitrate on it."

"What's that?"

"Blimey, don't you ever watch Discovery? Never heard of ANFO?"

Martin shrugged.

"I'm no scientist," she started, "but based on what I've heard, a quantity of that chemical mixed with a conveniently placed hole in a diesel fuel tank would make a rather effective explosive. Enough to punch a hole in the hull of a fair-sized ship, sending it to the bottom of the Gulf of Trieste. Wouldn't you say, Simon?"

"In a heartbeat," he agreed. "This one time on TV, I saw a little less than double that amount vaporize a cement truck."

Tumblers clicked into place in Martin's head, and his face dropped in shock. "That's where I've seen it!" he exclaimed.

"Welcome to the party," she mocked, before turning to Simon. "Is that something they would routinely order through Tessa?"

"Not likely," he replied. "I looked it up. It's used as a fertilizer, so unless they're growing their own coffee in that factory, they'd have no need for it. Definitely not that much."

"Let's get Taylor in here. We need him to dig up information about this Zanetti person. Interpol, local authorities, anything. I'd bet he has a record somewhere."

"I'll dig up what I can before he gets here. There was one other thing, though, ma'am. I found an email from an A. Tessaro asking to meet for a pint."

"A. Tessaro? You mean Alessio?"

"It only said A. I suppose it could be."

"That's very interesting. I'll need more details, though."

He tore the top sheet from his notepad and handed it to her.

She gave the page a once-over and smirked. "The game's afoot."

"What should I do?" Martin asked.

"Come upstairs for dinner, naturally."

"I mean, what can I do to help?"

"Simon, do you require Martin's assistance?"

He examined his boss's expression. His face seemed to say, "Please let me help." He remembered Martin had already made a significant part of his commute on a Friday night in London, so he wanted to make it worth his trouble.

"I suppose I could use a hand imaging the workstation. Who knows what details we'd find hidden away in there?"

"Brilliant! I'll get started," he said, bounding to his desk with excitement.

"Boys with toys," she sighed, and left the office.

"You didn't want dinner?" he asked Martin.

"If I were a betting man, I'd wager dinner will find us in an hour or so. Besides, I wouldn't miss the chance to give the Scouts a full shakedown."

"Can you believe it?" Alessio brayed in the half-empty bar. "I'm right, and you know it, Paolo."

"My friend," Paolo said, keeping his voice low, hoping to encourage his best friend to do the same. "Are you so positive that you're right? Maybe it got the result you desired, but it has caused a mess."

"Messes don't concern me. What bothers me is he shows me no gratitude. He casts me out of his home for doing him a favor."

"The *Capo* may have overreacted, but did you not? I told you my reservations about this plan. If you will not listen to me, who will you hear?"

"I will hear who thinks I should be in charge. I took decisive action, as a bold leader must do, and leading this family is my birthright. Be careful which side you choose, Paolo."

"I choose the side of Tessaro always. I have never been disloyal. You and your father have different methods, but you can find a way together. You will lead this family, but you must be patient!"

"Patience offers no rewards when our enemies sit in our port, biting their thumbs at us. We needed action, and I provided it."

"Was the embargo not action in your eyes? Your father said that they were on their knees."

"She should have been begging for mercy. After she stole the hostages back, we should have destroyed everything tied to the Five Pence name. Smug whore should have known her place."

"There has to be another way. Would you welcome the bloodshed from the old days?"

"I would invite the honor of the old days. You command

respect when your enemies fear you."

He realized appealing to Alessio's sensibilities had no effect on him when he was in a mood like this, so he sipped his beer and tried an emotional tack.

"Ales, is your father an honorable man?"

"Honorable? Without question, but he is weak."

"Why is he weak?"

"He shares these docks. The Tessaro name used to mean something here, and it will again."

"He is a pragmatist," he offered. "When your grandfather owned these docks, who did the police look to when they found a body? Who did the lesser families constantly try to overthrow? *Capo* united the port to everyone's profit."

"Are you on his side, Paolo? Are you against me?"

"I believe that there should be no sides, my dear friend. You are both Tessaro!"

The silence told him he'd gotten through, but the fire in Alessio's eyes said he would not change his mind. This meant more to him than defeating an enemy. It was now his crusade, and his cause was just and holy. He realized his words no longer held power, so he downed the remains of his beer and stood to leave.

"I must go home to walk the dog. Please consider what I've said before you do anything else. He may still accept an apology if you offer one."

Alessio grunted into his glass and wouldn't meet his eyes.

It was a cool, late spring evening, and he figured the walk back to his apartment would help to clear his head. Being Alessio's best friend had never been easy, even when they were children. He was impetuous, yes, but he grew cruel with the passing years. The unspeakable things Paolo had done on his behalf assailed him as he walked. What nagged him more, though, were the things he'd resisted. He earned countless beatings acting as his friend's conscience, but he knew his sacrifice mattered, especially to the *Capo*. To him, the elder Tessaro was more than the leader of the family: he was the father he'd needed when his own father spat on him. When he'd tried to teach them of business, of justice, of respect and honor, he listened when Alessio wouldn't. He would do whatever Giovanni commanded because he knew deep in his soul that, whatever it was, it was right.

He flipped a euro coin into the hat of the old man who often camped on his block and rounded one last corner to reach his building. The thought of a large glass of wine with dinner was the last to cross his mind before everything went unexpectedly black.

Geoff waved the smelling salts under the nose of the unconscious man until he stirred. His reflexes flung him away from the acrid smell and his eyelids fluttered, trying to gain his bearings. When he focused, shock and realization set in, and he struggled against his bindings. Geoff laid his meaty hand on the man's shoulder, looked him straight in the eyes, and shook his head slowly in warning.

"*Dove sono?*" the man said, then tried English. "Where am I?"

"You are safe, as long as you behave," a feminine voice said, which clearly didn't belong to the brick wall of a man in front of him.

"Who are you?"

"We've met before, though I'll forgive you if you don't

recognize my voice," she continued. "I recognized you at once."

"You must have me confused with someone else."

"Are you not Paolo Zanetti? Were you not in the Caffè San Marco when I discussed business with your *Capo*?"

He could see the pained expression of mental arithmetic, but since he likely had a mild concussion, it was little wonder that it hurt to think. He saw the man's thick eyebrows raise as the answer arrived.

"*Duchessa?*"

As rehearsed, he stepped aside, revealing the video conferencing terminal, the screen filled by his employer's smirking face.

"My apologies that I cannot question you in person, but the commute to and from Trieste has played hell on my transportation budget. I'm sure you understand."

"Question me? I know nothing, *signora.*"

"Games will only prolong this. We already know what we need to know. We just need you to confirm it."

"I'm afraid I do not know what you're talking about."

He cracked his knuckles. This was the part of the job he lived for, and Mr. Zanetti seemed like he may be tougher than he appeared.

"At ease, Geoff," she said. "Let's give our friend some time to think."

The screen changed from her face to the invoice they'd uncovered from Tessa Roasters. They watched him squint before he leaned back in his chair.

"How do you have this?" he said, his voice raised a panicked octave.

"Irrelevant, since it's obvious we do. It bears your name, your place of employment, and the materials that someone used to send my ship to the bottom of the gulf. I'm sure you understand why we might want to arrange this little chat."

The man's expression changed instantly from surprised to stoic. Geoff had questioned enough people through his employment with The Duchess to recognize his captive steeling himself, bracing for the punishment to come. It was clear this was not his first time under interrogation.

"My questions will be simple and brief. Giovanni impressed upon me how important honor is to his enterprise, so it must be to you as well. What I ask of you is not to betray your honor but to preserve it."

He said nothing, and Geoff rolled his shoulders. She'd instructed him to do nothing unless she gave a specific order, but she encouraged a little pageantry. A good show could make all the difference.

"Let's begin with an easy one. Did you order the ammonium nitrate on this invoice?"

He remained impassive. She gave him a full thirty seconds to change his mind on speaking.

"For this first question, I will take your silence as assent. I must impress upon you we will get our answers from you. Next question: I suspect Giovanni did not order my ship to be destroyed. Am I correct?"

Paolo looked at the screen in disbelief.

"Interesting. That's an answer, wouldn't you say, Geoff?"

"Yes, ma'am," he answered. He made a sudden move toward the prisoner, causing him to flinch, but only gave him a heavy thump on the shoulder. "Good man."

"Do you trust your *Capo*?"

"*Capo*? You mean the coffee?"

He knew that was a deflection, and he awaited the order. She had been generous with him, but he knew it only went so far.

"Geoff, level one," The Duchess ordered.

"They never learn," he said, crouching in front of the stubborn prisoner. With impressive speed, one hand darted up and grabbed his chin, while the other yanked several hairs out of his nose.

"Yaaaagh!" Paolo screamed, and his eyes watered instantly from the pain. Although he loved a good workout with the more stubborn sort, he had to hand it to her. The nose trick was her idea, and it produced results more often than not.

"Do you trust Giovanni Tessaro? Do you honor him? You will not enjoy it if you make me ask again," she repeated. She wasn't quite shouting, but her intensity was clear, and level two was imminent.

"Without question, *Duchessa*! He is like a father to me." Geoff saw him blink hard, trying to squint the tears away. With his hands tied, he could do little else.

"Good! You should. I have never met his equal in my years of business dealings. He is a shrewd and formidable man."

"More than a match for you."

He looked at the screen to see if there was an order coming, but she closed her eyes and shook her head slightly. *"She's giving him a lot of rope,"* he thought.

"You may be right," The Duchess replied, which deflated him. Not missing a beat, she continued, "How was your pint with Alessio?"

"He's a pain in my..." Paolo started, then froze. He'd answered her question without meaning to, which had been her plan.

"When did he tell you of his plan to sink my ship?"

"What makes you think he told me his plan, *Duchessa?*"

"Are you in the habit of purchasing 500 pounds of ammonium nitrate at your job? I have been patient, but I grow weary of these games. Although you are an executive at Tessa, there are always limits. You don't make a purchase that far out of your lane without orders. Even if I believed you, and he did not tell you his plan, you must have questioned the order. You must have understood what he would use it for."

"I told him to be patient! *Capo* would defeat you!"

"He almost did, Paolo."

Geoff was reasonably skilled at reading people's faces—perhaps not as good as The Duchess—but Paolo's became a puzzle at her last statement. He detected something that resembled pride, almost vindication, but he was also angry with himself for talking, almost against his will. He understood that feeling. It never ceased to amaze him how she could make people talk without threatening them.

"You must understand," she continued, "and Giovanni must also understand that I cannot abide this violence. An eye for an eye gets us nowhere, however, so I will arrange for your safe return soon. It should give us the opportunity to talk sensibly about business. I believe you have cemented your reputation with the true head of the family, and my enemy is only Alessio. Consider yourself my guest until I have arranged the meeting. Oh, and don't worry about your dog. I have an associate tending to him as we speak. He'll hardly notice you've been gone. Goodnight, my friend."

The screen went dark, leaving the room pitch black. Geoff flipped a switch, revealing a small room, complete with a bed, a washbasin, a refrigerator, and a hot plate. He untied his hands.

"You'll stay here. There's food in the fridge. You want anything else, you tell me, and I'll make it happen. Before you get any clever ideas, the utensils are plastic. You're her guest, so act like one."

"Alessio will kill me."

"Not if you stay here. You helped her, so she's in your debt."

CHAPTER EIGHTEEN

CASUAL CONFRONTATIONS

The mobile on Giovanni's desk rang, and he picked it up to screen the call. He saw the familiar face of Paolo Zanetti and smiled.

"*Paolo, come stai?*" he said.

"Sorry, he's not here right now," said the woman's voice.

"Who is this?"

"The person who is holding him until we've had an opportunity to chat."

"*Duchessa!*" he said in sudden realization.

"That's right, Giovanni. How have you been? It's been a while."

"Why did you take Paolo? What have you done with him?"

"He's fine. He answered a few of my questions and we've come to an understanding."

"What do you want?"

"A friendly chat, just as before. Only, you'll realize that now I hold the advantage. I expect you've known that since the unfortunate mishap in the gulf."

"And you think I had something to do with it, so you've taken poor Paolo?"

"Nothing of the sort! In reality, I'd already deduced you had nothing to do with it, and he only confirmed my hunch."

"You are familiar with this game. Nothing a man says under torture can be taken as fact. He'll say anything to make it end."

"There was no torture, my friend. I would say I didn't harm

a hair on his head, but that's not exactly true. In fact, his hair was the only thing we disturbed."

"He would never tell you anything. He is loyal to me."

"On that, we absolutely agree. He is a good man."

"Enough games. Say what you need to say."

"I know Alessio ordered the sinking of the *Barcola,* and I know he did it without your approval."

How could she possibly know this? Alessio must have involved Paolo, but why would he have talked? He calculated scenarios until she spoke again.

"I assume, by your silence, that I am correct. There must be recompense, but I do not wish for revenge, only justice. He must answer for his crime, and all you need to do is express your deep shock and disappointment in him. Offer him to the authorities, and our feud is over. We are even."

"You are mistaken! We will be even when you and your company leave Trieste and never return. You insult me by even suggesting that I give up my son. He acted against my orders, that is true, but it does not make it unwarranted."

"Alessio is in your employ. Therefore, by proxy, YOU destroyed one of my ships and cost me millions. He can serve jail time as a rogue operator, or the evidence I can supply will sink your entire family. You speak of honor and yet you show me none."

"You can prove nothing."

"Paolo can. If you will not deliver Alessio, I will take him to the GdF."

"He would never betray me."

"Can you be certain he would not betray your son? The son who has abused him since he was a child? He loves you like a father, but he is only loyal to Alessio out of fear."

He considered her point carefully. It was difficult to fathom how she'd discovered these private details about his family dynamic, but she had cut to the heart of it like a surgeon. He was far from beaten, but the power gradient no longer favored him. Softening his tone, he rejoined the conversation.

"*Duchessa,* I only regret that my son's rash actions have allowed you back into this game. We shall call a temporary truce and discuss terms face to face."

"Terms? You have heard my terms!" she shouted. "You accept them, or I will rain hell on you and your enterprise. What else is there to discuss?"

"Ah, but your quarrel is with Alessio, not me. I will plan for you to speak to him directly, but I dare say you will not relish the conversation. Bring Paolo with you as a show of your good faith. Convince me, and he pays for his crimes."

"If I don't?"

"Five Pence remains in business under new management, you understand?"

"I do, and I accept. If I were any less sure, I would not gamble my most profitable business."

"I will set the time and location."

"If you expect me to come alone to a location you select again, you must think me a fool. I will select the location this time. You may bring whomever you wish, but if Alessio does not come, there is no deal, and you will accept my terms."

"Agreed, *Duchessa,* but be wise. We do not want war."

"Nor do I. Good night, Giovanni."

He set the phone down on the desk and seethed. It had been a month since the explosion, and he had hoped that Alessio's mistake would not cost him. Even with supposed evidence, her sense of entitlement disgusted him, and he would own her business as well. He could imagine no scenario where he sided against his son. Still, the unforced error galled him, and he needed to shout at someone. The most natural starting point was with Alessio.

"Finally called to admit that I was right?"

"You continue to be wrong, and now you must answer for it. *La Duchessa* took Paolo and questioned him. She has found you out, boy, and you must face her."

"What? How is that possible?"

"You tell me, Alessio. If you are indeed ready to lead your family, then you tell me how she could know what you have done."

"I will kill her. If he told her anything, I will kill him too."

"That is your only solution? Your answer to everything? You continue to disappoint me."

"What would you have me do?"

"So, now you seek counsel from the *Capo*? I thought you knew it all."

"Don't toy with me, Giovanni. She has crossed the line."

"What line? Did you not cross the line when you exploded her shipment? Where is the next line? And the one after that? You see my point, boy?"

"What do you want of me, you feeble old fool?"

"You will grow up and present yourself at a time and place of my choosing to answer for your actions."

"Why should I?"

"If you renounce your name and compete against me, I will destroy you, rest assured. All along, you have mistaken my methods for weakness. I do not choose violence, but do not assume I am incapable."

"Enough of this bluster! Suppose I accept?"

"Convince me you were right. Your pride caused this, but you are still my blood, and I will not take her word lightly. If killing must be done, it will be on my order only. If you betray or defy me, I will not protect you."

"Protect me? From whom? I fear no one."

"So much to learn," he said, disconnecting the call. He would not give him the pleasure of the last word.

"ACP, Abernathy," Maureen answered.

"Hello, Maureen. I have a favor to ask." She recognized the caller as The Duchess at once and struggled to stifle the "ugh" on her lips.

"Business or personal?"

"Business, of course, else I wouldn't have called your office. I'm sure I've run out of personal favors, anyway."

"You're right. What do you want?"

"I need to take Veronica with me to Trieste, so I require you to convince Edwin to let me."

"Are you out of your tree? There's no way he'll allow that!"

"Surely, you could convince him of the importance."

"Explain. If I don't understand the importance, how am I supposed to convince him? Why is it so sodding important that you take her back to Italy? This had better be good."

"She and Martin are key to ending my disagreement there. Her talents are critical to our success."

"No."

"This is business. You can't say no."

"I bloody well can, and I have. This is absolutely out-of-bounds in terms of the trusteeship, and I won't allow it." True, she enjoyed pushing The Duchess's buttons, but as she'd said, this was business, and she had the legal high ground.

"I could get myself another trustee if you won't help me."

"Go on, you twat! Not one solicitor in the city would take up your cause. If you wanted a sycophant, you hired the wrong bleeding firm." Her raised voice and profanity had caught Nicola's attention, and she stood in Maureen's office doorway.

"Maureen, please see reason. This is crucial to our endeavors."

"See reason? OUR endeavors? This is for no one's benefit but your own, you miserable narcissist. You bribed them to go to Trieste last time. You want me to ask him like we're old buddies popping off down the pub? If you want to take her on this moronic crusade, go ask them yourself," she roared into the phone. "I fucking dare you."

"You won't help me then? Fine. I'll be in contact next week to dissolve the trusteeship. You've done a sterling job, but your services are no longer required." She caught the empty threat and refused to be cowed by her.

"Suits me fine, as your business is no longer welcome here, Ms. Nichols. I suggest you discuss the same with Mr. Fancourt when you talk to him, as all parties must agree to the dissolution."

She thought she detected a minute stammer before she heard, "Good day, Maureen." The line disconnected, and she placed the phone back on its cradle. She allowed herself a smile, bathing the office in her righteousness.

"Maureen, did you just fire our biggest client?" Nicola gasped.

"Technically, she fired me first, but yes."

"How could you do that?"

"She thinks she makes her own rules, but when she involved me, she etched them in stone. Contracts mean something to me, and I don't fucking bend."

Nicola's mouth hung open. "That was the sexiest thing I've ever seen," she said.

"I beg your entire pardon, Ms. Cobham?"

"I'm sorry, but I've always sort of fancied you, and I thought..."

She held her hand up. "Stop. I do *not* date co-workers, or anyone else, for that matter, so I suggest you change the subject if you want to save your pride."

"Er, yes, I understand. I'm sorry, I got carried away, and I'm very embarrassed right now."

"That said, if you and Henry would like to join me for a pint to celebrate the loss of our biggest client and this firm's newfound freedom, I'll be happy to buy the first round."

"Freedom?"

"Without her as a client, our destiny is finally ours. That deserves a celebration."

June had always been Francesca's favorite time of year in London. For one short month, the city shook off The Big Smoke and wrapped itself in a cloak of green, particularly here near Hampstead Heath. She reminisced about the times when her mum would bring her to the Heath and let her run in the fields. Perhaps this was why she'd had Geoff drop her off before they'd reached their destination. The fresh air (by city standards) was doing wonders for her mental state, which was not fantastic at present. It was nothing new for there to be a lot on her mind, but current events had her stretched to her limits.

Maureen was right, and she hated it, but her needs overruled standing arrangements. The conversation ahead had her worried, but not because she assumed it would be difficult or unproductive. The person with whom she needed to speak, Edwin Fancourt, was inclined to provoke her. Given the circumstances and her stress level, she couldn't guess what her reaction might be.

She inhaled deeply through her mouth, tasting late spring, then blew it out in a sigh. Countless hours spent in the tower, offices, and aboard the Speedwell had her sick of dry, recycled air. She crossed the street onto Wofford Terrace and started counting house numbers. The sun was just brushing the tops of the trees when she spotted Geoff stuffed into his preposterous compact car. She turned onto the garden path and up the steps to the entrance of Number 32 and rang the bell.

Jeanette Fancourt answered the door, and her jaw dropped. "Ms. Nichols, this is an unexpected pleasure. We were just preparing for supper. Would you care to join us?" Her cordiality was effortless, but her discomfiture was also plain.

"Thank you, Mrs. Fancourt, but I shan't be staying long. I wondered if I might have a word with you about Veronica?"

"Oh dear, I hope there's nothing wrong."

"Quite the contrary. May I come in?"

"Please," she offered before calling through the house. "Edwin! Veronica! We have company."

Edwin came out of the study, folding a newspaper. Upon seeing who the visitor was, though, his nose gave a slight wrinkle, as if she had brought several pounds of Camembert with her. Her attention turned to the top of the grand staircase, and she saw Veronica emerge from her bedroom. She didn't appear pleased to see her either.

"Shall we adjourn to the lounge?" he said, hospitable but

strained. He wasn't hard to read.

"That would be lovely, thank you." She was determined to keep the tone light as long as possible.

The lounge was far less palatial than her own, but tastefully decorated, comfortable, and cozy enough for conversation. She was sure the Fancourts entertained often, given their respective lines of work and their well-practiced welcome.

"How can we help you this evening?" Jeanette asked.

"First, please forgive me for dropping by unannounced at supper time. It's thoroughly rude of me."

"Quite," he muttered.

She noticed Jeanette mouthing something to her husband, which looked very much like "behave." The corner of her mouth ticked up.

"This is, however, of utmost importance and quite urgent. I'm sure that you both know that your daughter is more than special. She is, in no uncertain terms, gifted."

"Come to the point, Ms. Nichols," he huffed. "You've said all of this before, and we are obviously very proud of our daughter."

"Veronica has told me about her synesthesia. I believe it is no such thing."

Veronica's eyes doubled in size, and she stared at her, almost warning her.

"I will preface what I'm about to say by asserting that I consider myself a reasonable woman. I run multiple businesses, and I stick to provable facts, so I do not say this lightly. My research has led me to conclude that what she sees are, in fact, auras." Even Veronica seemed shocked to hear this last word.

"I'm sorry. Did you say auras?" Jeanette asked with a combination of confusion and skepticism.

"Human energy fields, emotion clouds, call them what you will. For her, people wear their personality traits like badges, which radiate from people as the colorful mists she has described. Each color describes the inner self."

"I say, Ms. Nichols," he said. "We've no time for this hogwash. Our supper is getting cold."

"She is also clairvoyant, Mr. Fancourt."

"There's no such thing!"

His face turned pink and blotchy, growing angrier by the second. Jeanette looked them over, trying to determine who to trust and what to accept. Veronica continued to stare at her, resembling an astonished porcelain doll.

"I would love to believe that myself, sir. My life would be considerably less complex if it were so. I trust you've both read her story, 'The Countess's Keep?'"

"Yes," her mother answered. "I have, at least."

"She has one of the most creative minds I've ever encountered, but that was no mere imagining. She was witnessing those events as they happened...to me."

"You? But..." he said, trailing off into unpleasant truth.

"Countess?" Jeanette asked tentatively.

"Duchess, in fact. Her skill with creative writing filled in the details that her visions omitted."

"Let's assume I believe any of this twaddle," Edwin interjected. "Why tell us any of this now? What is it you want?"

"I have need of her talents once more. The unpleasant events in Trieste involve me and my businesses, and she presaged it to me. I need her special sight as I try to conclude these dealings."

"Entirely out of the question!" he shouted, standing up, all decorum lost. "My daughter is neither a toy nor a tool. I trust you can find the door."

"Really, Edwin," his wife chided. "You should listen to yourself. Your daughter is not your property, either. I think we should ask her."

"She's a child, Jeanette! As her father, I have some say in what she does and doesn't do, and I'm not having her traipsing off to God-knows-where with this charlatan and her bloody fairy stories!"

"Veronica? Is there anything you'd like to tell us, dear?" her mother asked. "We've heard a lot of fantastical claims, but you haven't said a word."

"I hardly see the point in..." he tried to say.

"Shush! Veronica?"

"Er..." she started, hesitating. "She's not lying."

"She's filled your head with a load of nonsense!"

"I know what I see, Dad. I don't know if it's what Ms. Nichols said, but she's not wrong, either. Whatever it is, it's getting stronger...er, worse...I dunno."

"Have you told anyone else about this?" he asked, panicked.

"I told Bea. I didn't think anyone else would believe me."

"You could've told us, honey," her mother said in a soothing but regretful tone. "We would have believed you."

"Dad made me swear not to tell anyone after all the doctor visits when I was little. I thought it would get me in trouble."

Jeanette shot a sharp look at Edwin that caused him to sit down and study his twiddling thumbs. She could see his knuckles were white from clenching his fists. He was still furious, but he knew he'd made a mistake.

"Would you want to go with her? I'd like your opinion," she said.

Veronica looked at her again, this time with a hurt, searching expression. "Why haven't you called me or anything?

I haven't heard anything from you since we got back. Now you suddenly need me?"

"Ah, that explains why you didn't look pleased to see me," she sighed, caught off-guard. "I had other things to attend to. There were police inquiries and mountains of paperwork, but there's no excuse for my not checking in. I'm so sorry, Veronica."

"How can I help you? I haven't had any more visions since we left."

"I'd rather not explain it at present, but if I'm right, we can be more prepared and proactive rather than reactive."

"We?" he asked, rejoining the conversation. "Are you suggesting you're part of this rot as well?"

"It's fair to say I'm gifted in more than just business acumen, yes. I do not share her synesthesia, but my theories suggest it's what brought us together."

"You wouldn't put her in danger, would you?" Jeanette asked.

"My personal bodyguard has taken a sort of fraternal fancy to her. I dare say he might choose her over me if the choice needed to be made," she replied, winking at Veronica.

"You didn't answer me."

"I cannot promise an absolute absence of danger, but I would never put her at risk deliberately. I think you should know I've grown to care a great deal for your daughter. Family and friends have become so much more important to me of late, and I consider her a friend and equal. I hope she feels the same about me."

Seconds ticked, and the tension grew. Everyone looked at everyone else, waiting for a clue. The silence broke when a loud thump came from upstairs, followed by William shouting, "Ah, shit!"

"William! Language!" Edwin barked into the hall.

"Sorry, Dad!"

The women found this far funnier than he had. "Typical teenage boy," she laughed.

"I'll come with you," Veronica said.

"You will not!"

"I trust our daughter, Edwin! Yes, she's young, but she's old enough to speak for herself."

"Ms. Nichols, if anything happens to my daughter..." he said before she stopped him.

"If anything were to happen to her, I would never forgive myself, so I would not expect you to. In other words, I will guard her with my life."

"When do we need to leave?" Veronica asked.

"I can have Mr. Jenkins pick you up after school Friday. I apologize for the short notice, but this situation won't wait." After a thoughtful pause, she added, "So, who is Bea, and how much does she know about this?"

She blushed and looked at her sneakers. "Well, she's sort of my girlfriend."

"WHAT?" her parents said in shocked unison.

INTERLUDE: VACILLATING

Bea had not stopped asking questions since they left school, and Veronica's patience was wearing out—she'd passed wearing thin by the time they walked by the tube station.

"What is your deal?" she said, stopping in the middle of the pavement.

"What?"

"You've been on me since we left school. What's wrong with you?"

"I don't want to talk about it on the street. Can we go back to your house?"

"Ugh, fine!"

They walked on up the hill past where they usually waved and went their separate ways. Mrs. Fancourt was in the garden when they walked up.

"Oh, hello, girls," she said. "Bea, what are you doing here?"

"I need to talk to Vero. It's, er, about an algebra assignment," Bea said, not-so-convincingly.

"Can she stay for dinner, Mum?" she said, jumping to her friend's rescue.

"Sure, dear. It's always a pleasure to have you," Mrs. Fancourt said, winking at them.

Veronica groaned, knowing why and cringing inside. They hurried up the stairs, closed the door behind them, and she threw her half-full suitcase onto the bed.

"Here, you can help me pack."

"That was weird," Bea said. "What was that all about?"

"I kinda told my parents that you were my girlfriend yesterday."

"Oh," she replied, then it sank in. "Oh, ugh! She really winked! Why do parents do things like that?"

Veronica gathered things from her closet, folded them neatly, and put them into packing cubes. She loved the structure of a well-packed suitcase as a contrast to her usual disorganized spaces.

"So? What was your deal on the walk home?" she said flatly, staying focused on her suitcase.

"I'm worried. Scared, really. Every time you do something with Ms. Nichols, somebody blows up or something. Why did you tell her yes?"

"At least part of it was to spite my dad. He was talking down to me again in front of her. I wanted to do the opposite of *anything* he said."

"But…?"

"She said my synesthesia was actually me seeing people's auras and that my writing was clairvoyance. I've never believed in any of that stuff, but it's the first time any of it has ever made sense to me."

"*Madre de Dios!*" Bea said, covering her mouth. "Are you serious?"

"Super weird, right?"

"Yeah, but it also *does* make sense in a way. I still don't see why that made you say yes to this, though."

"She doesn't want me to hide it anymore. I dunno. It seemed really important to me then, but now I'm having second thoughts."

"Maybe you should listen to them. There's still time, right?"

"Yeah, I suppose I could back out if I wanted. She might

not sponsor me anymore, but then again, she's never said she wouldn't if I didn't do what she asked. Maybe I'm assuming too much."

"It's not like you'd stop writing if she didn't, yeah?"

"No, definitely not."

"So, it's settled. Should you call her?"

"Hang on, Bea. All that's true, but I think I'm still gonna go through with it."

"Why?"

"I can't explain it. It just feels like the right thing to do. When would I ever get to do something like this again? She said it might be dangerous, but she promised she wouldn't put me in danger on purpose. No, it doesn't make sense, but it *feels* right."

"If you think so, do it," Bea said, then wrapped her into a tight hug from behind. "Just come home, all right?"

CHAPTER NINETEEN

THE QUAY TO SUCCESS

Try as she might, Veronica could not sit still. She was no stranger to air travel—her family jetted across Europe for various work trips and vacations—and she had even flown first class once. It all paled compared to flying on a private jet. For as excited as she was, Mr. Alcott was twice that and then some.

"Is this your first time on a private jet, too?" she asked, trying not to giggle.

"Me? No, I've been on the Silver Speedwell a handful of times now."

"Why are you so excited, then?"

"I never tire of flying. I dreamt of becoming a pilot when I was younger, but I hadn't the aptitude, and the RAF didn't seem like my kind of place."

"Oh."

"Are you nervous?"

"No, I've flown loads of times."

"I meant about coming along on this trip."

"Well, sort of. I mean, I still don't know how I'm supposed to help."

"To be honest, neither do I. Technology is usually my role here, and this meeting seems very analog to me."

"You're both here as insurance," said Ms. Nichols from the galley.

"Insurance? Against what?" Mr. Alcott asked, echoing the

question in her mind.

She came back to the cabin with a tray of drinks and continued. "I trust the elder Tessaro, but the younger is unpredictable and violent."

Veronica gulped the large mouthful of cola she'd taken. "Violent?"

"I'm afraid I haven't told you the complete story, Veronica, and your parents would never have agreed to let you come if I had. What we're doing is akin to a hostage exchange, except we're holding the hostage."

"H-hostages? You mean you're the bad guys? But you seem so nice."

"It's not as simple as good and bad. It's rather hard to explain, but I'll try."

Ms. Nichols launched into a lengthy recap of events to date, including details she would not and, in her opinion, should not be privy to. To make it more unusual, she had a profound sense of déjà vu about the affair.

"The orange man blew up your ship?"

"I'd say that's the appropriate takeaway from it, yes."

"What about the dark red man? I saw them both on the street."

"The dark red man? I'm afraid we don't have a positive ID on him, but I have my suspicions, and I'm often right."

"How does this relate to us being insurance, again?" Mr. Alcott chimed in.

"It all comes down to Veronica's talent and the theory I've formed around it."

"And?"

"You recall our experiment in the lounge? Those without colors were unaffected; the ones with a faint color felt dizzy or experienced an auditory phenomenon. Our colors are the most luminous, so we're more susceptible to the effect, thus we were, for lack of a better term, taken."

"I think I see," she said. "The orange man is so bright that he might have some abilities too, but he doesn't know it."

"Remarkable! That's it exactly, Veronica. You may sense trouble before it happens. If events turn out of our favor, we will need any advantage we can find, and you're it."

"That still doesn't explain my role," Mr. Alcott said, sounding a little sad.

"You may have the most to do here, my dear," she said. "My offer to Giovanni may involve some of your talents, or at least the services of our security firm."

"This all boils down to a sales pitch?"

"Nonsense. This is very serious business, but it might sweeten the pot, as they say."

"If you say so. What else?"

"Your mind is the only one even close to as strong as Veronica's. If the situation becomes dicey, I need someone who can keep their head, so to speak."

"Now I'm worried."

"Don't be. The last thing I need of you is...well, you. Giovanni Tessaro is the only person I've ever met whose talents may exceed my own. You being there makes me feel more confident. Both of you and Geoff."

"Where is he, anyway?" she asked.

"Already in Trieste, tending to our guest. We'll all coordinate before we meet them."

"He probably needs a hug."

"More than you could know, I'd bet," Ms. Nichols said with a laugh.

"What about me?" Mr. Alcott said. "I could use a hug too!"

Veronica hugged him, although she knew she probably wasn't who he'd wanted it from.

The Duchess showed her Five Pence badge to the security guard at the main gate. She could see him tense when he recognized her, and she noticed the furtive glance into the car at the motley crew assembled within.

"Is there a problem?" she asked.

The guard snapped to attention and saluted her.

"That's unnecessary, young man. Just open the gate, please," she told him.

"*Si, signora!*" he replied, and fumbled at the switch on the wall.

The driver took them to a warehouse nearest to the end of the dock. The door opened and Geoff greeted them, followed by two of his security team. Veronica got out of the back seat, ran up to Geoff, and wrapped her arms around his formidable frame. He grunted and said, "Need to stay sharp."

"Sorry," Veronica said, releasing him and looking at her feet.

"But thanks," he added with something that resembled a crooked smile.

"Weird," Martin said.

"Everyone inside," The Duchess commanded. "We have a lot to go over."

Inside, more of her associates were minding Paolo, who was sitting in a folding chair, looking relaxed.

"Paolo Zanetti, it's good to meet you in person at last," she said.

"*Buona sera, Duchessa,*" he replied, quite casual given the circumstances. "I appreciate being treated well. Your people respect you."

"I inspire them to be their best. We have limited time, so I'll be brief. We will meet at the end of the quay, with our guests arriving by boat. I'm stationing a sniper on the roof of this warehouse, but only for surveillance and defense. This is not an ambush."

"Good thing," he muttered.

"You wish to assist, Paolo? I think you realize I know what I'm doing, but if you'd like to give us any advantage, I'm listening."

"He will expect a trap."

"Then I will disappoint him yet again. I want to resolve this peacefully. The girl will stay here at the warehouse with the rear guard. Watch through binoculars and tell me if you sense the situation has changed."

He chuckled.

"What is it now?" she asked, hand on her hip and losing patience.

"Your secret weapon is a child? It's a miracle he has not buried you already. You should play the Lotto with your luck, *Duchessa*. He must pity you."

"As I was saying, the rest of us will meet the party united. There is nothing more I wish to say in front of our increasingly rude guest. Gustav, will you please take him outside?"

Paolo followed his escort out of the warehouse with little drama. With the room clear, The Duchess continued her briefing.

"They will be armed and ready for a fight. Do not provoke them. Let me do the talking, speak only when spoken to. Everyone will have an earpiece and a call button. If you see something happening, press the call button, but don't shout. I like my eardrums where they are," she joked.

"I don't think this is a laughing matter, Duchess," Martin added.

"It's theater, Martin. A *danse macabre* with deadly weapons. You saw it just now with Paolo. He knows he's powerless, so he tries to get in my head. Giovanni inspires his people, and they will do nothing without his word, but not Alessio. He's the only person I can't predict. Veronica, when you spot the orange man, do not take your eyes from him, understand?"

"Yes, but..."

"Don't worry, sweetheart, you'll be far from anything you'd need to worry about."

"That's not it. It's the dark red man."

"Yes, I expect he'll be here anytime now."

"He's already here. It's that man, Paolo."

She stood stunned by the revelation. She had assumed it would be Giovanni. It made all the sense in the world to her: walking together in the city, their mental acuity being hereditary. Her error, minor in the overall scheme, created a small crack in her confidence, allowing droplets of doubt to seep through. "*Don't show weakness. Not now,*" she thought.

"I don't think that changes much," she said with some hesitation, "but thank you for telling me. It may come in handy later. Martin, you can stand behind the rest of us if you're worried."

"We'll see when I get there," he said.

"If everyone's ready, let's go meet our guests. Veronica, this is Danylo, our sniper. Do you speak Ukrainian?"

"Er, no, ma'am," she replied, eyes shifting to the man holding the long rifle.

"Neither does he," she said with a smirk, but the girl was unamused. "Just trying to break the tension. Please follow him to the roof and he'll give you the binoculars."

"Come along, young miss," Danylo said, and the pair took the stairs to a catwalk above.

"Duchess, can I have a word with you?" Martin asked.

"Always."

"I shouldn't be here, and I have a bad feeling about this."

"*Star Wars?*"

"Not the time! Someone is going to die out there tonight and I can't get the image out of my head."

"Oh, is that all?" she laughed.

"How you can be so calm about it?"

"It's not my first showdown, and I'm feeling good about our chances."

"You said yourself these men would come armed and looking for a fight. I'm not armed," he said, but stopped talking when she signaled to an associate. He knew what she was about to say, so he cut her off. "And I most certainly don't want to be!" he emphasized. "I've never even held a gun, much less fired one, and I'd prefer to keep that record intact."

"Suit yourself, but there's no point in panicking if you're not willing to protect yourself."

"Says the woman without a gun."

"I'm not defenseless. Besides, you should have considered that earlier."

"At the risk of repeating myself, I shouldn't be here. What am I supposed to do if shooting starts?"

"Play dead."

"Be serious!"

"I am serious. No sense wasting ammunition on a dead man. Hit the deck and play dead, if you want to know. I don't expect shooting, though. I have Giovanni intrigued, and he promised he would listen. If we can keep Alessio from being foolish for long enough, I think the math works in our favor, and we end this without a fuss."

"I wish I were as sure as you. I'm not psychic, but this has me worried."

"But you are psychic."

"Oh, shut up, will you?"

She threw her head back and laughed hard. "Trust me, Martin. Giovanni won't start anything. He would prefer to leave this episode behind him. Alessio has shamed him, and saving face is his best outcome."

"Are you prepared to be wrong?"

"I'm prepared for everything," she said with a wink.

Sea spray tickled Giovanni's face as the speedboat glided across the calm waters of the bay. Trieste from the water was his favorite view, especially at night. The bright lights of the docks, the warm glow of the old city, and the pinpricks of light in the distant hills stirred something in his soul. Any other night, he might enjoy it, but annoyance crinkled his face instead. He sat on the rear bench of the runabout, arm draped over the back, looking relaxed but disgruntled in his Armani suit. "*This should never have happened,*" repeated in his mind in various forms.

The boat slowed, and the bow dropped to level. Their own wake overtook them and lapped against the hull as he stood and straightened his suit. His crew moored the ship, and bodyguards climbed the ladder before and after him. When all had disembarked, they lined up in a formation around their esteemed leader and walked toward the line of people facing them, *La Duchessa* in the middle.

"Where is Alessio?" she asked, opening the conversation.

"I've not seen him for many days," he said. "We do not see eye to eye on this affair. I reminded him what was at stake this evening, so he will be here. Like you, he is so assured he is right that he would not risk me taking your side by default."

"Very well, then. We wait."

"Paolo, you are well?"

"*Si, Capo.*"

"*Duchessa*, something you said to me before, that I did not show you honor. I see now that was a mistake. Your actions mirrored my own. I am displeased that you took Paolo, but did I not take your Julia? Your sister? He has been treated well, and for that, I am grateful."

"Likewise, sir," she replied with a bow of her head.

"Do not assume that I have made my decision, though. My son acted against my wishes, but he is still my son, and I will hear him first."

"I would expect nothing less. Since we may be waiting for a bit, I'd like to introduce you to someone who may offer you a great deal, if you should agree with me. This is Martin Alcott, my Chief Technology Officer."

"It is a pleasure to meet you, Signore Alcott, but technology? Look around you, *Duchessa*. Technology is of no use here among the lines, ropes, and containers. What use do my men here have for computers?"

"Technology is how I discovered the connection and why we're standing here talking tonight. Trieste isn't immune to progress, and the rest of the world will move forward regardless of your opinion. It is inevitable. Do your men not carry mobile phones? Martin and his team can help you."

"You are being unfair, though. These negotiations will not start until everyone has arrived."

The standoff grew silent and tense, and he was becoming more irritated that Alessio had not yet arrived. The longer he waited, the less inclined he became to side with him, and he feared what his son might do if the judgment was not in his favor.

"Know any good knock-knock jokes?" she asked.

"What?"

"Too much quiet. Paolo, perhaps you would like to rejoin your family?"

He saw her nod at someone down the line, and the man untied Paolo's hands. Giovanni took a step forward, and Paolo walked over to embrace him.

"There is a sniper on the rooftop, *Capo*," he whispered in his ear in Italian. "She will not start a fight, but she means to finish it."

"Thank you, Paolo," he whispered back.

"Who are you supposed to be watching?" Danylo asked as he settled into position, adjusting his tripod.

"He's not here yet," Veronica said.

"Here they come!"

She trained her binoculars on the speedboat approaching the dock. It disappeared beneath the concrete platform, and nothing further happened until several men came to the top of the ladder, like ants coming out of a mound. Danylo's voice echoed both in her earpiece and unaided through her other ear, saying, "I have the target."

The scene unfolded silently, too distant to hear anything quieter than a shout. It fascinated her that everyone's colors were more muted through the binoculars; she'd never bothered to observe people this way. There was Mr. Alcott's light yellow, though he was less vivid. If she strained her eyes, she could make out Ms. Nichols's purple and Paolo's dark red. Interestingly, another man amidst the new arrivals also had a dark red color, and she wondered if it meant anything.

"What do I do if I want to say something?" she asked.

"If no one else is speaking, push the button on the earpiece, then say what you need. Keep it short and clear. Say 'over' when you're done."

"How will I know she understood me?"

"Our signal is when she scratches the back of her leg with her other foot. That means she copied the message. Go ahead, you've got this."

She pressed the button and said, "No orange yet. New guy is dark red too. Over." Through the binoculars, she could see Ms. Nichols's right foot tuck behind her left leg and scratch.

"Well done! What does that mean, though?"

"The colors are important. I don't know why, but I guess she has it figured out."

The gulf beyond the jetty was blacker than the sky, which glowed a faint orange from the city's lights. Out at the edge of sight, she spotted running lights on two large container ships, but nothing closer yet.

"Do you see anything?" she asked.

"Young miss, I have my target and I must not change my focus unless she signals me. Anything else is your charge."

"I understand," she said, feeling a little dumb for thinking they were both scanning the sea. She allowed the binoculars to dangle from her neck, looking out over the harbor with her naked eyes. Conflicting thoughts flooded her mind, and she struggled to process them all. Phrases like, *"I shouldn't be here,"* crashed into others like, *"This is so cool."* She wondered how aghast her parents would be if they could see her now, standing as lookout on a rooftop next to a sniper. It reminded her of what Mr. Alcott said on the flight, being unclear about their roles, and she felt as lost as he did. Perhaps more so, since he seemed less surprised by the requests. Maybe Bea had been right, and she should have backed out.

Though it wasn't late—maybe only 10 pm—the port was quiet. Even the congregation on the jetty had gone still as a tableau. She hadn't spent a lot of time near any sort of harbor, so she didn't know if it was normal, but it didn't match her expectations. She was suppressing a yawn when movement caught her eye to the left. The faint lights drew closer, so she brought up her binoculars and spotted another speedboat aimed toward them.

"There's another boat coming. Left side. Over," she spoke into her microphone. The people below turned their attention to the sound of the motor. The sight confused her at first, because she'd have sworn the boat was on fire. As it got closer, she realized what she was seeing.

"It's him," she announced. "The orange man is here."

The magazine slid smoothly into the pistol and clicked into place. He was above cliches such as etching *"La Duchessa"* into a bullet, but he intended for one of them to find her. It crossed his mind that one of these instruments of death may end the traitor, Paolo, and another could spell his ascendancy by killing his own father. It mattered little to Alessio. This was business. They had shown him who they truly were: weak, cowardly, and expendable.

His cruiser pulled alongside the dock where the *Barcola* might be sitting were it not rusting thirty meters below the surface. It brought a wicked grin to his face, despite what his father thought of it. He lacked the entourage that his father commanded, but the men who climbed the ladder ahead of him had sworn complete, unquestioning loyalty to him. Quality mattered far more than quantity.

When he reached the top, he saw the two contingents—his enemies—lined up, ready to meet their judgment. He gave their judgment, which he wore on his hip, an absentminded pat, and walked toward them.

"Where have you been?" his father asked with a growl.

"Am I late? Oh, I can't be late because you can't start without me," he drawled.

The stony faces that greeted him suggested they didn't appreciate his wit. "*Their loss,*" he thought.

"It's been a while, Alessio," *La Duchessa* said, rubbing the back of her neck. "I haven't seen you since the cafe, but you've been a busy boy."

"Shut your whore mouth," he spat. "I am no boy. You know nothing of men."

"If I know nothing of men, I imagine I'm a pretty poor whore, as you say."

He seethed. This woman's audacity would make her end sweeter. He could almost imagine the surprise on her face as his bullet pierced her heart. Soon.

She continued. "I know what you did, Alessio. Given your

family's status, if you admit your crime, the local police will give you little more than a slap on the wrist. You preserve your name, your family's honor, and we end this feud."

"I did nothing. Neither you, this tired old fool, nor this traitor can prove anything."

He saw his father's bodyguard inch his hand toward his holster, but no more. In his mind, he'd already identified the priority targets were, and prepared to execute his plan.

"Alessio, end this!" Paolo shouted. "Conspiracy gets you three months, and they'd suspend most of it. This has always been a financial matter. It is not worth the blood you would spill."

"SHUT UP!" he screamed. "I decide how we settle this, and you will be lucky if yours is not the first blood spilled, Paolo. *Duchessa*, take your people off this dock and never return. You've lost, and if you admit that, you walk away with your life."

"Mine is not the life in danger. Look around you, Alessio. You stand on my dock, outnumbered five-to-one, accused of sinking one of my ships, insulting your father, and threatening the only friend you've ever had. There is no advantage left for you to play, and your only risk is jail time. Take the loss."

His hatred surged across every nerve, heart pumping righteousness through every blood vessel. "Loss? I have already won! Giovanni could not defeat you, but I did. Walk away now or die."

"LOOK AROUND YOU!" she bellowed. "If you fire a single round, you're dead before you pull the trigger a second time. Shoot your father, and his bodyguards will empty their clips into you. Shoot me, my sniper takes the top of your head off."

That rattled him. He looked for any sign of a shooter or the glint of a scope, but the high-intensity lighting made it impossible. She had a point, damn it, but he steadfastly refused to let her win the day.

"Say what you must say, boy. Swallow your pride," Giovanni said.

He recognized the sympathetic tone his father had used, and his resentment of it was visceral. *"How dare he talk to me like a child, here at our family's triumph,"* he thought. *"You make me appear weak in front of a common adversary."*

"I was justified in what I did," he said in defiance.

"Perhaps, but you answer to me!"

"Would you have listened, Papa? Would you have agreed to act so decisively?"

"I listened, boy, and I told you why you were wrong. It is you who did not listen. Your thirst for violence blinded you to reason. You are still wrong, but you can atone for your misdeeds. A *Capo* must be decisive but must also be humble—we are not infallible. It pains me to say it, but *La Duchessa* is correct. You should surrender now and preserve what honor you still cling to. I will speak with the police and negotiate a shorter sentence."

"She is not correct and I will not surrender! You say I will be dead before I shoot twice, but there is one person here who no one will avenge."

With almost superhuman speed, he pulled his pistol and shot Paolo in the chest. Time slowed as his eyes swept the crowd, searching for the next target on his well-rehearsed list.

A distant scream floated through his ears before the world, as he knew it, exploded into thousands of shards.

CHAPTER TWENTY

LIGHTER THAN AIR

"What is this witchcraft?" Alessio shouted as he hung suspended above the crowd. His arm remained pointed ahead of him, aimed at her heart, but his gun was nowhere to be found. She floated in space opposite him next to another man whom he did not recognize. He looked below and saw Paolo and one of her men laying motionless on the concrete. His father kneeled in his circle of protectors with his hands cupped over his ears. Bodyguards and henchmen scrambled to their aid. The scene was unmitigated chaos, but it surprised him that no one had started shooting. Sudden movement to his right drew his attention, and he sputtered as a spectral girl flew toward them.

"Are you okay?" the girl asked, drifting up to his foe.

"I'm fine, Veronica. What happened?"

"I heard the shot, and I panicked. I was afraid he would shoot you next."

"You may have saved his life, believe it or not."

"Saved my life? Who are you? What's going on?" he demanded.

"Just a moment, Alessio," she said calmly, suggesting this was a run-of-the-mill occurrence. "Veronica, aren't you still on the rooftop?"

"I suppose, but I had to make sure you hadn't been hurt."

"Very thoughtful. We'll have to explore how you did that."

"I just thought that I needed to be here," Veronica said,

"and then I was here."

"That's good to know, but I'm afraid this isn't the time. We have more pressing matters to attend."

"I'm fine, thanks for asking," the other man uttered.

"Not helpful, Martin," she told the man before turning back to him. "Now, Alessio. I imagine you're a bit confused. Our young friend here has a special talent. As you have unexpectedly joined us, it would seem that you do as well."

"Make it stop!" he ordered.

"The only person who can stop it is you, I fear. If you would lay your gun down, we can negotiate a truce. Hopefully, we can still help Paolo."

"He is dead. I do not miss. When this ends, you will die too."

An immeasurable pain wracked his brain, and he cried out.

"What was that?" she asked, looking at him with concern.

"He was going to hurt you, and I got angry," the girl said.

"That's...terribly disturbing. Please stay calm, dear, for everyone's continued well-being." He saw the slightest flicker of fear on her face, but it was gone as soon as it appeared.

"I didn't mean to hurt anyone!"

"I'm sure you didn't. It's not in your nature." She turned to face him. "But it is in yours, Alessio. Since you and I cannot hurt each other in this state, but apparently our young friend can, it seems like an opportune time for us to talk."

"Is that a threat? Would you use this child as a weapon?"

"If the facts threaten you, take it as you will."

"Talk, but be quick about it."

"Why do you hate me so much? I shipped two crates of coffee per month through this port, so I would never compete with you, really. Your father has understood this. Why can't you?"

"I don't care about coffee! That was his worry. This started between us when you took my hostages. I vowed I would see you dead."

"For that? You've got an overdeveloped sense of vengeance."

"*Princess Bride* again. I'm impressed," the man called Martin said.

"Not now!"

"My family means everything to me," he said proudly, "but it means nothing to you or the other families. All of Europe used to tremble at the sound of our name, and they will again. This is my destiny, and it begins with my victory on these docks tonight."

"I've already told you how that would end, and you still choose your pride over common sense? You have your guards, but killing Paolo has almost certainly turned your father against you. Please surrender. I don't wish to kill you."

"No, no, you misunderstand, *Duchessa*. You do not get to predict how this ends. You cannot touch me, and neither can your sniper. I will succeed."

"I am begging you, Alessio. Lay down your weapon and let's talk. We can find a peaceful solution."

"I have my gun aimed at your heart, and you are defenseless." The surrounding air glowed an incandescent orange, a manifestation of the hatred he felt toward them all. He'd never been so certain of anything in his life. This was his moment—his ascendancy—and no one would steal it from him.

"I told you to bring a gun," Martin said.

"Hush!"

"You will die and then my father. You are all already dead. I am invincible!"

"Very well," she said, bowing her head. "Veronica, let's get back into ourselves, just like we've done before."

"No!" she screamed. "He can't hurt you up here."

"It's all right, sweetheart. Let us go."

"But..." Martin said.

"Relax. It'll all be over soon."

He felt a sinking sensation as his body drifted closer. His enemy's eyes were closed. *"So, she has accepted her fate,"* he thought, preparing for the kill shot and evasion maneuvers. His entire being sizzled with power. He could picture their defeat, watching himself moving at superhuman speed, ending his foes until none remained to challenge him.

A jolt shot through him as his soul reunited with his body. He blinked twice and focused his eyes down the length of his arm to his gunsight. When he found her heart, he saw her arm already outstretched toward him. The impulse to pull the trigger traveled down his arm until...

He felt a sudden, fleeting pain, then bewilderment, as her dagger pierced his throat. *Impossible!* He staggered backward, firing his shot into the sky, and crumpled onto the deck. As he lay on the concrete, he watched his future swirl out into the ether. The stars blinked out one by one, and Alessio Tessaro ceased to be.

"I'm all right," Giovanni told his guard as he struggled to his feet. "What happened?"

The guard's eyebrows were knit, and his eyes shifted. He saw the guards all standing with their guns drawn, but frozen in shock, waiting for an order.

"What has happened?" he said, turning to find Alessio. His son lay on the ground with a knife protruding from his neck.

"Alessio, my son..."

"I'm sorry, Giovanni," she said. "There was nothing but evil in his heart. I could neither sway nor reason with him."

"I heard nothing! How could you know that?"

"You could say I asked his soul, but you'd never believe me. He left me no choice, so I had to defend myself." She would not look at him. Instead, she stared at the ground, no doubt waiting for the shot that would punish her for what she'd done.

"You killed my son! Tessaro blood has been spilled on this night! Give me one reason I should not kill you where you stand."

His men snapped back to their senses, training their guns on her party.

"He would have killed us both. He betrayed you, claiming it was his destiny."

"*Assurdo!* No one heard him say this."

"I heard him, sir, and she is telling you the truth," Mr. Alcott said. "His exact words were, 'You will die and then my father.'"

"You lie for her! Why should I trust your words over my own eyes?"

"Because I'm too terrified to lie to you."

He searched his heart as he looked at the lifeless form of his boy. He knew Alessio's ambition was strong, but he never truly believed his own son would kill him to get what he wanted until now. With Paolo also dead, he felt his empire slipping from his fingers. His heart screamed in ultimate suffering as the truth of their words sank in.

"*Signore!*" one of his men shouted. "Paolo, he is alive! Barely, but he breathes."

"Call the paramedics, Tomas. We must save him."

"But Alessio said he was a traitor."

He sighed. His men needed their leader to be strong, and

they awaited his order. More death would neither assuage his pain nor change what was true. "Alessio was the traitor. Paolo is innocent."

"*Signore?*"

"Do as I tell you, Tomas."

"*Si, Capo.*"

"*Duchessa,* I can never forgive you for the death of my son." His men sharpened their aim.

"Please, Giovanni, this is not..."

He raised his hand, motioning for his men to lower their guns. She stopped talking at once, and his men complied. "But I believe you. For many years, he has plotted to end my reign, but you forced him to act. In his misguided mind, killing me was his only way to become head of the family. You have saved my life, so I will spare yours, but I will always hate you for it. I will not avenge myself upon you."

"Isn't that how it is done?"

"You dueled with him on a field of honor, but he proved he had none, so I must accept that. Because of you, I found who my true son is, even if he is not my own blood."

"I see. If there is anything I can do..."

"You have done enough! Take your people and disappear. If there are guards on duty, send one out to me with orders to talk only. Paolo and Tomas were trespassing, and your guard did his proper duty. That will be the story, yes? I will take Alessio home with me, where he belongs. I will contact you when I am ready. Our quarrel has ended."

"I understand," she said, motioning her people toward the warehouse. "I am truly sorry."

"GO!" he shouted through the tears welling in his eyes.

"Are we safe?" Martin asked as they hustled through the warehouse. The catwalks above clanged with the hasty footsteps of Danylo and Veronica as they ran down to join the party.

"Move your arses," Francesca bellowed. "We can argue whether we're safe once we're away from here. I don't want to be around in case he suddenly changes his mind."

"Do we have time for me to be sick?"

"No!"

The team burst through the front entrance to the warehouse and hustled to the waiting cars. Well, most of them hustled. The two unfortunate souls who had to support Geoff only managed a trudge. They loaded him into the van with Danylo, Gustav, and the other heavies, tearing off without another word.

"In!" she ordered the remaining pair.

"I'm sitting up front unless you want me to redecorate your interior," Martin stated, looking rather green.

"Fine, just get in."

With the passengers secure, the driver made haste as he carved through the streets of the industrial district, dodging the occasional lorry. She kept her eyes out the back window to ensure that they hadn't picked up a tail along the way. It wasn't until they got on the dual carriageway that she relaxed and turned her attention back inside the sedan.

The moon cast a judgmental light over the car as it sped along, bound for Trieste airport, the Silver Speedwell, and the safety of the skies. She sat with Veronica, but no one had said a word since she commanded the driver to leave town with all haste. There were so many questions to ask, but she wasn't sure the answers were palatable just now. It made no sense that she was still here, respiring, leaving town without a consequence.

"I'm so sorry," Veronica said, unprompted.

"My dear girl, why?"

"I ruined everything."

"Now, stop that. It's likely that you saved all our lives tonight."

"But what I did..."

"Yes, that's caused me more than a little worry. It was a benefit in that moment, but your talent has now become a danger. I don't think you'd misuse it, of course, but when you attacked Alessio...well, let's just say I'm not eager to see that again."

"It was an accident. I'm sorry."

She took a deep breath. What she needed to say didn't come easily, but it still needed to be said.

"No, Veronica, I'm sorry. I should never have put you in this situation. It was my arrogance that got us here, and I used you. I would say a mere child, but you are no such thing. I think it would be best for all of us if we said goodbye when we return to London. Our association awakened something that should not have been disturbed."

"Forever?" she asked, crying.

"For now. Nothing is forever."

"Even my writing?"

"Oh, dear, yes, I will happily continue to support you. I'll just do it from afar now. The only thing I ask in return is that you tell me if any of your dreams or stories involve me before you publish them."

"I can do that," she said, wiping her eyes with her sleeves.

"Martin, are you all right?"

He didn't answer, staring straight ahead and breathing

deeply as they exited the highway. The driver took them through the security gate and straight to the bottom of the steps of the waiting Speedwell. Martin sprinted from the car and into the jet, and Veronica came around the car from the far side.

Francesca pulled her into a powerful hug. "I won't let you down again."

CHAPTER TWENTY-ONE

THE HANGOVER

The familiarity of the lavatory from this angle bothered Martin. In four flights aboard the Silver Speedwell, he'd vomited on two of them, which was far too high a percentage for his liking. The scene on the jetty played through his memory in a torturous loop, and each time it reached its climax, he heaved. Since they'd met, he knew intrinsically that The Duchess was dangerous, but it had always been an implied danger. The more he got to know her, it seemed less real and more cartoonish. She toyed with her foes as Bugs Bunny would with Elmer Fudd, plugging their guns with her fingers. But seeing her strike Alessio Tessaro down with her own hands, with the same knife she'd thrown at him in her office, was unbearable. Another wave of nausea wracked him, and he retched again, helpless.

A knock at the door startled him, and he responded with a raspy shout. "Go away!"

"Martin, I want to help."

"I'm fine."

"You are not. Let me in."

"Go. Away."

"We're landing in under an hour, so you need to return to your seat. Do you need a bag?"

"Yes."

"Please talk to me! This isn't airsickness, and you haven't

been drinking."

"You killed him."

"I had to."

"Go! Away!"

"I'll send the captain back here if I must. When we start our descent, I expect you in your seat." From the change in her tone, it was obvious he'd irritated her. Good. He said nothing more and wiped his mouth with a towel. A few minutes later, he had gathered himself up and sat in one of the forward-facing seats, an emesis bag on his lap.

With their hasty, late-night departure, they couldn't return to the Speedwell's home field at Farnborough, which was not open overnight. She announced their diversion to London Luton Airport, and he could see her conferring with the members of the crew, presumably to make arrangements for them to get home from their unplanned destination. She proved him correct when she reached the rear of the cabin to talk to him and Veronica, although the latter was asleep on the sofa across from him.

"Our car will head for The Cathedral. It's far too late to drop Veronica off at home, so I figured she could stay in one of the guest suites. You're also welcome to the facilities, Martin."

"Hounslow isn't too far out of the way, is it?"

"No, but I was hoping we could talk."

"Later, please. I still don't feel well."

"Very well. We'll be descending soon, so buckle up."

The landing was textbook, and they taxied to their temporary position on the apron. Three cars awaited them, and he recognized Mr. Jenkins, her personal driver, standing outside of the largest. They loaded Veronica onto the rear-facing bench and let her return to her slumber. As they merged onto the

M1, he felt ready to have the conversation.

"How could you do it? Why?"

"Mr. Jenkins, would you mind giving us some privacy?" she asked her driver. Without a complaint, he raised the divider, and they were alone. "For whatever it's worth, I didn't want to, Martin. I tried to talk him out of it, but you heard him in the dream state. It was him or me, and it would have been a bloodbath if he'd killed me. It was an impossible situation, and we're quite fortunate that it didn't escalate."

"I understand that empirically. I was there. But I've never seen anyone die before, and knowing you did it..." An urp from his gurgling stomach interrupted his sentence. When he'd settled himself again, he said, "Would you kill me like that if you had to?"

"Don't be ridiculous."

"Duchess, would you kill me if you had to?"

"I can't imagine any reasonable scenario in which I'd need to, honestly."

"How many people have you killed? How many people have you *had* killed?"

"Would it make you feel any better if I told you?"

"Probably not."

"Then don't ask a question you don't want the answer to."

They rode through the dark countryside in silence until she asked, "So, are you coming to The Cathedral?"

"I miss my cat."

"I'm sure you do." She pushed a call button on her console and said, "Mr. Jenkins, please take us to Hounslow."

"Aye, ma'am," he said through the intercom. The limousine diverted onto the M25, heading west.

"I assume this is the part where I'm supposed to plead with

you and say nothing has changed, but I can tell it already has," she told him. "What can I do to improve the situation?"

"I'll need some time...and therapy."

"That's fair, and, given the state of things, that's a request I can honor. How much are you likely to need?"

"Maybe a week. Maybe forever. I don't know. Thinking about it is still making me queasy."

"We'll change the subject, then. I don't think the upholstery could stand the abuse." She smirked, but he found the joke ill-timed. "Veronica seems to have found a new talent, and I'm worried it could be devastating without some control."

"Control? Are you in control of yours? Because the only way I've found to get you out of my head is to drive halfway across the country."

"There must be something we can do. I refuse to believe we have no agency in our own minds. We've been able to harness it and send messages, but it's taken time. That must mean something."

"Are you proposing becoming her spirit guide or some such?"

"I haven't the time, but I was considering you for the job."

"As a counterpoint, I've been pondering on these mind connections quite a lot lately, and maybe we're going about this all wrong?"

"How do you mean?"

"Well, er, did you ever wonder why or how it started? The dreams, our meeting, her knowledge of the Owen Affair? You and I have always lived in London, and best I can figure, so has Veronica. Until three years ago, we were all complete strangers. I'd never even imagined you. What led to our connection? Why us? It keeps me up at night sometimes."

Her forehead creased, and she tilted her head to the side.

It became clear she had never considered this aspect of their gifts, and her face lit up with realization. "My God, you're right! I assumed it was some latent, long-dormant psychic ability, but something activated it. No warning, just boom. Some shift in energy or ley lines or other new age nonsense I don't actually believe in."

"Wonderful. Now you're going to lose sleep over it as well."

"That's possible, but I may have some ideas. My theories have proved correct thus far, hence why I brought you both with me to Trieste, but they're only informed hunches. Do you think you could research it further?"

"I wouldn't know where to begin."

The rear compartment of the limousine was almost electric with her plotting.

"I recommend you take a leave of absence. Simon is more than capable of maintaining the status quo in the catacombs, and he may even be ready to take an apprentice of his own. He's quite brilliant, as you know. Any information you need, ask Taylor or Mr. Adkins from the command center. We need to study it before it overtakes us all."

"And what will you do?"

"What I always do, Martin. Run my businesses. Just promise you'll call me once in a while and check in. Tell me what you've found or just say hello. I would hate to lose you."

They said little else until they arrived at his flat in Hounslow. Before he reached his front door, he realized he couldn't leave things this way and turned toward her.

"Duchess, I…"

"Good evening, Martin," she said, and closed the door. He watched her limousine drive away, wondering what he would have said had she let him.

Zaphod was indeed happy to see him when he walked inside. Martin scooped him up and carried him to the sofa. He sat staring at the walls, emotionally numb, but mind racing on his new task, and he wished it would stop. Zaphod walked across his legs, rubbing his face on his stomach, before circling and curling up on his lap. All seemed right with the world. His travels over at last, everything collapsed in on him with the weight of a dying sun and he sank into a black hole of sleep.

She watched the car disappear around the bend of Wofford Terrace, leaving her alone on the pavement in front of her house. The sun had risen above the trees, and she watched the colors of the sunrise. Color played an outsize role in her day-to-day life, but it had gained a different meaning of late, and the sunrise reminded her. For now, she took a deep breath and appreciated the atmospheric artistry. The sky harbored no agenda and needed nothing from her. For now, that would do.

What would she tell her parents when she got inside? The unfiltered truth would guarantee she would never see Ms. Nichols again at best, assuming her father didn't sue her for child endangerment or some such rot. She'd told too many lies and half-truths already, so her guilt made that option even less appealing. Intermingled with her worry and guilt was the familiar refrain of wondering how her world had become so convoluted in such a short span. She should be worried about her coming GCSE exams and her evolving relationship with Bea, whatever that was. A fifteen-year-old girl from posh Hampstead shouldn't care about matters of life and death half a continent away. She took another deep breath and proceeded to her front door, deciding to figure it out as she went.

"I'm home," she announced in the foyer.

She heard the scrabbling noises of her family rushing to meet her.

"Veronica!" her mother said, rushing up and scooping her into a rib-cracking hug. "Are you all right, dear?"

"I'm fine, Mum."

"We worried about you the entire time. You're not hurt?"

"Honestly, I'm fine."

"They didn't have you committing crimes, then?" her father asked between sips of coffee.

His flippant comment caused her to panic, and she was about to crumble when her mouth acted of its own accord. "Silly Daddy! They took me to the docks, where they load the container ships, and I got to meet some...interesting people."

"*Where did that come from?*" she thought.

"Hmph," her father humphed. She recognized it as meaning that her answer satisfied him, but he wasn't interested enough to ask follow-up questions. Score.

"We didn't know when to expect you. I've just started breakfast. Can I make something for you?"

"That'd be lovely. I'm famished. Can I tell Bea I'm back?"

"You haven't already? She's called several times, wondering if we'd heard anything from you. I dare say she's worried sick. Word to the wise, dear. Family first, then loved ones. Breakfast will be ready in about fifteen minutes. She's welcome to join us if she hasn't already eaten."

Her mother had always been a little distant and wrapped up in her career, but here and now, it was clear she'd gotten it all along. She gave her another big hug, hoisted her bag onto her shoulder, and ran upstairs to her bedroom to make the call.

"*¡Ay Dios mío!* Are you okay?" Bea said upon answering her call.

She laughed. "I'm fine. I just got home."

"Let me get my shoes on. I'll be there in ten minutes."

"Mum said it's okay. See you," she replied and disconnected the call.

The lack of drama surprised her. Her parents had threatened no punishment. William hadn't even shown up to troll her. If this was what being an adult was like, she thought she might just be okay. Ten minutes elapsed in the wink of an eye, and hurried footsteps thumped up the stairs. She rose from her bed and moved towards the door, but Bea burst in before she could open it.

"Oi, you could knock!"

She ignored the quip. Veronica opened her arms for a hug, but Bea walked up to her, grabbed her face with both hands, and kissed her hard. Satisfied, she wrapped her arms around Veronica and held on tight for a very long time. If there were any remaining doubt about their being a couple, it was erased in that instant. Bea loved her, and perhaps the feeling was mutual, but the timing was abysmal. The kiss was inevitable, and it felt right, but it was overwhelming. She had to slow this down.

"Bea..." she said.

"Why didn't you call?"

"I was only gone for two days! It was pretty hectic anyway."

"I'm so glad you're okay. So, what happened in Trieste?"

"I don't know if Ms. Nichols would want me to tell anyone. It was a little intense."

"What can you tell me, then?"

"Well, erm, I met a nice man named Danylo, and a less nice man named Paolo. He, er, sort of got shot, but they said he's going to be all right."

"WHAT??"

"Yeah. I won't be seeing much of her for a while. I think I helped her, but I don't belong out there doing things like that. If she still wants to support my writing, that's super, but that's all. I guess you were right, after all."

"Does that mean we can spend more time together?" Bea said with a hopeful smile.

"Erm, I mean, yeah, but things are confusing right now. She helped me learn some things about myself, and now I have to figure out what to do with them."

"Oh."

How had she interpreted that as a rejection? She had to fix it. "You're my best friend, and I really do like you. I just I need some time to think about everything."

"I understand, I suppose. If you saw somebody get shot, you're probably a wreck. When did your life turn into a James Bond movie?"

"Reluctant chosen one. I answered the call, and I've changed my mind."

"What can I do to help?"

"Just be Bea. Help me have a normal summer."

"I promise."

Bea kissed her again, and since it wasn't a surprise this time, she welcomed it, but it was still too fast.

"You know what else I need?" she said, changing the subject. "Breakfast. Did you eat?"

"No, I ran out as soon as you called."

"Mum said she made extra. Let's go."

They enjoyed a delightful family breakfast together, and she regaled them with stories from Trieste, leaving out the violent bits. Later that morning, she and Bea walked down the High Street together to get gelato, holding hands the entire way.

The walls of her office were closing in on her, and she could see the light dimming through the conference room windows. After returning Veronica to her family, she had orchestrated getting the Speedwell back to Farnborough, dealt with police inquiries regarding the incident on her docks late last night, and she decided she'd had quite enough for a Sunday.

It required every ounce of effort to remain upright, yet Francesca opted to visit the pub before turning in early. A quick slug of something strong and some good vibes might help her stay asleep—getting there wouldn't be a problem. A light but raucous crowd had the pub abuzz. She recognized most of the patrons, and many of them nodded a greeting in her direction. She then spotted Taylor, but it shocked her to see him on the drinking side of the bar.

"Taylor? What are you doing here? It's your night off, isn't it?" she asked.

"Yes, ma'am. I didn't want to be alone in the flat tonight."

"What's wrong?"

"D'ya have a mo to chat in private?" he asked.

"Of course. Let's go upstairs."

They re-boarded the lift and ascended to the lounge. Taylor brought the remainder of his pint, but she had not yet gotten the drink she wanted. She sauntered behind the bar and poured two fingers of an aged sipper, neat.

"Now, what brings you back up here on your night off, Sebastian?"

"Lovesick, I suppose."

Of the thousands of ways he might have answered her question, this counted among the ones she least expected.

"Smitten by Cupid's arrow. Who's the lucky girl?"

Taylor stared at the bottom of his glass, silent and blushing.

"It's not…me, is it?" she asked.

"What? No, ma'am!" She must have appeared hurt, because he scrambled to qualify his statement. "I mean, you're brilliant, but you're my boss, and that just wouldn't be cricket."

"Not at all cricket, but why won't you tell me who it is?"

"It's a bit embarrassing, and I've no idea if she feels the same about me."

"Taylor, you were the one who wanted to chat," she said, patience waning. "I see no reason to hold back now. How does this involve me?"

"It's…well, it's your sister, ma'am."

"Tajana??"

"Yeah, I'm mad about her. I've been unhappy since she went home."

"Have a little crush, do we?" she said, smirking. "I didn't realize you'd spent that much time with her."

"Just once, when she came to my flat for the research you'd asked for. Things sort of happened, and there was a big spark. At least, I felt like there was."

"I understand why you wouldn't want to discuss this in the pub," she told him. "I hope you know I hold no influence over her. In fact, I don't think she's eager to talk to me again."

"I know, and I wasn't hoping for a good word or anything."

"Then why tell me at all?"

"Well, as she's your sister, I wanted to make sure it was all right with you first."

"You're one of the last true gentlemen, Sebastian. It's fine with me, but I fear you may face a challenge if you wish to woo her, especially considering the distance."

"That was something else I wanted to discuss with you. I wondered if I might take an Italian vacation?"

"Hmm," she said, considering his request. "You're due some time off, no doubt."

"Thank you, ma'am," he said, standing up to take his leave.

"There's nothing tying you to London, really," she continued.

"Beg pardon?"

"As luck would have it, we've had a recent opening at Five Pence in Trieste. You're well respected on those docks, it seems. Perhaps we could make it a temporary reassignment, so you could find out if our Imports Manager fancies you? I may still assign research projects for you from time to time, if you'd be interested in continuing that portion of your job."

Taylor perked up. "I think that would be more than satisfactory!"

"I'll start the paperwork tomorrow. And now, a toast," she said, raising her glass. "To chasing love, wherever it may lead us."

"To chasing love," Taylor repeated, raised his glass and drained it.

Giovanni Tessaro no longer had an heir to his empire. It was not his son he mourned as much as the loss of what might have been. He could not run the family forever, and his daughter had made it exceedingly clear that she had no interest in it herself.

He had visited the hospital every day since the incident, ensuring that Paolo was receiving the finest care available in Trieste. He remained unconscious, but the doctors seemed confident that he would come around soon. The chaos of that night brought clarity, and he realized Paolo had always been everything a son should be, even if he was not his own. The future of Tessaro depended on his recovery, so he would leave nothing to chance—that was not his way.

He stood outside the hospital, mobile phone to his ear, trying the number once more. This time, to his surprise and relief, the call connected.

"What do you want?"

"Vittoria, your brother is dead."

"What?"

"I am glad you answered the phone. There was a conflict—a duel—and your brother died."

"Will you take revenge on his killer?"

"No."

"Papa, what do you mean? How could you let his killer walk free?"

"Alessio meant to kill me, Vittoria. He was a traitor to our family's name. Although I hate her for it, she has done us a service."

"She?"

"I did not think you cared about such details."

"They matter when you tell me I've lost my brother. How did he betray you?"

"At first, he shot Paolo."

"Paolo...Zanetti?"

"I am surprised you remember."

"I always liked him. He was more sensitive and brighter than Alessio. Did he die also?"

"No, I am with him at the hospital. The shot only narrowly missed his heart. He will live, but his recovery will be long and difficult."

"Who is this woman that murdered my brother?"

"It was not murder. She defended herself well. It was a fair fight, and she was quicker. She is *La Duchessa* Nikolić, a family from the old empire in the south. We will be enemies no more."

"I cannot believe he would have killed you."

"He'd gone mad with power, and said I was in his way. I cried for us, not for him."

"Why do you stay now with Paolo?"

"He has shown me loyalty, but more, he has shown me love, so that is why I stay with him. I see now that he learned everything I ever tried to teach your brother."

"Did he ever marry?"

"No, Alessio always stole his girlfriends."

"He would never have allowed him to date me."

"You would have had him for yourself?"

"He was the only man I ever met in Trieste who was worth my time. The others are all impetuous, like Alessio. Men in Venice are pretentious and think only of themselves."

"Vittoria, please come home for the funeral. I feel there is much to discuss. God willing, Paolo will be awake to meet with you."

"Are you matchmaking, Papa?"

"This is business, my daughter. If you were to marry this man, he would be my son and heir, and Tessaro will live on."

CHAPTER TWENTY-TWO

ALONE AGAIN, NATURALLY

London sweltered that July, and The Duchess barely left her keep. No one had been to visit her in weeks, and Taylor's cheerful face had been absent from the pub since he'd departed for Trieste. Martin hadn't spoken to her for days, and she doubted he was interested in the task he'd agreed to. Tracy and Duncan were so wrapped up in little Aidan, she'd heard nothing from them since the break-in. Julia took a sabbatical, and she'd sent pictures from the wedding in Kingston, as well as her travels throughout the Caribbean with Ian. If she was honest, she couldn't be sure Julia planned to return to this side of the Atlantic, given how badly shaken she was after her abduction.

Veronica was a different problem. Francesca still supported her needs as she pursued her writing career, because she'd committed to that, and she always honored a commitment. Their communication grew less and less frequent, though, since she'd effectively banned her from The Cathedral. They were still friendly, and did a video chat now and then, which soothed her soul, but she could tell things were different. The girl's eyes always seemed to dart from side to side, looking for a reason to wrap up the call.

Her empire was ceaseless, and something always required her attention, which usually was enough to occupy her. Simon, who was a tireless worker and a sweet kid, wasn't a close friend by any means. Geoff, her sentinel, was as close to her as anyone could be, but she tried opening up to him and he simply walked away when he'd heard enough. It made her angry, but that was never meant to be his role, so she forgave it.

When she thought of all the others, a troubling pattern emerged from the noise. Had she pushed away the only family she'd ever known? Had she used them callously beyond the point of no return with no hope of repair? Her throat tightened at the thought. As she told Martin when they returned, she still had her businesses to run, and they'd made immense improvement since the feud with Giovanni ended. Tajana elevated their sourcing of coffee beans to expert levels, and the partnership with Tessa Roasters created an exemplary product—she drank little else these days.

She could no longer take the silence and grabbed her mobile phone from her kitchen counter. The double-chirp of the call went off four times before Martin's voicemail answered. Ordinarily, she wouldn't leave a message, but he hadn't answered her calls for days.

"Martin, it's me. Listen, I don't need anything from you. I'm not asking you for updates or anything business related. Please, just call me back. I need to hear a friendly voice."

She sipped at her latte and stared out over the London skyline from the window over her sink. Even as high up as she was, the heat refractions coming off the sizzling streets and buildings below were still visible. The bending, wobbling reality outside was hypnotic, and she didn't know how long she'd been staring when her mobile rang, startling her from the reverie.

"Hello?"

"Hi, Duchess."

"Martin, thank goodness."

"You sound dreadful. What's wrong?"

"I'm a mess," she said with a catch in her voice. "I've pushed everyone away."

"Beg pardon?"

Her voice got shakier as she fought to hold the tears at bay. "I've nothing left. No family, no friends."

"You still have your vast empire. Sounds like business is booming of late."

"Before I met you, that would have been enough."

"Are you saying you're lonely, Duchess?"

"Yes," she said, tears breaking loose from the corners of her eyes.

"I'd love to help, but I can't get away from home right now."

"What's going on?"

"Erm..."

"Be honest with me, Martin. You don't want to see me, do you?" It took tremendous effort to stop herself from sobbing.

"It's not like that, really, but I'm tired. I can't come running every time you call. Perhaps my time isn't as valuable as yours, but I have a comfortable life here. I enjoy my space. I've no appetite for the lavish lifestyle or the international man of mystery bit."

"Would you see me there?"

"What, here?"

"Yes, Hounslow's not that far."

"I'm really in no fit state to entertain right now, I'm afraid."

"Have you got someone over?"

"No, why would you ask that? I've got a lot of work to do, I haven't cleaned the flat in days, and, if you must know, I could really use a shower."

"I don't mind. I'll get my shoes on."

"The answer's no, Duchess. Not today. I just…can't."

"Right," she said, furious and devastated all in the same breath. "Right, well, I won't keep you from it, then."

"Er, I…" he said, but she didn't hear him because she ended the call.

She had to move, scream, fight…something. She boarded the lift and went down to the pub. With fewer people about to run the place, she'd had to reduce its hours—even she couldn't tend the bar all the time. The lights were off, the stools and tables stood empty, and the only sounds were the whirrings of air filters and refrigerators. She went behind the bar and found the nearest bottle of Irish whiskey, poured a solid two shots into her latte, then took a seat at the bar. Her afternoon had just gotten all booked up.

EPILOGUE

It was possible Edwin Fancourt had partaken in too much Christmas cheer at his firm's holiday party. He'd passed the merriment of drunkenness and slipped into melancholy. He sat at the opulent hotel's bar, brooding over a tumbler of scotch and water and desperately avoiding conversation with an enthusiastic junior partner. As a vice president, he'd become accustomed to younger members of the firm trying to impress him, hoping to schmooze their way up the ladder, and most times, he would let them. This was the third such interaction on this evening, however, and he'd become weary of it. The partner repeated his name, so he realized he may not have been listening, and rejoined the conversation.

"I'm sorry. What did you say, Bartlett?" Edwin said with a thick tongue.

"It's Braxton, sir. I was asking about your family. Have you any children?"

"Yes, a daughter just turned sixteen, and a fourteen-year-old son."

"Jolly nice. Got plans to follow in their dad's rather impressive footsteps, have they?"

"My daughter wishes to become a writer, but there might be hope for William yet."

"What's so wrong about being a writer?"

The poor kid never saw it coming. That simple question

triggered him. With all filters dissolved by alcohol, he banged on about Veronica being headstrong, flighty, and the extra sprinkles of pride flags bedecking her bedroom. The junior partner sat enthralled, hoping that the sudden outflow of candor might ingratiate him, but he was growing uncomfortable with the details.

"...and then there's the nonsense with her synesthesia or auras or whatever she calls the bloody thing."

"I beg your pardon, sir, but did you say...auras?"

"That's what she called it. It's all balderdash, if you ask me. Insane notions planted in her impressionable brain by that infernal Ms. Nichols or Duchess or whatever."

"I can see why all of that might upset you, sir," the partner said, looking over the crowd. "My deepest apologies, sir, but I'm afraid the group I came with appears to be leaving. It's been a pleasure meeting you, Mr. Fancourt, and I hope we might get the chance to work together soon."

"Likewise, Bradley."

"Er, Braxton. I really am sorry, but I must be off."

He resumed brooding, but pushed the tumbler away from himself.

Braxton, the junior partner, walked out of the holiday party alone, and proceeded to his car in the hotel's garage. His hands-free connected, and he input a number quickly on the car's touchscreen.

"Hello?"

"The Light will guide us, and those who see it must lead the way."

"Good evening, my son. What can I do for you in this festive season?"

"Archseer, I have information to share. I have unmasked

those who share The Light without your blessing."

The line went silent, and he closed his eyes.

"Fancourt and Nichols. They are not names among the families of old. It is indeed a mystery, Braxton of the Eighteenth Cycle. Proceed to the temple at once, where we shall cast our minds across the land to learn all that is learnable."

ACKNOWLEDGMENTS

I guess it wasn't a fluke after all! Last year, when I released *The Duchess and the Accidental Thief*, I already had about a third of this book completed. To be honest, I didn't know if I had another book in me, but I had ideas. Fortunately for me, and hopefully for you too, my characters told me they had more to say. They still do, and I have some fun things planned for Book 3, but it's not fleshed out enough for a preview this time. Fret not, though, because I will post snippets on social media, and possibly send out full chapters on my newsletter.

This year has been a whirlwind, and I've gotten to do some things I never dreamed would be possible. With four GalaxyCons under my belt, Louisville Book Festival coming up, and many more events to come, it was definitely not something I had on my bingo card. I must thank C. R. Rice, Just Cory, Danielle M. Orsino, Leslie & Janice Sommers, Brandon Hoy, Heidi Nickerson, A. K. Ramirez, and everyone else from the Pop-Up Bookshoppe for accepting me into the community. It makes being an author not feel so lonely. Also, gotta thank J. V. Hilliard for introducing me to the group, as well as so many other bits of advice. You all believed in me, and I can never thank you enough for that.

There wouldn't be an *Indigo Child* without my editor and best friend of twenty-eight years, Becka Lloyd. Her savagery has really pushed me to be a better writer. She also knows more about the publishing industry than I could ever hope to forget, so I hope she doesn't mind continuing to share. If you want to see just how good she is, read the preview at the back of *The Accidental Thief* and compare it to this one.

A special thanks to a special beta reader, Martha Hall. Her feedback was critical in the later phases and really added the polish this one needed. I'm not just saying this because she's my mother-in-law.

I think I said something similar in the original *Her Violet Empire* acknowledgments, but it's worth repeating. My mom and dad are truly my biggest fans and cheerleaders. They always told me I could do anything if I tried, and I knew they would be there to dust me off if it didn't work out. Of course, I also have to thank my rock star sister, Becci, and my soon-to-be rock star niece, Graysie B, for admitting that I'm kinda cool. (I can almost hear Becci saying, "Hey, I never said that!")

In Hollywood, you always put the biggest stars last, and for me, there are no bigger stars than my wife, Elizabeth, and the coolest kid on the planet, Cecilia. I hope, when they read this, they understand how much I appreciate them and all the family time they sacrificed to allow me to write and travel. It fills my heart to bring them with me on these wild adventures, and I hope there are many, many more to come.

And thank you to you, kind reader, for getting this far. I hope you have enjoyed these books, and if you have, I'd be most grateful if you'd leave me a review somewhere.

The Duchess, Martin, Veronica, and the rest of the gang will return in *The Duchess and the Dwindling Stars.* I've always wanted to do one of those *James Bond*-style endings. :)

—*Scott*

Milton Keynes UK
Ingram Content Group UK Ltd.
UKHW040113231024
450028UK00022B/55